Salvation Run

To Michael & Martha—
warm memories!

Mary Gardner
Oct. 21, 2005

BOOKS BY MARY GARDNER

Keeping Warm
Milkweed
Boat People

Salvation Run

a novel by

Mary Gardner

University Press of Mississippi
Jackson

www.upress.state.ms.us

The University Press of Mississippi is a member of the Association of American University Presses.

Manufactured in the United States of America

First edition

∞

Library of Congress Cataloging-in-Publication Data

Gardner, Mary.
Salvation run / Mary Gardner. — 1st ed.
p. cm.
ISBN 1-57806-716-2 (cloth : alk. paper) 1. Fathers and daughers—Fiction. 2. Children of clergy—Fiction. 3. Pregnant women—Fiction. 4. Motorcyclists—Fiction. 5. Minnesota —Fiction. 6. Lutherans—Fiction. 7. Adultery—Fiction. 8. Clergy—Fiction.
I. Title.
PS3557.A7142S25 2005
813′.54—dc22

2004029462

British Library Cataloging-in-Publication Data available

for

Butch (R.I.P.), Gaylord, Mother Mick

– real bikers –

one

From the outside, it could have been just any frame duplex in Moorhead, an up-and-down one, shabby in a modest Minnesota way, built almost to the sidewalk to take advantage of all the square footage the lot had to offer. Upstairs someone had nailed an Indian blanket, one corner hanging loose, across the front window. The door downstairs had a sign on it that said JESUS MISSION KEEP OUT. It made you stop and wonder.

But around the back the wondering stopped. A row of Harleys had been pulled into the alley. It was night, and the light from the streetlamp on the corner reflected off their chrome, shooting lines of silver when a gust of wind rose. The big bikes looked like stabled animals resting close to the ground.

Inside the duplex, a glass splintered, then another. Someone laughed hard. A TV blared, the blue light flickering through the big window next to the door. Then a tall shadow passed in front, cutting off the sight line for a moment before disappearing. Up the block, another Harley, ape hanger handlebars spearing up into the summer darkness, rumbled up to the curb and turned into the alley. A broad-shouldered figure slammed through the door to greet the newcomer.

"Hey, Rocker, you're fuckin' late."

"So?" The rider swiped with one hand at his sissy bar as he swung off the bike. "You brothers can't teach a prospect a few things without me being there to hold you all in line?"

"Largo's pissed at him."

"Largo drinking again?"

"One or two."

"Never could hold it."

"Better than he used to be."

"That's not saying much."

The two men walked into the clubhouse, where shouts rang out in greeting. The Iron Riders were celebrating. Last night they'd partied with the Angels, or at least some of their members had, the ones the Angels respected. Now it was their club's turn to take care of all of its own.

Inside, the men had gathered in a ragged circle around the perimeter of the big central room. There were about two dozen of them, the older ones with bikers' guts. Gold rings flashed. Beer that had spilled from one of the tables splashed onto the floor in steady drips. No one was paying any attention to it.

A skinny Chicano man stood in the middle of the room, thumbs hooked in his belt. "Largo, what the fuck you got against me?" he asked. He had a heavy accent, but the words were clear.

Rocker moved up to the speaker. "Stop running your mouth, Little Juan," he growled, his gut arched out against his black Harley T-shirt. "Largo's been an Iron Rider since you was still a fucking rug rat. Long as you're our prospect, we tell you what to do. You wanna hang around, you follow the instructions."

"Shit, man."

With his eyes squinted, Rocker looked Juan up and down. "Truth is, you're looking like a dirtbag right now. Bad enough to be a fuckin' greaser, I'd say. At least you gotta keep that vest clean, know what I mean? You're not going to earn your colors that way."

Juan grimaced, cocked his head to one side. He looked birdlike, a frowzy adolescent eagle, but one with a mean streak. Rocker had a good six inches on him. "Fuck, I *am* clean," Juan grunted, cocking his head in the other direction. His vest was bare now except for the bottom patch, but it wasn't dirty.

"You ain't one of us yet," said another biker, a big man with a black cascade of hair knotted down his back. He stepped forward, fists tight. "You ain't got your colors. That's just a fuckin' vest."

"Let it go, Largo." Rocker lifted his hand.

"No, I ain't gonna let it go. Little Juan's gotta get cleaned up." Largo's voice lowered. "Take it off," he said.

"Take it off?" Juan looked down at his black leather vest. He couldn't figure out what was going on. "It is not dirty," he muttered.

"You heard me right."

"Sandy, she washes my shirt every day."

"You should fucking well wash hers."

Rocker put his hand on Largo's arm. "Cool it, man," he said. "You're hammered."

"One beer."

Rocker looked Largo in the eyes. "OK," he said. Then he turned back to Juan. "Take it off like he said," he ordered, his enunciation crisp as a knife edge. All the other bikers were paying close attention.

Hesitating, Juan hunched his shoulders backwards. He let the vest slip down, then pulled it off and held it in front of him. "I end this prospect shit next month," he said, staring defiantly.

"Maybe."

"You know the deal."

"*We* make the deals. Throw that vest on the floor."

The black leather hung from Juan's hands. "What for?" he asked.

From behind Rocker, Largo loomed up again. The two men were the same height, but Largo's bulk was rangy, squared off at the shoulders. His jeans hung low on his hips. Rocker was square all the way down, his gut the only divergence. His Harley shirt cradled it as if it were a separate entity grafted onto his body.

"*Throw it.*"

Lips tight, Juan tossed his vest. It flopped flat on the dirty boards. Rocker made a little gesture with his right hand, and a biker stepped forward. He had a shit-eating grin on his face. With a quick movement, he unzipped his fly.

"Nice dick, Dinger. Let 'er rip."

A sharp yellow stream arched out, splashing off the leather. Juan's face blanched. "Jesus, you guys are fucked!" he said.

Red Harry stepped forward. Another stream. Around the demeaned vest, a dark puddle was stretching across the floor. Mixed with the smell of beer, the hot odor of piss rose into the air.

Juan's fists tightened. His shoulders rose. The bikers straightened themselves. Nobody said a word.

Another shot of piss, Largo this time. He put out a tremendous amount. No surprise there, though. Largo always did things bigger than others.

Outside, an old car was pulling up. The muffler or something that sounded like it was banging off the pavement. Then the motor cut off. The men looked at each other.

"The old ladies ain't due till eleven."

"Some of 'em ain't learned to tell time yet."

Swinging his shoulders around, Largo looked out the window. He was tucking his shirt in. "Sandy," he said. "Little Juan's Numero Uno. Until she wises up, that is."

Dinger took a look too. "Gettin' fat," he said.

Comanche was next. "If she ain't stretched out enough, the wetback ain't goin' to be able to find where to put it."

It was teasing, but it was mean teasing. Despite his dark skin, Juan's face had gone white around the mouth. He looked like he had been going to punch someone but had thought the better of it.

They could hear Sandy walking along the side of the clubhouse. Now she was at the door. "Pick up your goddamn vest," Largo said to Juan.

The knob turned. "Goddamn fuckin' bitch," Juan said, the soaked leather in his hand.

"Watch your mouth," Largo grunted, his whiskey voice in an angry growl. "She's a preacher's kid."

"How the fuck do you know what she is?"

For a moment, it looked like Largo was going to attack, but he didn't. "Put that vest on," he said.

The door was opening. "What the fuck," Juan croaked out. "This goddamn thing is covered in piss!"

And then Sandy was inside. She was a very young woman, her hair a mass of dark curls. Next to the big men, she looked almost like a child. Her blouse hung over her jeans. She had a casserole dish, covered with tinfoil, in her arms.

"I made lasagna." She looked around. No one made eye contact.

"Pee-eeww. This place smells. Is the john plugged up?"

No one said anything. Juan stepped toward her in a gesture of ownership. She leaned in his direction, then pulled back.

"You guys having bladder problems?"

Juan grabbed her upper arm. The lasagna wavered. "Shut the fuck up," he said. "Just shut the fuck up."

Sandy's small impudent face faltered, but she spoke right back. "You got the pre-wedding blues?" she asked. "Is that your problem?" To show him she wasn't really angry, she moved up against him, her curls brushing his shoulder.

"Fuck the wedding."

"You guys can bring your own beer. As long as it stays outside in your saddlebags. My mom will see that there's lots of food."

Juan fell silent. The circle of men was breaking up. Someone changed the channel on the TV, and two musclebound wrestlers sprang forward. Rocker and Comanche leaned up against the wall, watching them. Outside, another car pulled up. More old ladies. They were the ones who brought the food. By now, everyone was getting hungry. The smell of piss didn't make much difference.

With his fingers tight around her upper arm, Juan was pulling Sandy into the little kitchen behind the counter. She bit her lower lip. Suddenly Largo was looming over the two of them, reaching out for the lasagna. "Gimme that," he said.

Sandy looked up at him but didn't argue. She handed it over.

"And let go of her."

Juan relaxed his fingers. Largo was a loose cannon. Even a prospect knew that. With the tinfoiled dish in his big hands, he could be dangerous. Especially if he decided to throw it.

Sandy reached over and pulled up a corner of the foil. "It's still hot," she said. "I drove up fast from Littleriver. And it's got sausage too. Like the real Italians do it."

Largo nodded. Juan moved around them back to the bigger room.

"You're all invited to the wedding, you know," Sandy said loudly to the group. "We didn't send invitations or anything, but you're still invited. It's at my dad's church, out by Eagle Grove. In just two weeks. Everyone from the church'll be there, even the two gay guys. But no faggot jokes. They're OK."

Largo slid the lasagna dish onto the counter as another car pulled up. Outside, women were talking. The real party was about to start.

"Somebody should clean that up." Sandy gestured toward the puddle in the middle of the room. She started toward the sink.

"You don't do that." Largo blocked the way.

"Who else is going to do it?"

Largo looked down at his own chest. It wasn't going to be him, for sure.

Suddenly Rocker was in the center of the room, a blanket in his arms. "This'll do it," he said, and he swung the blanket like a bullfighter's cape. His fingers let it loose at the last moment, one biker boot pirouetting on its toe. If he hadn't been the Iron Riders' president and a tough dude to begin with, it could have been looked on as funny. But no one laughed.

Muffled under the wool, the smell diminished. Rocker stalked into the kitchen where Sandy was peeling the tinfoil off her lasagna. He grabbed a fork, speared a chunk, and raised it to his mouth.

Sandy grinned. "Like it?" she asked.

Rocker nodded, chewing. "You gonna make some man a good wife," he said. "Only I got second thoughts about that taco bender Juan."

two

Englund Lutheran Church was one of the small Lutheran churches that had been established more than a hundred years ago around Eagle Grove, a northwestern Minnesota town that lay between Littleriver on the one side and Moorhead on the other. Despite the passage of time, most of the congregations persisted, even if in diminished form. Each church was surrounded by a sweep of farmland so profound that, even from a low-flying airplane, the church itself would have been almost invisible in the summer stretches of green and brown.

Approaching from the west along Highway 10 or I-94, a visitor to Englund would pass through the flat Red River Valley, then into the first range of hills, the old shore of glacial Lake Agassiz, which had formed the valley after the Ice Age. The second rise marked where the Scandinavian and German farmers had settled in the 1880s and 1890s, homesteading their small acreages, then expanding, finally coming to own pig farms, chicken factories, rolling fields of grain, sunflowers, corn.

In the old days before automobiles, a Sunday trip into Eagle Grove for a church service would have been difficult. So the settlers had created the grid of little Lutheran churches to provide for everyone. Eagle Grove Lutheran, of course. Hegland Sygne Solem Rural. Immanuel. Then Emmanuel, spelled with an "E" and slightly more liberal in its theology. Peace Lutheran. Then

Englund Lutheran. A church could not be more than an hour's buggy ride away from at least ten farms. Each little congregation drew its boundaries for practical reasons. All the churches were painted white.

And whiter than usual with the new steel siding, thought Ed Olson, the pastor of Englund, as he turned his aging Oldsmobile off the gravel road and down into the parking lot. The surface there was so hard-packed by parishioners' cars that even in the driest summers, little dust rose. On the north side, the woodpile for the barbecue pit, scene of the July pig roast, was topped off by the Myhres' old dock and a garnish of scraps from Ed's own carpentry shop. The pit itself was hidden under a sheet of plywood, to keep the Sunday schoolers safe.

There were only nine Englund Lutheran Church children now. It was primarily a congregation of old Norwegians. The children were almost a disruption to the scrubbed, compulsively neat church building, polished and arranged by Ed's wife, Grace, and by Mildred and Rose and Gertrud, when Gertrud's knee wasn't swollen. The hired helper, Mrs. Swenson, vacuumed on Thursdays, and Burton Rogers came in at least once a week to dust obscure corners to his own satisfaction. How many little Lutheran churches could boast an English teacher as a volunteer custodian? And a politically correct one as well, since Burton was gay.

Even sitting behind the wheel of his Oldsmobile, gathering his thoughts together, Ed fantasized the aroma of Fantastik and bleach. Once he was inside the church, however, the only smell came from the gladioli on the little organ. There were white ribbons tied around the backs of the two front pews on each side of the aisle—Grace had clearly come by earlier. He thought of the wedding guests, the curious from the congregation, all to arrive in a spasm of Lutheran promptness in exactly half an hour.

And Sandy. Who was never late.

Except the one time, when she'd been in the sixth grade at the Eagle Grove school, and she'd missed the class trip to the movie in Moorhead, even though it had been *The Sound of Music*, her absolute favorite. She had slept late despite the alarm, despite her mother's tapping at the door of her bedroom. The bus had left without her. Down across her brown eyes, a sheet had fallen. "I don't care," she'd said.

Her mother had nodded, taking her cue, walking delicately. "Of course," she'd replied.

Sandy hadn't spoken another word, had gone up to her room, had begun to throw things out her window. Grace hadn't realized at first what she was doing, and neither had he. Sitting in his study on the first floor, copying over the Text of the Day for the third time in an attempt to coerce his mind into a sermon, Ed had seen a shoe tumble down outside the window like a disoriented black bird. Then two books. Then three more. He had watched, fascinated, hearing everything thump scratchily into the forsythia below. Then Sandy's music box, glittering in the descent.

Grace had gathered them all up, put them outside their daughter's door. She'd never said a word about the incident, and neither had Sandy. On Monday, sermon safely behind him, Sandy off on the bus to school, Ed had gently opened her door, curious about the carnage. Nothing seemed to be missing. Even the music box sat on the bureau, secure. Only, when he looked at it closely, he saw that its lid had been reattached by delicate wires through its bent hinges.

He had been afraid to wind it up, to see if the mechanism had broken too. And Sandy had taken it with her when she'd moved out last year. So he would probably never know.

The music box hovering in his mind, Ed walked to the vestibule of the church and leaned his forehead against the window. Across the road, the corn rose so high that the landscape seemed to be bounded by a green wall, faintly alive, leaf moving against leaf. The Andersons, who owned the field, rotated what they planted: soybeans, wheat, corn. This was the corn year. Back in the buggy days when Englund had been founded, in 1882, the great-grandparents of today's Andersons had already owned the land across the road, even before the road was there. Joel, the current Andersons' twenty-year-old son, with eyebrows so blond that they left no observable mark on his forehead, was at the ag college now and would farm the land when his parents retired.

When she had been in grade school, Sandy had played with Joel before the service, running in a burst of giggles out the door, tearing between the gravestones scattered in the yard around the church, tromping over the barbecue pit plywood so loudly that the earth seemed to shake. The other children, more of them present in those earlier years, came and sat with their parents. If Grace hadn't been able to corral Joel and Sandy outside, they simply kept on giggling and running, dancing over the dead with joyous disrespect.

And now Sandy wanted him to perform her marriage ceremony. But not to Joel. To a man Ed had only met once, and a Mexican as well. He wasn't sure about the Mexican part. Latino. Hispanic. Something not Norwegian.

Outside, at the edge of the glass, he could see the rise of dust that signalled an approaching car. That would probably be Grace, in their Ford Escort, jolting over the gravel to join him, to try out the organ, to rearrange the gladioli, to stand at the door in her pink linen and greet the curious parishioners trickling in to see Sandy given in marriage. Grace was the one who had put the announcement in the Sunday bulletin, despite his own ambivalence. "She grew up at Englund," she'd said. "People will want to come."

"Sandy may prefer it private."

"Ed." Grace had lost weight recently, and it had narrowed her face as well as her body. Even her benevolent words seemed narrow to him. "I spoke to her about it. She wants people here. Why wouldn't she? They love her."

In recent years, the word "love" had become as charged for Ed as Mrs. Dean's onion pickles, the only flavor at church potlucks to lift itself above the mashed potatoes and processed ham. "I suppose they do," he'd said.

Bouncing ahead of its cloud of dust, the car emerged in front of the church. It wasn't the Escort, after all, but Sandy's nasty little Mustang, old before its time, with its engine roaring and its tailpipe banging off the gravel. At the hump into the parking lot, the pipe clanged ferociously but stayed attached. The first of today's miracles, thought Ed, as he opened the church door to greet his daughter.

"Hi, Dad."

"Hello, sweetheart."

She looked askance at him. "It's only a wedding."

"Sorry for the sentiment."

She'd been named Sandra after his mother. The nickname Sandy had nothing to do with her complexion. Even as a baby, she'd never been blond like he was, never shown any signs of Norwegian bone structure, and now, with her long cotton skirt, skeins of beaded necklaces, and a blouse which seemed to have toppled to her breasts and hung there precariously, she looked like a gypsy.

"Don't apologize."

He tried to remember what he'd apologized for.

"Lutherans spend too much time being sorry."

She has no idea, Ed thought, and bent his head. "But it doesn't make us much better than anyone else," he said. "Unfortunately."

Sandy spun around, her skirt like red petals. Then she took his arm and led him to the front pew. "I have some things to say to you," she whispered, and she pushed her father down gently, then arranged his hands in his lap.

"Is that the skirt you're going to wear for the wedding?"

"What's wrong with this skirt?"

"It's awfully bright."

She snorted, then sat down tight against him. "I've made my scarlet letter a fashion statement," she said, her eyes narrow with humor, her hands busy rearranging his collar. "Shh. Mom will be here soon, and then everyone else. I'm marrying Juan so he can get his green card. We're not going to live together. We've already tried that. Oh, maybe just for a little while. So when I say my vows, I'm going to have my fingers crossed. So it doesn't count. Just don't be surprised, OK?"

"Why didn't you get married at the courthouse?"

"Because I wanted to do it this way."

Ed's brain jangled. He was surprised at his own anger. "The wedding ceremony isn't a joke, Sandy," he said.

She leaped up, spun again. The skirt swept against his hands. "Daddy! Mom wanted it this way too. It gives her a chance to be unprejudiced, Juan being Guatemalan and all. This isn't Vietnam, you know. Everyone's not the enemy anymore."

Ed looked up at her face, then jerked his eyes lower. Her belly curved heavily against the red cotton of her skirt. He didn't want to think about it. He looked down at her feet, in built-up sandals made of some kind of woven straw. The polish was peeling from her toenails. Behind her, above the altar, an ascending barefoot Christ seemed the only safe vision in the sanctuary.

Sandy moved back to him. "Some of my friends are coming too," she said. "Juan is riding with them."

"Of course."

Now beneath the altar of the church, Sandy leaned up against the organ and broke off one purple gladiolus flower, which she thrust into her hair. The splash of color against the dark curls looked like an O'Keeffe painting. "I'll bet that when I was little, you had no idea who I'd turn into," she said. She adjusted her blouse, grinned, showed her one crooked tooth on the left side.

“Sandy.” Ed rose and put his arms around her. She reached behind her back and grabbed his thumbs, the way she used to. “I’m not good about talking over these things,” he said.

“I know.”

“Your mother’s bringing two sheet cakes. And some hot dishes. There’ll be coffee in the basement afterwards. Plenty of coffee.”

“Enough for them too?”

At first he didn’t know what she meant, but he looked back towards the door of the church, following the incline of her head. There was a faint rumble in the distance, as if the Andersons were making the corner swing with their combine, only it wasn’t the right time of summer. Thunder? But the sky was clear.

The rumble continued, unchanged, then sputtered and increased. Ed moved to the window and saw the cloud of dust.

“What’s that?”

Sandy sat in the front pew cross-legged. “I told them to come early,” she said.

“Who?”

“The Iron Riders.”

“Who?”

“The Iron Riders. On their Harleys. The motorcycle club. Juan’s a prospect there, and we all party together.” She grinned; her tooth sparkled. “I don’t think they’ve ever been to a country wedding.” The grin absorbed her face. “Maybe not even to a church.”

The roar was astounding. From the window, Ed saw the first bike turn into the parking lot, heaving itself over the hump. Another followed, then another. Even from the hard-packed lot, dust rose and settled.

“Don’t worry, Dad.” Sandy grabbed his elbow, rubbed the palm of her hand around it through his suit jacket like she used to do when they had played together on the lawn. “They bring their own beer.” Desultory roars still declared themselves from the parking lot, joined by the arrival of the Escort, blue and pure, and then Mrs. Lund's Chrysler, pulling into the handicap space. She always came early. She hadn't been truly handicapped since her hip surgery two years ago, but she was fond of the sticker.

"And I don't know how they feel about the sheet cakes either," Sandy said. "But most bikers will try anything."

three

Of course this was the bluff side of Weed Lake, and a good thing too, what with the high water in the spring, which had now extended into the summer, and the cabins on the south that were teetering on the edge of innundation. But when they'd bought this place, he and Alex, they hadn't paid any attention to the hill, so taken were they with the old peony bushes and day-lilies edging the yard and the birch grove down near the shore, situated so that from the back of the house, one could imagine a stroll in the treetops. "Me Jane," Alex had whispered, goosing Burton in the tush when the realtor wasn't looking.

Originally it hadn't even been a house, just a cabin with some pitiful pretensions. Insulation around the foundation but not under the roof, only loose attic boards and a colony of flying squirrels that died in succession between the rafters and dripped unpleasantly in a line from the kitchen counter to the linen closet. That had taken some doing, extricating the little corpses and discouraging the living. The two of them had spent the first summer there, working like leathermen, Alex actually developing quads from the endless heaving of lumber, and he, Burton, losing ten pounds without even noticing for what was absolutely the first time in his life.

But when October came, he'd insisted on calling a halt, because the baseboard heat was a fire threat with the bad wiring, and until they had excavated some kind of a cellar, they couldn't install a proper furnace. Alex had sulked all winter in town, and by February, he was starting to spend almost every night at the Flagpole Café, coming home just before dawn and settling in on the far side of the king-sized mattress. On March 1, Burton had reached out at six a.m., goosed Alex back (though he knew Alex wouldn't remember the time with the realtor), and said, "You win."

Alex couldn't turn over without coming nearer, so he'd grunted into the pillow, "What?"

"You can call the contractor. He'll have to use dynamite. He'll tell everyone that the Weed Lake fairies are out of their minds."

Alex had laughed so hard that his gut rumbled. "All is forgiven," he'd said.

"*I* should be the one saying that." Burton had handed him the bedside phone. "Get him before he puts his cute little tush into those enchanting overalls and sets off to install someone else's furnace."

So they'd had the basement dug through the half-frozen soil at astronomical winter prices, and they'd moved in for good on May 10, the grass only beginning to green up, the goldfinches already at the bird feeders. As May wound down, the orioles had come, and the hummingbirds. Alex dyed the sugar water red, then maroon, then finally lavender. "A gradual transition," he'd said, "since they may not be as color sensitive as the books say." But nothing had changed the small, buzzing, ferocious greed.

And now, now! Summer of 1998, another July eight years later, the daylilies fluorescent with flower. Alex wouldn't pick them because they died so quickly, but he allowed Burton to garner a bouquet or two for the hallway. The birch leaves were a carpet of green into which it still appeared one could step as casually as onto a dance floor. But sensible men, among whom they counted themselves, walked down the well-laid treated-wood steps, nineteen of them, to the stone table and bamboo chairs, shades of Italy, or at least the Cape, and then on down thirteen more to the tiny beach and the dock.

"So what excitement met you in town today?"

Burton pulled his thoughts back from the treetops. Alex was standing just behind him, wearing their favorite shared Vikings T-shirt, his cell phone hooked on his belt.

"Nothing special."

"No encounter with Elvira at the bank? Students planning your assassination in the fall? Some real tofu at Jim's Market?"

"None of the above." Burton smiled back at Alex. His own nature wasn't ironic. He appreciated Alex's sharpness as a replacement for a part of himself that was lacking.

"People still talking about Sandy Olson's wedding?"

"It seems to have died down."

"I thought Mrs. Lund was going to die when that biker offered her a beer."

Burton shook his head. "I actually thought she was amused. In an elderly Norwegian way."

"Did you get a good look at Sandy? She seemed a bit preggers to me."

"I don't think one can be just a *bit* preggers."

"Well, let's not argue gradations." Alex looked out over the birch tops. "We could get tens of thousands more for this place than we paid for it," he said. "Especially on a lovely summer day."

Across the lake, the light echoed fiercely off the Ericksons' aluminum rowboat, tied up against their dock. The next cabin was the Grafsgaards', who wintered over in Tempe. They had a martin house painted in exact imitation of their own house, even to the blue blinds, but the martins all nested and produced infinite broods in Sven Nystrom's dilapidated martin house down behind the swamp at the east end of the lake.

Around the other end was Pastor Ed's house, near the heron rookery, and beyond that were the Melchoirs, the Olsens-with-an-e, and the rentals from the Bald Rock Resort. People waved hello, and chatted when they went to town. Alex and Burton's being gay didn't seem to make much difference as long as they didn't march in the Gay Pride parade. Actually, they would have been allowed to march, but not to talk about it with other Lutherans.

"Ooops." Alex grabbed his waistband. His phone was ringing.

"Aren't you going to answer it?"

"Burton, dear, you know that technology makes me nervous. But yes." He pulled up the phone, held it to his ear, whispered a greeting. Then he turned back to Burton. "For you."

"Me?"

"With how many others do I share my life?"

"Who is it?"

"The art teacher with the excessive red hair. No doubt she wants you to model."

Burton grabbed the phone and walked back towards the house. He despised people who babbled on cell phones when they were doing yard work, driving their cars, supposedly interacting with the outside world. It had always seemed a gross display of egotism to him.

"Evelyn?"

Her raspy voice affirmed her identity. She had given up on smoking last Valentine's Day, but her larynx was still in recovery. "Burton, how are you?" she asked, her voice thick with innuendo.

"Just fine. In the yard admiring the view."

"Your place is so lovely."

"We work on it."

She paused. He waited. She cleared her throat. It was almost like a theatrical rehearsal.

"Did you read the paper yesterday?"

"Not the local one."

"Did you hear about the accident?"

"Some of the kids from school?" Adolescents were always damaging themselves, some of them seriously. The roads were less crowded out in the country, but the space encouraged recklessness. Last year two seniors had been killed going the wrong way on Highway 10. He'd known them, known most of their friends.

"Yes. Jimmy Dement and Richard Hagstrom. Jimmy broke both legs in the rollover. No seat belts, of course. Richard smashed up his shoulder. Out by the intersection going to Wishbone. They must not have been paying attention. The car is a complete loss. Jimmy was driving."

Burton knew Jimmy, a skinny chess player from his junior English class. He knew Richard too. Richard's folks lived in the best-maintained house in the township, every window agleam. "What a rotten shame," he said.

"That's not all."

He couldn't imagine what other details she had yet to reveal.

"Hold your breath."

Instead, he looked at the semi-Victorian table that stood beside the couch, with his mother's crocheted doily draped across its top.

"They were naked."

"What?"

"Naked. Or almost. The paramedics weren't sure at first because it was such a mess."

Burton couldn't think of how to respond. "It's summer," he finally said.

"That wasn't why."

There was a long silence.

"I knew both of those boys," Evelyn said, "and I had no idea."

Something was stuck in Burton's throat. It was one of the times when the right comment was needed. He wished Alex were standing next to him, flip and articulate and sure of himself.

"Burton?"

"I'm here."

"Did *you* know?"

He pulled himself together. "They're kids, Evelyn," he said. "What's to know? Even kids have private lives."

"There's more."

Burton's breath was speeding up. His throat tightened. "I can't imagine what, Evelyn," he said, forcing out the syllables.

"Richard's parents have disowned him."

"People stopped being disowned back in the Middle Ages."

"Well, maybe you'd call it something else. But they said he couldn't come back home. He's in the hospital now. The sheriff wasn't going to tell them the details, but you know Einar. Somehow it slipped out."

Einar, the enormous slow-moving sheriff, hadn't kept a secret in his entire life. And how he would relish revealing this one, Burton thought.

"What will happen to him, Burton?"

Although during the whole conversation, Burton had been casting Evelyn in the role of country gossip, he heard the edge of genuine sympathy in her voice. Inside his head, he tried to focus on Richard—tall, pimply, a good writer, but without objectivity. Not a favorite, not a nonfavorite. Just another neutral kid, putting in his time during adolescence until he could escape and have a life. He hardly knew the family, even though they lived only a few miles from each other. He had no responsibility in the matter.

Evelyn's voice cracked with urgency. "Could you?" she asked.

He pretended he didn't know what she meant. "Could I what?" he asked back.

"You know, Burton. Take him in. You and Alex. You've got the extra bedroom. Everyone respects you." She paused. "And you could probably teach him some things," she said.

Dear God. Burton set the phone down on the doily, from which Evelyn's voice nattered on obscurely. What was she thinking about? The name of a politically correct lawyer? The right magazines to look at? Sexual techniques? He taught teenagers all the school year. Living with one seemed like some kind of undeserved punishment.

"Burton?"

He heard his name and picked up the phone. "I'll talk to Alex," he said, before she could utter another word.

"I'm sure he'll agree."

Alex, who loved crises, probably would. "Richard's at the hospital in Littleriver?" he asked.

"Yes. His doctor is Mathison. Who else? I'm sure he'll fill you in on the details."

"Will there be any legal problems if we decide to do this?"

"Oh, I don't think so. His parents are just terribly upset. It'll probably blow over in a few . . . weeks."

She had been going to say "months," Burton knew. He only hoped her original thought hadn't been "years."

"I'll check with Alex," he said again.

She actually breathed a sigh of relief loud enough to be heard over the phone. Then she changed gears. "Were you at the wedding?" she asked.

"In back. We came in late."

"An amazing event. I was sorry I didn't bring my sketchbook."

Matchbox, their brown and nasty little cat, crept out from under the table and swatted at Burton's ankle. He only wanted to get off the phone. "Grace seemed happy," he said.

"She certainly brought enough food."

Before his eyes, Sandy's bright face danced. He nudged Matchbox away. Even at Englund, most brides got dressed up. Sandy's red skirt had been a first.

"Did you have a good look at her?" Evelyn asked, her voice lowered.

"As much as I could see from the back."

"She certainly didn't look like a virgin bride to me."

My God, Burton thought. Can't we be allowed to deal with one crisis at a time?

"Like maybe four months along. Or five."

Already Burton's mind was running through their linen closet, the food in the refrigerator, his skimpy medical knowledge. If Alex agreed, they should go visit Richard later today. He didn't want to do this, but what choice did he have?

"Burton?"

"Evelyn, I have to go. And you know that gay men don't have the *faintest* idea about things like that."

four

"Shit, I didn't think nobody was here!"

Largo stood at the entry of the clubhouse, so caught in his surprise that the doorknob still lingered in his hand. Through the opening, hot summer air poured into the dark room. Not that the clubhouse was all that cool, but the one window air conditioner was rumbling and struggling to make a difference. In the midst of the feebly moving air, the big room with its discarded bottles, cigarette butts, and torn *Easyriders* magazines looked more like a stage set than a real place, something waiting passively for the next act to occur.

Sandy glanced up at him from across the room, where she was scrubbing the counter. "I'm cleaning," she said.

"You got no need to clean. We can do that ourselves."

"But you never do. It's a mess. In the summer, there's bound to be bugs." She dug away at the corner of the counter where it met the wall. "Besides, I like to clean," she said.

Largo stood mystified, still hanging on to the doorknob. He glanced down at it, then slammed the door shut. "Where's Juan?" he asked.

Sandy didn't answer. She was squatting now, swabbing at the front of the counter.

Largo waited, thinking maybe he'd missed something. All that cleaning made him nervous. He wanted a beer, but he'd be in Sandy's way getting it. The circles of her cleaning seemed like a ferocious barrier.

He searched for a topic. One flew into his mind. "Nice wedding," he said.

"It's already a long time ago."

"Not so long." Why was he arguing? He couldn't even remember how long ago it was, nor why he'd felt the need to say it was nice. The frosting on the cake had made his teeth hurt. And the church had been so clean he had hated to wear his boots inside. Maybe that was why Sandy was scrubbing. People learned things like that when they were young.

Now Sandy had edged around the counter into the kitchen and started on the stove. It was filthy. Even Largo knew that. She had tied her tangled curls back in a big bunch that stuck out on her shoulders. They shook back and forth as she scrubbed.

Largo struggled for more conversation. "Your dad sure looks like a preacher," he said, thinking how stupid that sounded the minute it came out of his mouth.

"No, he doesn't."

"What?"

"You heard me, Largo." She turned around and glared at him. "And how do you know what a preacher looks like anyway?"

This wasn't going well. Largo wanted his beer more than ever. That was the only reason he'd stopped by anyway. But Sandy was looking at him with such rage that he didn't dare approach the kitchen, much less the refrigerator.

"And anyway, you can't tell a thing about a man by the way he looks!"

Her voice sounded funny. Maybe she had a cold coming on. Summer colds were the worst, Dan the Man had always said, though Largo couldn't remember him ever having any kind of cold at all.

They were both silent. Then Sandy clanged something against a stove burner. Largo realized she had a spatula in her hand, but she sure wasn't cooking.

She banged it again. And again. The noise was deafening. Largo put his hands up to his ears, but it didn't make any difference. He couldn't even hear the air conditioning through the banging. And now Sandy was screaming too.

"Fuck off, you stupid Indian! Just fuck off!"

He had never heard her swear. As far as he knew, he hadn't even done anything. She was beating at the stove as if she wanted to split it into pieces, and Largo was afraid she'd hurt herself. The spatula cracked in two and flew up in the air. Now she was using her fists and screaming without words, just a wild sound like a chopper's brakes screeching.

"Sandy!"

She didn't pay any attention.

Largo leapt over the counter, pivoting on one hand. He hadn't done that in years. Through the snarl in his head, he thought about grabbing her, but the way she was, she'd probably fight back, and he might hurt her by accident. He really didn't want to do that.

Lying next to the refrigerator on the counter was a pile of tools that Red Harry had left. He never put anything away. Largo thrust out his hand and grabbed the lug wrench. He raised his arm and brought it down on the stove with all his strength. The crash was outstanding, and satisfying too. He did it again.

For a moment they both stood there, whamming the shit out of the old stove. Sandy stopped first. She was panting. There was a big bruise on her cheekbone, though she had tried to cover it with some powder or something that ladies used. "Are you crazy?" she rasped out, leaning back. Her legs were trembling.

Largo gave the stove one more bang. The impact shot through his wrist. Then he threw the lug wrench aside.

"Maybe."

He could tell she was forcing herself to stand straight. She put both hands on her stomach. She caught her breath. "Don't tell anyone," she whispered.

"I guess we all got shit to get mad about," Largo replied. "And the stove don't tell no stories."

five

She hadn't meant to blow up like she had. Juan would kill her if he found out. Getting so mad, pounding on that stupid stove with Largo. She'd even said the F-word.

Not that Largo hadn't heard the F-word before. He was a biker, after all.

In her grubby little apartment, Sandy stood as straight as she could hold herself. She touched her cheek. If Juan came home and saw it, maybe he'd be nice. Half the time when he hit her, he was nice afterwards. He didn't know his own strength. She'd always thought strong men would be good in bed, but Juan really wasn't much. And when he was drinking, he couldn't always get it up. Then he got really pissed, but he usually just yelled at her. Twice the people downstairs had pounded on their ceiling.

Starting at the far end of the little living room, Sandy began straightening things. She liked everything at right angles to everything else. It wasn't her fault—she'd inherited it. When she'd been living at home, she'd tease her folks about their being Norwegian and wanting everything in order. Sometimes she'd been down-right mean about it. But they were always so kind that it just made her feel like being meaner. How could she ever learn to be her own independent person if they kept her wrapped up in kindness like that?

Of course, they weren't perfect. At least her father wasn't. He spent a lot of time driving around in the country when he probably should have been building something or preaching to someone. He read those books about Vietnam all the time. Even if she kept after him, he couldn't talk about anything important with her. Not that her mom could either, of course. When she'd told them about Joel and what he'd tried to do when they parked at the quarry, neither one of them had had a single sensible thing to say. "You know how to do what's right," her father had finally croaked out. What kind of advice was that?

Not that she didn't know about sex. She wasn't stupid. But it wasn't sex so much. She just wanted to try things she hadn't done before. And Juan had told her they'd do a road trip down south, across the border on the Harley, back to Guatemala and the jungles and everything. She'd never seen a real jungle with vines and all. She was light enough that she figured she could grab one and swing out through the air until all the birds swooped around her.

Of course, they'd never made the trip. All Juan wanted was to have an old lady to screw and give him a green card. And even when she'd bought rubbers, he wouldn't wear one. She didn't want to mess with her system by using the pill or anything like that. So she shouldn't be surprised he'd knocked her up.

Halfway down the living room, Sandy kept on straightening. Her music box stood in the middle of a bunch of little framed pictures from when she'd been in school at Eagle Grove. One year at the church Halloween party, she'd dressed up like Pocahontas. She'd even worn a long black wig, but it had just looked fake.

She wondered what tribe Largo belonged to. Chippewa, probably. Most Indians in Minnesota were Chippewa. And he wasn't all Indian, she was sure. There weren't many full-bloods left anymore.

When she'd been growing up, she hadn't even known there was a motorcycle club in Moorhead. Of course, her family didn't go up there all the time. They did most of their shopping in Littleriver. But she'd seen the Iron Riders on Highway 10 one day, a whole line of them going straight west like they were riding to meet the sunset. One of the guys had seen her too and held up his hand. Not a wave exactly, but an acknowledgment. And then later that same year, some of them had been out to the Fall Festival where the Lutherans were selling those awful chicken rolls. That was the first time she'd talked to a biker. He'd asked her how old she was. She'd just graduated from high school, so she didn't have to lie. And then Juan had come up and whistled at her. She'd thought about adventures all her life, and before she knew what was happening, she was having one. Sort of.

Now everything was neatened up. She'd gathered Juan's gear into a pile next to the sofa. Her plants didn't need watering. She couldn't get the carpet clean no matter how hard she scrubbed. And her pants were too tight for her to bend down anyway.

Then she heard the knock. People could just come inside downstairs because the lock on the big door was broken. At first she thought it was Juan, come back from wherever he'd gone, but he would have just blasted into the apartment like he was going to explode the place. Still, she went to open the door. She couldn't stop trusting people no matter how hard she tried.

"You OK? I took a run down from Moorhead to check."

Sandy stepped back. She didn't have a single idea how to respond.

Largo took one step into the room. When the apartment door closed behind him, he leaned back against it as if he were holding it shut. He had his leathers on, and his shades too. His hair was newly braided. In the little hall with the dirty cream-colored paint, he looked like the dark angel from some TV series.

"You OK, Sandy?"

It was her name that did it. Juan hardly ever called her by her name. She didn't like to think about the names he did call her. Her eyes filled. She pretended she had a cold and pulled a Kleenex from her jeans. "Sorry," she said, turning away and blowing her nose.

"It ain't my business, I know that. Just tell me fuck off if you want." He pulled his dark glasses off, squinted his eyes.

"Don't swear."

Consternation passed over his face. "I won't do it no more," he said, though Sandy wasn't sure that he even knew what he was promising. Most bikers used swearwords without thinking about it.

"You're not supposed to mess with another biker's old lady." Sandy made her voice as harsh as she could. Largo was looking at her cheek. He wasn't stupid; he must know what was going on. She had to lay down the boundaries fast.

"I ain't *messin'*." He paused, reached back to grab his braid as if to pull strength from it.

"Then why're you here?"

"Jesus, Sandy."

She was relentless. "Just a good Samaritan, right? Did you take care of lost animals when you were a kid?"

Largo shook his head. "I only had this one dog," he said.

But Sandy tore right over him. "I'll bet you rescued them from the pound and fed them hamburger. I'll bet every mutt in the neighborhood loved you. You just get off looking after the poor and helpless."

"Sandy, leave it be. I'll go." He was leaning back so far against the door that she expected it to collapse under his weight.

Her fists clenched. She moved forward, ready to shove him. But everything she touched turned to dust. Instead, she just glared into his face. "Don't you ever fight back?" she snarled. "No matter what people say to you?"

"I don't fight no women."

It was all just too crazy. Sandy turned away. If Juan came back, he'd kill them both.

"If you're OK, Sandy, I'll head on out."

Sandy looked at him, his black hair, his skinny mustache that appeared to have been charcoaled in. "What tribe are you from?" she asked.

"What?"

"Your tribe. You *are* Indian, right?"

"Half." He reached for the knob. "Chippewa," he said. "My ma."

"Does she live in Moorhead?"

"Died a long time ago."

They both stood silent. "You better leave," Sandy finally said. "Juan'll be really pissed."

She could see the color rise in Largo's face even under his tan. "He says one word, I'll stomp him dead," he growled.

"Largo." Sandy moved closer. "Go."

He hesitated.

"I don't need any more trouble."

That he understood. He turned the knob and stepped into the hall. In his throat, his Adam's apple went up and down.

Sandy reached out to close the door. She knew that she had to work this out for herself. If you made your bed, you slept in it. Biker or preacher's daughter, it was all the same.

Largo was starting down the stairs, two at a time. She called his name. He swung around.

"Largo," she said again. The syllables felt salty in her mouth. "Thank you for coming."

six

No one else in or near Eagle Grove gardened with raised beds. Everyone planted on flat ground, preferably on the extended rectangle of a former barn foundation, luscious with manure, or on a plot lovingly tended since Grandpa's time. Only Lighty Stuart had made gardening into a deliberate architectural act, her herbs and annuals and vegetables perfectly contained two feet above ground, each bed edged with walls of flat stones from the woods around her small house. She had three compost piles, each one in transition to the next. Every year she expanded her territory and built a new elevated bed.

Well, not every year. Not the year Eugene was born.

Today the mail must have come early, because although Lighty hadn't seen the mailman's car at the Hendricksons', her little red flag on the box was already down when she got far enough along her driveway to see it. The dented silver mailbox stood just slightly askew on its post, weeds reaching up to scrape at its bottom. She'd bought the second-biggest one at the hardware store, prepared to house any amount of message the world might send her.

But there were only ads in the box, and the Englund Lutheran Church newsletter. This year they were using yellow paper. Ed's pastoral message was shorter than usual. He'd probably been thinking about other things. He hadn't been out to see her for almost a month.

She'd known Ed for more than six years, Lighty thought, as she folded the ads and the newsletter into a tight wad and started back up her driveway. When they'd first met, he'd been building a house with the local Helping Hands project. She'd gone by to bring lunches, tuna salad made with olive oil instead of mayonnaise so it wouldn't spoil in the heat. And her homemade wheat bread. He'd been the first one down his ladder, and she'd thought he was a carpenter by profession, with his tool belt slung comfortably around his waist. His square Norwegian skull had pushed angles into his facial skin, but no one could doubt that he was a good-looking man. Then he'd had more hair too, slicked back into a smooth blond mat on his head.

She laughed, reached down to pluck a seed off a basil plant. That was what he liked best about her, she sometimes thought. Her hair. "I won't wash your feet with it, though," she'd said the first time, and he'd blushed, a bright spreading of color that went all the way down his chest. "I'm doing nothing I need forgiveness for."

She knew how she appeared to others. An older woman, long dark hair graying at the temples, body broadening. Clothes that hung loose, weren't stylish. Someone who went beyond salt and pepper and the dash of paprika, who used cumin and basil and lemon thyme, who dried her own herbs in bunches along her kitchen wall. Someone who had never joined the church, though she did go when she felt like it. Someone who walked in the woods at night, who swam in the creek, and probably not wearing a thing, though even the Dilmer boys couldn't get close enough to be sure. Someone who had had her suffering, and still had it, but didn't whine.

Through the self-portrait she was weaving, a sound inserted itself. A car, not his. Whose then? A sputter and bang out by the mailbox, then a reenergized rumble as if all the tenuous parts had taken a deep breath. Along the driveway behind her, the engine coughed and grumbled. She didn't give herself the indulgence of looking back.

"Lighty?"

She turned. A rusty old Mustang, window rolled down, driven by a young woman. For a moment she didn't recognize her. "Yes?" she asked, waiting.

"Can you help me?"

So sudden. No beating around the bush. And at the same time, though Lighty hadn't seen her for years, she knew who it was.

"Sandy. I didn't know you knew where I lived."

"I've been here before."

Lighty couldn't remember when. But she probably had. On a semipastoral call with her father. When the youth group had gone camping. Any number of possibilities. And why would she lie?

"I suppose you have."

The car door slammed shut behind Sandy. Her tooth glinted, her face stubborn and sharp. Only she was wearing makeup now, at least foundation. And dark glasses. "You raise stuff, don't you?" she asked.

"Quite a lot of stuff."

"And you know about herbal medicines and things like that?"

"Only what I've taught myself. Teas and things."

Sandy put her hands on her hips. She was wearing something loose and Mexican looking, so wide that her body seemed to run down the center of it without making contact with the fabric. Her hair was in two ponytails sticking out on each side of her face, every curl at war with the restraints. "Show me," she said.

"What do you want to see?"

"Show me the most interesting thing you grow."

Lighty smiled. "Plants don't operate preferentially," she said. "They're like children—all of equal worth."

"That's not true."

"What?" Lighty looked at her. Nothing came through the dark glasses except her own reflection.

"Not true. Some children are worth more than others."

"Oh, Sandy, I don't think so."

Sandy didn't reply. She bent down and broke off a spear of rosemary, rubbing it between her fingers. Even at a little distance, the smell colored the air. "I need something," she said, rubbing the rosemary harder. "I need you to help me with something."

Lighty said nothing.

"I need it right away." She leaned back, the round ball of her belly suddenly shoving against the Mexican tent.

"Sandy."

"I figured you'd be the one to ask. Because you know my dad and all. And live by yourself. You know how to keep things private."

Inside her chest, Lighty's heart thudded. "How far along are you?" she asked.

"Maybe four months. Five." She dropped the rosemary, a tiny crushed green ball. "Or a little more."

"Oh, Sandy." Lighty put her fingers out, almost touching Sandy's recalcitrant hair. "There are some things, yes. But you're too far along."

"So?"

"It wouldn't work. And it would be too dangerous. You might die."

"So?"

"Sandy. Your folks will help you. And what about your husband? You're not alone."

It was like a translucent sheet of plastic had fallen in front of Sandy's face, smoothing out all her expressions. She stuck her finger into her nostril like a child. "You didn't try to get rid of Eugene, did you?" she said.

"Why should I have? I wanted him."

"Did you know what was wrong?"

"Nothing was wrong until the end."

Sandy turned away. "I knew you wouldn't help me," she said.

"I would help you in any way I could. This is not a way I could." Lighty moved forward, holding her hands at her sides. Sandy looked so small. If she let herself reach out, she feared she'd damage her in some way.

But Sandy had made her own decision. She opened the rusty door of the Mustang, slammed herself into the seat, let the door clunk shut behind her. On her upper lip, little blobs of sweat were forcing themselves out through the makeup. "Thanks anyway," she said, her chin tilted up, her ponytails vibrating. "I just thought I'd try." She turned the key in the ignition as the old, poorly maintained motor rumbled into life.

"You know you can talk to your folks," Lighty said, raising her voice. "They'll help." She paused. "I know your father would help."

Sandy swabbed under her eyes with her fist. "You damn sure know more about that than I do," she said, and gunned the Mustang until it all but rose on its haunches as it circled around, tore through half of a peony, and headed back out to the road.

Eyes narrowed, Lighty stood watching her. The mail in her hand was sweaty under her fingers. Should she talk to Ed? Or would that betray a trust? Still, how innocent could he be?

In the house, dropping the crumpled mail on the kitchen table, its soft wood waxed to glowing, she heard Eugene cry. Along with everything else, his voice had been affected, and he sounded more like a machine than a person. It made it easier to think that he wasn't really suffering, and that was what she made herself think as she moved away from the table's glow and opened the door to the bedroom where he was kept.

When he'd been born five years ago, she had known something was wrong. Known it on some level beyond medicine, felt it even during labor, a savage attack that she'd endured with all the silence she'd accumulated in her independent life. And when Eugene had been thrust into the world, blue as the sea and attached to a ship's rope of umbilical cord that oozed around his shoulders and chest, he hadn't cried, not even this strange cry. His Apgar had been a three—not good, but not desperate. He hadn't nursed properly. Passive as he was, his eyes were seldom shut. His hands twitched. He made only a few clear sounds, up until he was a year old. Then he didn't make them any more.

Now he was sitting upright, strapped in his special chair from Social Services, meant to keep his blood circulating properly. They thought he heard things, so she kept the radio playing, but she no longer made sure it was tuned to talk stations. If children didn't learn speech by age three, it was too late. He didn't care if the music was country or jazz or classical. But he sometimes seemed to incline his head toward the sound. On top of his flaccid body, his high-cheekboned Norwegian face with its roof of white-blond hair seemed an ironic contrast.

She changed his diaper. Because he ate only pureed food through the tube in his stomach, his stool was always soft, a velvety green. She knew she was supposed to be revolted by the smell, but she had come to like it. It reminded her of the garden, where everything, no matter how lumpy or buggy or smelly, contained the magical possibility of growth.

seven

There had appeared to be no end to the boxes. But now, bending down for what seemed like the hundredth time in the hot early afternoon, Ed gathered the final armful from the closet in what had been Sandy's room and pulled himself upright, just barely remembering to carry the weight in his knees and not his back. Last year he'd had muscle spasms after every construction day if he'd exerted himself at all. This summer had been better. Perhaps he'd taught himself to move without strain, or at least to distribute the strain properly. Perhaps muscles could function independent of thought and feeling, both of which struggled tumultuously inside him.

"These last ones will fit in the cabinet in the garage."

Grace's face was as clear as the moon. Her hands stayed at her sides. Ed, tottering under the boxes as he edged his way downstairs, could barely keep himself from leaning the heap against the banister and wrenching every cardboard top open. What did he expect to find, he wondered? What relics could an eighteen-year-old have left behind to engender such savage hunger in him?

"I think that's the final trip." Grace held the door into the garage open, flattening herself so he could move past her without their bodies touching. "Then we'll have it all cleared out." She paused, her voice unchanging. "Once you're married, you're not likely to come back," she said.

Ed couldn't help himself. "But what if Sandy wants to retrieve any of her things?" he asked, dumping the boxes on top of the cabinet, then beginning to shove the smaller ones inside. "Will she know where to look for them?"

"We can tell her."

They'd only heard from Sandy once since the wedding, and that had been a brief phone call. Ed assumed she was still in the same Littleriver apartment. She and her husband. The word "husband" pushed itself out through his lips in a little hiss, though he hadn't intended to articulate it at all.

"What?"

"Nothing."

"All right."

If he hurried stowing these boxes away, Ed thought, he'd have the rest of the afternoon free. He could take a drive, ostensibly for church business. He could visit Lighty. He could make the veterans' meeting in Tomsville. He could abandon these relics of his daughter, stored tightly behind the plywood doors he'd built and hung himself, each box glowing with a heat that threatened to scorch the cardboard. He'd thought that once Sandy was gone, once she'd truly moved out, the tension of her presence would depart too. He had been dead wrong.

Grace stood looking out the window above the cabinet. A fine sheen of sweat veiled her forehead. "I didn't realize she'd accumulated so many things," she said.

"We could have just left them where they were."

Grace shook her head. "Sandy had already packed most of them away," she said.

"We could have called her to ask."

"We *have* called her, Ed. She's never home."

"Or she doesn't answer the phone."

"She has her own life now. It's hers to choose." With one finger, Grace touched the plywood door, then turned and walked back into the house.

And of course she's right, Ed thought ten minutes later, powering the Oldsmobile up Highway 10 to Tomsville and the veterans' meeting. It made perfect sense to pack the boxes away. Sandy wasn't coming back. She was as stubborn as he was, and braver. Somehow she had grown up a preacher's kid without being festooned by guilt. She could make her mistakes and not condemn herself for them.

Two deer were standing in the road up ahead, unusual for the afternoon. He braked. They watched him for a moment, then recognized the threat and sprang for the underbrush, tails alight. Beyond them, he caught the first glimpse of the Tomsville water tower, crisp and white against the sky. In less than five minutes, he had turned in under the railroad bridge and was pulling up next to the American Legion building where the veterans held their monthly meeting. Father Paul stood on the curb, talking to a bearded man in a wheelchair. Jim Edgars, from Jacoby. A mortar had torn his back apart in Hue. Now he was the town drunk, or one of them. People were tolerant, though. And Father Paul was always kind.

"Afternoon, Ed."

He slammed the car door shut, walked up to them. Jim's greasy hair hung below his collar. Father Paul, as always, was perfectly groomed. Ed had used to think it would be impossible to use that prefix of "Father" when talking to his friend, but now it had come to seem so natural that he couldn't imagine it otherwise.

"The rest of them are inside already."

"Any particular business on the agenda?"

"Fall Festival parade. Donation to the monument fund in Fargo. The young guys are carrying most of the responsibility. They may not attend many meetings, but they can bring the cash in."

Ed slid behind Jim's wheelchair and pushed him over the threshold. Inside, the meeting still hadn't begun. It always seemed to him that people moved aside when he entered, turned their heads slightly, watched his back when he passed. But perhaps it was just the preacher phenomenon, that peculiar midwestern response to the chosen. The response to Father Paul was different, he thought, though he recognized that his judgment might be clouded.

The group was smaller now, in summer, when there were so many other interesting things to do and decent weather to do them in. Only three men were left from the Second World War, and today only Hans Eckstrom had made it. A few from Korea. Then their group from Vietnam. At their picnic ten years ago, Sandy had started calling them all "Grandpa," though she was certainly old enough to know better. Grace had scolded her about it.

None of the Gulf War vets came. Times had changed.

"You were at Cu Chi, weren't you, Ed?"

Ed turned around. Miller Rembert, the pharmacist, was talking to him. He'd spent his year in Nam typing news releases for his Marine unit, but it wasn't fair to scorn him for that.

"For six months."

"You weren't a chaplain then, were you?"

"No. Medic. I went to seminary after the war."

"Did they let you get away with not carrying a gun?"

"Usually."

Ed realized his voice was fading. He stepped back. As if in response, Father Paul joined him.

"Chaplains didn't carry guns either, Miller. Ed and I were defenseless together." He smiled.

But of course it hadn't been so simple. He'd been trained to shoot, but instructed to keep his .45 in his rack. Except for the day when the village, full of shabby huts and tiny closed-face women with cone-shaped hats, had sent out the child with the bomb under his shirt. He didn't want to think about that now.

Father Paul touched his elbow. "Let's sit down and get this over with," he said. "I have to be back at the rectory in an hour. Jeremy Knutsen and his fiancée are coming in for counseling. Not that I'll have much to tell them—they've been living together for six years."

"I shouldn't be staying too late either."

They settled themselves into the back row. The folding chairs creaked. Hans Eckstrom rose from his place, turned toward the flag, and led them all in the Pledge of Allegiance. Ed heard his own preacher's voice rising with the rest, promising liberty and justice for all as if it were conceivable that, if all the boxes were properly stowed away and all deceptions revealed and reconciled, such beneficence might be possible.

eight

"Missy, do you know anything about adolescents beyond your own poignant memories?"

"Are you crazy?"

"What a simple solution that would be." Alex turned from the pile of unfiled records on his desk in Memorial Hospital's admission office and drank deeply from a stunning alabaster mug with tulips carved in bas-relief on both sides. For reasons no longer clear to him, although he suspected they had once had something to do with getting off the farm, so to speak, he volunteered three evenings a month, driving down to Littleriver to help put things to right in the paper world of Memorial. He shared most of those evenings with Missy, the regular nurse, an ageless Norwegian with such white skin and blond hair that Alex had often wondered with the mildest of curiosity whether or not her privates were decorated in the same milky way.

"Is Burton asking you for advice about teaching the high schoolers?"

"Would that he were. But it's still summer. He puts them out of his mind until the first clang of the bell in September."

"So what adolescents are you talking about?"

"You haven't heard?"

Missy sighed. "Alex, dear heart, I hear quite a few things. Occasional gossip about the Reverend Olson, I fear. Discussions about whether Einar will actually go on a diet. Some talk about if the Littleriver Fourth of July celebration this summer will produce a record-breaking number of April babies. I must have missed your tidbit. Sorry."

"Burton and I have adopted."

"What?"

"Not adopted. Taken in. An adolescent. Richard Hagstrom."

"Is that the family with the perfect house?"

"Yes indeedy."

Missy stuffed a shaggy pile of photocopied forms into her top desk drawer. "How did that come about?"

"You don't want to know the bloody details. Literally. But his family has disowned him, at least for the moment. Burton and I, softhearted fairies that we are, have taken him in."

"You really are a nice man, Alex."

"Missy, I am deeply appreciative. But instruct me. I know he doesn't have to eat his Grape-Nuts. Those ghastly pop tarts are full of nutrients. But shouldn't he make his bed? It's doable even with only one functioning arm. And clearing off the table? Should we insist? Also the cat. Is it normal to torture a small furry creature, even one that bites you at every opportunity?"

"Does all this have to be answered immediately? Won't he be going home soon?"

Alex shook his head, swung his chair around, pulled out a file drawer. "Actually I would miss him if he did," he said, his fingers flipping through the folder labels. "He fills his space in such an interesting way."

On Missy's desk, the phone rang. She picked it up. "Dr. Mathison isn't here," she said. "But I can call him." She jotted something down on the notepad.

"Are we having a crisis?"

Missy waved her free hand, shushing him.

"I absolutely *love* crises. Notice that I understand the plural form."

Missy hung up. "They're bringing someone in. A 911."

"Crime in the heartland?"

"A domestic. Even the heartland has domestics, Alex. And not everyone's crisis is down around the pop tart level."

"Naughty, naughty."

Missy was punching in Mathison's number. She spoke quickly, then hung up. "He was on his way already," she said. "Another few minutes. They'll probably get here the same time." She stood up, brushed back her hair, anchored it in her neck. "I don't like these domestics," she said. "Half the time the woman goes right back after she heals up. More than half the time. Don't they have a brain?"

"Some people *like* pain, Missy."

"Oh, don't give me that S-M stuff."

"My, MY!"

Outside, a siren pushed through the air. An aide rounded the corner and hurried to the door. In a hospital as small as Memorial, the functions of Admitting and Emergency blended together in the low traffic hours. Anything too complicated could get transferred out to Fargo.

Alex stood and walked to the table by the pop machine, where a Mr. Coffee was bubbling. "Do you want a cup of the best to fortify yourself?" he asked. "It's glorious tonight. I ground the beans before I came in."

Through the big glass doors, the red lights were already revolving. "Afterwards," Missy said, pushing the button. The glass slid open. Two EMTs began to wrestle the gurney in. Half of it was covered with a blanket, which was heaving up and down.

"I don't need this stretcher!"

Missy and Alex looked at each other.

"I want to walk!"

The bigger EMT leaned over and put his hand on the woman's shoulders, trying to keep her flat. "Nothing so bad happened!" she yelled, her feet churning. "Keep your hands off me!"

The gurney rolled to a stop in front of Alex's desk. Behind it, the doors closed, then came open again. An older man, slightly frayed looking, hurried inside.

"Let me take a look."

"You couldn't even give me my shots right when I was a kid!"

Alex raised his eyebrows. His hand halfway in front of his mouth, he whispered, "I know who that is."

Missy looked at him, eyes wide open.

"It's Ed Olson's girl. Sandy. *That* little till-death-do-us-part didn't last very long at all."

Dr. Mathison was leaning over the girl, the blanket flung aside. His hands were on her belly. "Did you try to abort?" he asked, snapping the restraints on her wrists.

"No! I'm too far along!"

"Well, you're bleeding vaginally. And someone worked you over pretty well. What happened?"

The defiance tempered into a choked sob. "He got mad," she said.

Mathison shook his head. "We'll have to admit you," he said. "You need to be checked over. We'll try to stop the bleeding. Just let yourself relax."

For a moment, the blanket quieted. The EMTs were pushing the gurney toward the elevator. Then the voice rose again. Alex shook his head and shrugged.

"I need to make a phone call," Sandy yelled out. She was yanking her wrists against the restraints. "One phone call! Even in jail, for Christ's sake, you get to make one call!"

nine

The ride down from Moorhead had never seemed so far. Largo swung into the soft curve outside of Tomsville, leaning forward over the handlebars, pushing his Heritage Softail toward the east with all his 190 pounds, with all the tight muscles in his legs, with his boots gripping the foot pegs so hard that he felt the vibration of the pavement rising up through the soles. There wasn't a car on the road, and a good thing too, considering the speed he was going.

The roar of the Harley motor rose around him. Sandy loved that sound. Juan, that dipshit, gave her a hard time because she liked it so much. "Harley Mama," he'd said at the club last week, giving her a shove. "Harley Mama, kiss my fucking biker ass."

Largo chewed on his lip. The rushing air dried the spit before he could even feel it. Dan the Man had always been good to his women, kept a clean tongue in his mouth when he was with them. Largo had tried to give them his best shot too, at least when he wasn't wasted.

Those years were gone. Largo twisted the throttle, and the big bike screamed down the highway. And Dan was gone too.

Buried him in his colors, though. More than a hundred choppers made the run to lay him down, all the old strokers and the new ones too. Dinger's Knucklehead from before the war. Like thunder. So much black leather you could smell it.

Shame. Goddamn shame. Even the tattoo couldn't bring him back, and, fuck, Largo had known that all along. All the girls in Whiskey Corners thought that Dan was *his* name, not Largo, when they saw the big blue letters on his arm. If he could of swallowed Dan the Man up and become him, he would of. But it didn't work like that. You were stuck being who you were.

Sandy had never called him before. Didn't know she had his number. Probably got it from Rocker at the clubhouse. She hadn't sounded so good when she'd asked him to come down. Her voice was kind of thick, like she was hurting.

Why in the hell had she got herself mixed up with that Juan, who couldn't even talk to her like she was human? He must of been smashed to hit her. Sandy could hold her own with words. But she listened good too. Preacher dad and all, she could listen just as good as she could talk.

He was afraid she had been crying. Women crying made him crazy.

The Softail coughed once, then again. Shit. Something was running rough. Time to rebuild the goddamn engine before the run to Sturgis next year. Forty-five thousand and counting.

The powwow at White Earth was the last time I came through Littleriver, Largo thought, as he saw the city limits sign flash by on his right. I was just one more breed, one more city Indian. I'm in the tribe, but I'm no skin, and they don't let you forget it. At least I can get my teeth worked on for free, if the dentist at the rez ain't pickled. He ran his tongue around his mouth. Need a new bridge one of these days, he thought, shifting on the seat. And a new back too, if they get smart enough to work that out. Like Ole Waylon said, "If I'd of known I was going to live this long, I would of took better care of myself."

But, oh man, them days. Partying right on through. Every trooper in the western part of Minnesota had our number, but they never *got* our number. Dan the Man and me, we was running at the front of the pack. The new guys in the club, the prospects, they still ask about it, tongues hanging out. Never be like that again.

Jesus. This was supposed to be the corner. He'd forgotten how near the lake it was.

Largo shook his head. Last time he'd been at Memorial Hospital, he'd still had his ground pounder. Pecos had cut him right down his face. Nearly lost his ear, but they sewed it back on. Both of them had been drunker than ten bears.

The hospital loomed to the right. Largo dynamited the brakes, tilted the big bike into the parking lot. The carburetor sputtered as he slowed down, and two orderlies in white at the emergency room door turned to look. Why wasn't they taking care of the people who got hurt?

Sandy'd said Juan beat her up. Maybe she was going to lose the baby. Jesus. No biker hits a woman unless she likes it, and some do. But not Sandy. And her pregnant and all. Little gook baby. Shit, not gook. Wetback.

That Juan was probably in Tijuana by now. Hauling his sorry ass back where it came from.

Largo swung off the seat, put the kickstand down. The men were still looking. "You want you should put *your* ass on some class?" he snarled as he stormed past them, through the door, up the hall past the information desk to look for Sandy.

ten

Ed had always thought that Grace was at her best under fire—even her appearance stayed serene, from her forehead down to the long line of her neck. If turmoil had been engendered, she internalized it. But he had realized in the last years that she simply deflected turmoil, that it never came to her internal being at all, but slid off her into the earth, like lightning off a rod.

Now Grace sat looking up at the doctor, Mathison, that idiot, so strictly Lutheran that he attended the Missouri Synod church in Littleriver even though his family had been Englund members back from the days of its founding. Her face was clear. A beautiful woman, Ed thought, startled. She was that when I met her, and she still is.

"Most of it is superficial," Mathison said. "It looks worse than it is. What I'm concerned about, however, is the vaginal bleeding. That's why I took the liberty of calling you in. Sandy's only six months along—too early to save the baby. I've got her on some medication. She's up in 307, and I'll want to keep her there a couple days, at least." He ran his hand through his graying hair. "Maybe we'll get lucky," he said.

Grace nodded. Mathison turned to Ed. "Any questions, Pastor?" he asked.

"No." Ed tried to think of a further sentence, but nothing came. Then one did. "We respect your judgment," he said, sacrificing truthfulness for civility.

"You can see her once she's settled in." Mathison paused. The air was rich with the question that wasn't asked, and then, gleaming with righteousness, he asked it. "Where's her husband?"

"We don't know."

"Traveling?"

"He may be *now*," Ed said. You could get a distance in a few hours, particularly if you were guilty of something.

Mathison shook himself, a brief back-and-forth twist of his neck and shoulders. "I ought to report this," he said.

"Go right ahead."

"The police will investigate."

Ed envisioned Einar Hilsrud, flesh lapping his six-foot-five frame, unfolding from the Eagle Grove squad car. "Better get the state patrol if you want to find out anything," he said.

From her chair, her back bent slightly forward, Grace reached out her hand to the doctor. "We appreciate your kindness," she said. "I'm sure Sandy does too. We want to support her in every way we can."

Mathison looked pleased. "Why don't you go talk to her now?" he said. "I'll finish my notes." He looked at his watch, the kind that held every conceivable bit of information. "It's Saturday night," he said. "Got your sermon written, Ed?"

"Not when I last checked."

"A good Bible chapter will do."

"Unfortunately, Lutherans have to follow the order the Synod prescribes," Ed said noncommittally. Mathison knew that as well as he did.

"But there's always room for *some* personal inspiration."

When Ed had been a child, sermons had seemed to appear from the pulpit like acts of nature. He had never thought of them as being composed. When he built something—the cross on the Englund organ, their house overlooking the lake—*those* things were composed, structured by human hands. His hands.

Right now, however, as they stepped into the elevator, those hands felt separate from his body, attached only tentatively to his arms. Grace touched his elbow. "She'll be all right," she said.

"I had no idea she was pregnant."

Grace looked up at him. "Well, Sandy didn't officially tell us," she said. Her voice was soft, but as the elevator shook to a stop on the second floor, her tone lowered even further. "She's so young," she said.

So maybe she'll lose it, and we'll all be grateful, Ed thought, trying to remember Sandy at the wedding just six weeks before, trying to recall her body. Her belly had looked full in that gypsy skirt, but it had never registered any special meaning to him. Just like any Eagle Grove slut, knocked up on the backseat of that awful Mustang or God knows what else. Just like those little Vietnamese women with their endless babies.

The elevator hit the third floor, bounced, sank, came to rest. The doors opened. As Ed walked out, Grace slightly behind him, one figure appeared.

"Pastor Ed?"

The voice was breathy. He turned. "Alex Lacy," he said, reaching out for the hand of his parishioner, grateful for a normal interaction. "How are you?"

"Fine." A pause. "I saw her come in," Alex said.

"You're visiting someone?"

Alex rose just slightly on tiptoe. "I was volunteering at the desk." He settled back. "I hope she's all right," he said.

Grace gave him a little smile and moved forward next to Ed, her body inclined back toward Alex so that it seemed as if she were bidding him a lingering farewell even as she abandoned him. "We'll see you later," she said.

The door of 307 was ajar as they approached. The TV was on, but softly. "Go ahead, Ed," Grace said, stepping to one side.

But the gulf between him and the inside of the room held him back. Then an image of the nine-year-old Sandy dropped into his brain. She had been at the drugstore in Eagle Grove to buy something for Grace. What? He couldn't remember. And she had stolen it instead. "I wanted to," she'd said when confronted, her tongue between her teeth.

A jar of cold cream. That's what it had been. A jar of Pond's Cold Cream.

"Go in, Ed."

This time he could do it. Sandy was sitting on the bed nearest the window. Her brown curls were pulled into a snarled cascade on the back of her head.

"Hi, Dad." She raised her chin to focus on Grace behind him. "Hi, Mom. The doc said you were coming. I was mad at him for bothering you."

At first Ed couldn't see anything that marked her, nothing at all, and since she was wrapped in a hospital gown, he couldn't make out the outline of her body either. For a moment he wondered if the doctor was wrong about the pregnancy, if she'd been fooling him. Sandy, who didn't even like her little cousins.

She saw him looking. With both hands, she reached down, grabbed the cotton, and yanked it hard to each side. The little bowling ball of her belly came clear. "Yes, indeed," she said, releasing the fabric and patting herself. "It's the worst-case scenario."

Grace touched her shoulder. Sandy lifted her head, tilted her chin up. For the first time, Ed saw the marks.

"What happened?"

"I never learned Spanish."

"What?"

"That pissed him off."

"Sandy, that doesn't make sense."

She reached for the glass of water on the bedside table, raised it to her mouth with both hands. "He just got really mad," she said. "And I was stupid enough to laugh at him."

She's just another person in the hospital, Ed thought, someone we're calling on. Now he could see the black and blue marks on her neck, running up each side, and the big bruise under her chin.

She saw him looking. "I'd rather be strangled than punched," she said. "As long as it doesn't go too far. Though I have to admit I really don't like the kicking."

"Sandy!"

"Juan isn't much of a puncher. He likes his pretty hands." She looked at her own, lines of gray under the nails. "I know they're not clean," she said to her mother, her head tilted. "I was planting a fall garden when he came home. The landlord said it was OK. The hardest part was getting the broken glass out of the dirt. I just wanted some fresh lettuce before the frost came." She winked at her parents. "Vitamins are good for breeders," she said.

They could only nod.

"I figure that's maybe what I want to do to earn a living. If Juan decides not to come back. I could garden. Lots of old people have houses and gardens and can't do the work any more. I could hire out." She grinned, her tooth glinting. "I could probably earn quite a lot," she said, her hands resting on her belly.

"I thought you never intended to stay with him," Ed said, his voice rising into its preacherly mode.

"Hey, Dad. You married us. I said we might for a little while. It seemed like the right thing to do."

At that, Ed turned to his wife. But Grace was hurrying into the hall, her head down. Something had broken through her serenity at last. He felt a surge of sympathy, then struggled to push it aside. Someone was shouting down by the elevator.

"Who's that?"

Sandy turned too. "We'll know soon," she said, and smoothed the wrinkled gown over her belly. She swung her feet up on the sheets, then pulled the thin hospital blanket over her legs, but not before Ed saw the bruises on her calves and thighs. He *had* kicked her.

The noise from the hall continued. "Who's that?" Ed asked again.

"Don't worry, Dad." With the blanket pulled up over her breasts, Sandy looked like a tomb figure. "It's probably Largo," she said.

"Who?"

"One of my biker friends. He was at the wedding. But this damn hospital made me wait a long time before I could call him."

At that, a crash resounded from the hall. Sandy swung her feet out of bed, wincing. Ed reached toward her. "Don't get up," he said.

"I'd better."

"I'll go see what it is."

"I *know* what it is." She slid to the floor in her bare feet, pulled her gown around her.

Ed reached out again. She eluded his hand. Stomping feet banged toward them. "Sandy, that you?" said a voice, low-pitched and fierce.

In the doorway, hands on each side as if he were spreading the frame wide enough to enter, a man stood. Even from across the room, he smelled of sweat and oil. His hair was black and hung down past his shoulders. Deep lines slashed down on each side of his mouth, and even though it was night, his eyes were covered by silver-rimmed dark glasses.

Shades, Ed thought. They call them shades now.

"Sandy." The man moved his arms outward as if to embrace her, but he didn't. Instead, she stepped toward him and pushed the bush of his hair back. "You lost your braid," she said. "How long did the run take?"

"Forty-five minutes." He seemed to be trying not to look at her body.

"That was pretty fast."

Suddenly he looked modest. "The Harley is awesome on the open road," he said.

"I'll bet."

They inspected each other. Sandy put her hand on his arm, which was covered with tattoos. Ed saw some letters, a circling bracelet, a splash of red and blue. Then she pulled him around. "Largo, this is my dad," she said.

Holding his breath, Ed extended his hand. Largo looked at it as if questioning its identity, then held out his own. "I don't go to no church," he blurted out. "But when me and the brothers go after that Juan, we're going to do some surgery that he won't forget in this world or the next."

eleven

No moon. No stars either, because the sky was blanketed with clouds. But the yard lights stuck up from almost every yard around Weed Lake, and their patches of illumination ran ahead of the Oldsmobile as if on a board game, one square almost contingent to the next. The road sent up clouds of dust as they passed, each one golden in its splash of light, then dissipating into the darkness.

Ed glanced at Grace. Her eyes were shut. They hadn't said more than half a dozen sentences since they'd left the hospital. She clearly was accepting everything, carefully adrift on God's grace. The irony of her name had never seemed more vivid to him.

"Here we are."

They pulled into their driveway. In their hurry to get to the hospital, they'd left the garage door open. A small, belligerent, black-and-white creature stood precisely in the middle of the space, glaring at them.

"We've got a visitor."

Grace's eyes opened. "We should have closed that door," she said, but without rancor.

"Shall we just wait?"

"Try honking."

Ed pushed the horn. The little skunk stiffened as if it had been injected with a chemical agent. It lifted its tail, stamped its back feet.

"Oh dear."

Ed honked again. The tail went higher. Impasse.

"I guess we could spend the night here."

"Eventually it'll go. She'll go. The ones rummaging around are all nursing mothers this time of year."

Ed supposed she was right. "Should I walk around to the back and get my gun?" he asked.

"Let's wait. And we'd be smelling her for weeks."

Sandy had always been madly interested in small wild animals. The flying squirrel that had fallen and knocked itself out. The two raccoon babies. Endless chipmunks who came and went like solicitors. A turtle with a cracked shell that had never healed, and which finally gave up the ghost, legs and head sprawling limp in its cardboard box. Her mercy had been without limit.

"We could leave the car in the driveway."

Which they did many nights anyway. But the passage around the skunk still had to be negotiated.

"Let's just sit here for a few more minutes."

I suppose we could pray, thought Ed. For Sandy, for her baby, for that misbegotten biker crashing around in the hospital room. For all the lost and destroyed children of the world.

But what to ask?

Grace was leaning against the side window, watching the skunk. It had lowered its tail and was looking uncertain, if such an emotion could be assigned to that particular creature. Grace tapped the glass with her fingernail. It raised its head.

"She knows we're watching."

Ed glanced up at the sky. It was as inscrutable as ever. It asked nothing, gave nothing, trafficked in nothing. Perhaps, in a global sense, that was the definition of the divine.

Grace tapped again. The skunk started to walk away, toward the shrubbery. It made a point not to hurry. At the edge of the drive, it looked back. Its tail twitched. Then it was gone.

The Indians had believed in totems. What would a skunk stand for?

"Respect," said Grace, as if she had read his mind. She opened her door. "To an Indian, skunks represent respect earned through the evidence of the senses. Isn't that a curious thing, that a little creature could have such a big meaning?"

twelve

"If Rose insists on measuring the chicken roll contents this year, I for one am resigning." Alex hitched his jeans higher and slammed another tinfoil cookie tray down on the counter in the basement kitchen of Englund Lutheran Church.

"She doesn't measure them."

"Then what exactly is she doing when she puts her fingers around the finished product like pincers?"

"Shhh." Burton put his hand on Alex's shoulder, feeling even now after so many years a lift of the heart at the wiry gathering of muscles through the L. L. Bean shirt. *His* shirt, actually. Which made the contact all the sweeter, their two beings layered together in a sandwich of intimacy.

"What?"

"Shhh. Rose is coming. I can see her largeish ankles through the window. That means Mildred and Gertrud Chilson too. They always ride together."

Alex rolled his eyes, then lowered his head onto his arms, folded together on the counter next to a vast deposit of ground poultry for the Fall Festival chicken rolls. "I can't do it," he wailed. "We made the chicken rolls with them last year. I even got rubber gloves from the clinic so we could meet the county's standards of sanitation. Then we drove to the festival with frozen chicken rolls in untold heaps in the back of the van. We baked them in infinite quantities and fed them to further infinite hordes of festival goers, along with real mashed potatoes from the Amish and vats of carrot sticks from the Hutterites, and massive mountains of brownies produced by the confirmation classes of Englund, Grove Lutheran, Hegland Sygne, Immanuel . . . I'm forgetting some of them. But surely no more is required even of the Gay Lutheran Brotherhood. Surely . . ."

"Alex. Control yourself. We're only here for two hours."

"I should go home and check on Richard."

"I'm sure he's fine."

"How can you be sure? He's got a huge slice in his chest from the windshield glass. It took two incompetent doctors to stitch it together. His collarbone is broken. He's sleeping in that awful bed with the humps in the mattress that I keep telling you to get rid of. His parents aren't talking to him . . ."

"That's not true any more."

"Screaming over the phone is not talking."

"Yes, but . . ."

Like a phalanx of late summer bloom, the three heavy women entered the basement, each wearing what might have been called a housedress in the previous generation. Behind them, clinging to the banister with both hands, was a small figure with a funny blank face.

"Mildred, who'd you bring with you?"

Mildred, her hair a tight bouquet of permanent from Rural Beauty, turned back toward the stairs. "Hildegard Solem's girl," she said. The little woman, childlike but not young, took another step downward.

Alex raised his head from the table. "She lives around here?" he asked.

"Lives with her mother. Mongoloid. Doesn't get out much." Mildred leaned forward secretively. "Has a *past*," she said as she began to scrub her hands with surgical intensity. The water steamed and bubbled while the red crept up her arms.

Burton stepped forward. "Shouldn't I help her?" he asked.

Mildred cast an eye back. "She does most things herself," she stated, turning to Rose and Gertrud Chilson, who were sinking their hands into the first bowlful of chicken roll mixture.

"Is she a relative of yours?" The small woman was on the second-to-last step.

"Distantly." Mildred began to slam the chicken rolls onto a tinfoil cookie sheet.

"Can she cook?" Alex asked.

"Probably a little." Mildred lowered her voice. "She's not *bright*," she said. "But she wants to see the graves."

Alex's hands paused in midair. "Graves?" he asked. "Here?"

"Outside." Mildred shoved a finished tray to Gertrud Chilson, who slid it into the far corner of the kitchen counter up against the industrial-sized refrigerator. She lowered her voice. "Her grandmother was an Englund," she said, as if that explained everything.

"But if she wants the graveyard, why is she coming to the basement?"

"I have no idea," Mildred replied, her hands dancing among the chicken rolls.

The little retarded woman had completed the final step and begun shuffling her way around the basement walls. She stopped in front of each picture—Jesus in the garden, Jesus entering Jerusalem, Jesus in the temple. Pastor Ed hadn't chosen them, Burton knew, because they had that tinny brown look of old prints from back before his time as minister. The woman was examining each one.

"Pastor Ed and Grace have had their troubles lately," said Rose, suddenly seating herself on the stool in the corner. Her chicken rolls, though neatly rounded, did not seem to meet her standards of perfection as she glared at them.

"It's that Sandy."

"She's just the same as always."

Three more cookie sheets of chicken rolls went in the corner of the counter. Alex, stepping high, began bagging them and storing them in the big freezer. "I've always liked Sandy," he said. "Such an interesting young woman. Makes things exciting around here, I must say. A bit of excitement is always welcome."

The little woman had turned and was starting up the stairs slowly. "Shouldn't we help her?" Burton asked again, suddenly nauseated by the smell of chicken on his hands, by the steamy air of the kitchen, by the bulk of the three good Lutheran ladies.

"She can do it," Mildred said.

"Shouldn't I ask her?"

"She's deaf as a post."

"My goodness!" Alex slammed the freezer lid. "Doesn't her mother know about hearing aids? They're so *cheap* now. And insurance covers practically the whole price. They don't whine anymore either. Somehow the makers have managed it so that the batteries amplify only the important sounds, not the wind, or . . ."

"Nobody talks to her much anyway."

Alex sputtered. Burton kicked him from behind the counter. Alex yelped. The ladies looked up.

"Mosquitoes," Burton said, kicking Alex again. "*So* hard to get rid of them completely."

The chicken rolls were accumulating. The Fall Festival at Wish-bone was still a month away, but there was security in early preparation. "I hear you have a guest," said Mildred, unwrapping one of the last packages from the butcher. "It was kind of you to be hospitable." Her antennae were quivering. She clearly knew a good part of the story already.

"Richard's no trouble." Alex was holding his leg out of Burton's reach.

"Still."

Gertrud Chilson had begun to swab the countertops with an old dishrag from the drawer. She didn't believe in sponges. "His parents have blue sheets," she said.

"Do they really?"

Now Gertrud was working on the stove top, edging the dishrag beneath the burners. "Children should live at home with their parents," she said, scrubbing hard.

"Well, yes. Of course."

"He should be there now."

How could she be so sure? The need to justify their actions grabbed at Burton. "But we do have the extra room," he said. "Because, naturally, Alex and I occupy only *one* of the bedrooms." He couldn't believe those words had come out of his mouth rather than Alex's, and he looked for him to see if possibly their identities had become confused. But Alex had disappeared. "It was Richard's choice," he managed to stutter out.

Mildred thrust the last pan of chicken rolls into his hands, flattening him against the refrigerator. "Your friend went upstairs after Hildegard's girl," she said. "Helpful of him, I'm sure."

Burton rushed to a basement window, peered upward. He could see a bit of leg, a pair of heavy generic sneakers, and Alex's Nikes, all lined up neatly in the hostas that bordered the south side of the church's foundation. Then they all moved outward and disappeared among the gravestones.

"I'd better go see what they're doing."

The Three Fates nodded. Burton raced up the stairs, through the little church lobby, and down the outside steps. Pastor Ed must have mowed just the day before because the yard was perfect, cut to a low-napped carpet of green on all sides, and even the hydrangeas against the front of the church had been groomed into neat circles. He rounded the first bush and crashed into Pastor Ed himself.

"Sorry!"

"It's all right, Burton." Ed stepped to one side. "You're clearly in more of a hurry than I am."

"I didn't know you were coming today."

"Well, obviously the chicken rolls are in better hands than mine. I just brought a load of firewood for the pig pit. We took down the old maple that was hit by lightning last year, and I thought I might as well cut it up before I got involved building the Regersons' guesthouse." Ed looked at his hands, square and tan, with one blackening nail on his left thumb. "The hammer is usually a friendly tool," he said, smiling.

"Not one that *I've* ever become intimate with," Burton replied. He started to blush, an adolescent pattern he'd unfortunately retained. He swept his gaze around the churchyard, into which Alex and the small retarded lady seemed to have disappeared. No, they were in the far corner, where Alex was kicking aside some encroaching brush.

Ed started walking toward them, and Burton followed. They passed the Halverson stones, grass trimmed to stubble around each one. The white lamb, from which the inscription was almost worn away, was an Olsen-with-an-e. The Lessers, the current Mrs. Olsen's parents, were under matching granite rectangles, unusual pink stones that had been shipped in from Montana, as Mrs. Olsen had announced to everyone more than once.

At the edge of the graveyard, the wire fence was eaten up with wild morning glory and poison ivy, tangled together in malignant embrace. In the corner, Alex was still kicking at the ground. "How could there be a baby under there?" he asked, bending down to wrench away the undergrowth.

"What?"

"A baby."

Ed bent his head. His forehead creased. The wind lifted his hair, then laid it down slightly askew. He doesn't look like a minister, Burton thought. He looks like he got caught up in something a long time ago and went through the wrong door, then couldn't get all of himself back out again.

Leaning forward, Ed reached out and cupped his hand under the little woman's elbow. She turned and looked up at him. "Baby," she said, her voice so scratchy it sounded as if she hardly ever used it. Her smile was uncertain.

"This might be the base of a stone," Alex said, throwing handfuls of leafy detritus around him. "It could have been broken off."

"Baby," the woman said again, pointing. It seemed like the only word she knew.

Behind them, Mildred appeared, panting from her hurry. "Is she after that baby again?" she asked, wiping her hands on her apron in a businesslike way.

"What baby is she talking about?"

Mildred shook her head. "I didn't think she remembered about all that," she said, dusting off the back of the woman's blouse as if she were a piece of furniture.

By now Alex was standing upright. "Is it *her* baby?" he asked.

"Baby!" exclaimed the little woman, her smile widening. She slapped at Mildred's hand, then walked over and pulled up some artificial roses from where they stood impaled on the Erickson grave. She smelled them, then dropped them in a red clutter on top of the pile of disturbed weeds.

"It was hardly even a baby yet," sniffed Mildred. "Good thing, considering. Her mother had no idea how it happened."

Ed looked at them both. The little woman's smile was fading. He put his arms around her delicately. "Babies are important," he said, enunciating with abnormal clarity. "All babies go to God when they die."

She's deaf as a post, Burton thought, and retarded to boot. She isn't going to get any comfort from those words. But the little woman nodded and started back toward the church. One untossed plastic flower stuck out rakishly from her fingers.

The rest of them followed, Mildred in front. "Well, at least we finished the chicken rolls," Alex said, slapping the leaves off his hands.

"We always do."

At the church door, Ed stepped back and let Alex and Burton go in ahead. "I'll drive back home," he said. "Thank you for all your work."

"How's Sandy?" Burton hesitated. "You know that Richard Hagstrom is recuperating with us, don't you?" he asked. Somehow the two topics seemed related in some peculiar way.

"Word is out about Richard."

"It just seemed the right thing, considering." Burton paused. Oh, hell, Ed was a preacher who knew everything. "Considering that his parents more or less disowned him for being gay," he went on.

Ed nodded, but seemed distracted. "Sandy's in the hospital," he said. "Mathison says she's stable." He shook his head. "What a word."

Burton held the brass doorknob in his fingers. "I hope she's OK," he said. Then, "None of us is truly stable, I'd guess."

Ed turned toward the parking lot. "The Bible recommends a lot of things," he said. "Love your neighbor. Take care of those in need. Be honest and good. Love the Lord. Spread the word. But it doesn't say anything about stability, as far as I know. Even in the newer translations."

Behind them, in the cornfield across the road, four geese rose into the air with a great crashing and bickering. Too few to make a proper V, they fluttered clumsily toward each other, then set off in an irregular rhythm, honking unhappily. The men watched them rise, their hands lifted for shade against the sun.

thirteen

The bleeding had stopped. They didn't really know why, but it had stopped.

Sandy sat as straight up in bed as she could, the mattress back raised high behind her. It seemed like she'd lost weight; the bones of her pelvis stuck out on each side of her body, with the baby cradled in its lump in the middle. Even her belly button had started to stick out. Her body was being taken over, like with those flesh-eating bacteria, only she would get it back again all in one piece. If she was lucky.

She'd sent Largo down to the cafeteria to get her a salad. The look of mystery on his face had made her laugh. He knew what a salad was, she was sure. He'd just never had the responsibility of putting one together.

Last night he'd still been there when she fell asleep, straddling a chair backwards next to her bed. When she'd woken up this morning, he'd been yanking at the venetian blinds on her window. He said he'd slept. She had no idea where.

Her neck hurt. Other places too, if she thought about them. She didn't intend to.

There was a sound at the door. She thought it was the nurse. Her mom had left an hour ago to get supper for her dad. He wouldn't come in until tomorrow. There wasn't likely to be anyone else visiting.

"Sandy?"

She pulled herself up in bed, but she was already as high as she could get.

"Sandy?"

Not a nurse.

"Sandy, may I come in?"

Almost everyone said "can." The door was already opening. Lighty stood there, a small package in her hand. They stared at each other.

"I heard you were here."

Sandy pulled her hair back. "Word gets around," she said.

"Not just any word."

"Probably not."

There was a long pause. Lighty was wearing something that looked like a bathrobe, belted in at the waist with a tasseled cord. Her sandals were built on heavy soles, rubber probably. She'd tied her long hair back so that it swooped down over her ears. Everyone wears their hair back, Sandy thought, reaching for her own. I wonder why that is. Maybe because it's still summer. Maybe when the snow falls we'll all disappear under great blankets of hair.

"This is for you."

Sandy reached out her hand.

"I grew it. Them. Sage and sweetgrass."

"What's it for?"

"If you hang it in your house, the air smells better. Like the wind was blowing from the prairie. Also, you can burn it, a little at a time. In a clay dish. It brings good luck." Lighty hesitated. "I don't want to sound like I'm preaching," she said. "It just works better in a clay dish."

Sandy passed the package from one hand to the other. It was so light it seemed as if the paper covered nothing. She let it come to rest on her belly. When she looked up, Lighty was smiling.

"Are you all right?"

"You mean, is the baby all right?"

"Not just the baby."

Sandy lifted the package to her nose. The faintest green smell came through. "The bleeding stopped," she said. "I didn't try anything to hurt it."

"Don't go back to him."

"How do you know about all that?"

Lighty tightened her belt, moved towards the door. "Your father told me," she said. Her chin was raised.

With her thumbs coming up from underneath, Sandy pushed against the brown paper. The smell intensified. "I don't know yet what I'm going to do," she said, so softly that Lighty, who was already in the hall, had to lean back to hear her.

"Just be careful. You'll figure it out."

Sandy nodded. She shifted herself slightly, let her hands fall on her belly. A crooked smile came over her face as she shut her eyes. The paper parcel slid to the floor.

"I can get it!"

"Largo!"

"Who was that lady?"

"Someone my family knows. Give me that salad before you drop it."

Largo slid the salad into Sandy's hands, then knelt for the package, his colors stretching tight across his back. "They got more junk to put in salads," he sighed, rising with the parcel in his hand. "This smells weird."

"It's just plants." Sandy pressed harder on her belly. "Lean over, Largo," she said. "Feel this."

His neck turned red. "Shit, Sandy. This ain't none of my business."

"I just want you to feel it. They kick. Didn't you know that?"

"Man, Sandy, I don't like doin' this."

"Worried what Juan would think?"

With an explosion of hair, arms, his whole metabolism, Largo pulled back and sat rigid on the end of the bed, eyeing the salad. "It ain't none of my business, that's all," he said, looking around the room until his eyes focused on the window. The sun was tottering just above the small line of stores that led down to the center of Littleriver. He stared at it.

"You're not supposed to look at the sun."

Largo's face took on an air of desperation. "Why don't you just tell me to fuck off, Sandy?" he asked. "Maybe pull a job and do a little time in the joint? I'm just trying to do what you tell me to."

"Why?"

Largo put his big hands over his face, rubbed his eyes. He looked out the window again, then shook his head hard, as if to rearrange its contents. "Must be that stove," he said.

Sandy giggled.

Largo took out his wallet, opened it. He pulled out some snapshots, small square black-and-whites with grainy backgrounds, and handed them to her.

"Whose pictures are these?"

"Who do you think?"

She held them up to the light with both hands. "Someone with Indian hair in an awful short crew cut," she said.

Largo raised his eyebrows.

"And here he is, sitting on the steps waiting for somebody."

"My ma. Spent half my life waiting for her."

"Is this the reservation?"

"No. I grew up in St. Paul. East Side. Six months on one block and then we'd move. I could make you a map."

Sandy's face turned serious, and she handed the pictures back to Largo. "I know I called you," she said. "I was scared, and I knew you'd come. Rocker or Red Harry would've probably come too, but I was sure about you."

Largo blushed.

Sandy began to pick at her salad, after setting aside a large chunk of eggplant that had been perched on top. "Anyone can ride a motorcycle," she said, "but there aren't many real bikers." She looked over at Largo, a piece of lettuce gleaming against her tooth. "Who was Dan the Man?" she asked. "The name on your tattoo."

Largo looked at the blue letters on his arm. "A brother," he said.

"I've got a tattoo too."

"You got one?"

"Yup."

"It ain't the Marine Bulldog, I bet."

"Nope."

"Gonna show me?"

Sandy slid down to the floor, wincing as her bare feet hit the cold tiles. She hiked up her hospital gown until her legs were bare almost to her crotch. "Right there," she said.

"Jeez, Sandy."

"Right there." She jabbed with her finger. "See?"

"Looks like a mosquito bite."

"I didn't have enough money for a big one."

"Where'd you have it done?"

Sandy giggled, one hand over her mouth. "There was a booth," she said. "At the Hansford County Fair. I was still in high school. I think I even had a 4-H entry that year. Yes. A Brown Swiss heifer. I raised her at my cousin's place. Got honorable mention. Ten dollars, and I spent it on this tattoo."

"Can't even tell what it is."

"Do you really want to know?"

Largo shifted his position, his knees cracking. "Well, it ain't Betty Boop," he said.

"It's a magic carpet."

"What?"

"A magic carpet. And I wouldn't let the man put anyone on it. I wanted it empty. Ready to go anytime. For me."

"Where'd you think it was going to take you?"

Sandy was walking across the room, running one hand through the curly snarls of her hair. "Wherever I wanted," she murmured as she reached the closet. "With a little help from a friend and his main jammer. And right now, what I want is to get out of this hospital."

fourteen

It was one of those clear nights where the stars spilled light down the sky. The Milky Way truly seemed like a path to or from something. Sandy could never remember the names of the constellations except for the Big Dipper. And on the Harley, everything moved too fast to pick even that one out.

"Did you ever read Shakespeare, Largo?"

"What?"

"Did you ever read Shakespeare?" Sandy hunched herself up a little on the bitch seat and pushed her mouth against Largo's ear. The bruises on her neck hurt. Beneath her, the Harley's motor made such a roar that she wasn't sure he heard her this time either.

"What'd you mean? I didn't even get my G.E.D."

"But everyone reads Shakespeare. We did *Romeo and Juliet* in sixth grade."

Largo shook his head, sent his black ponytail into her face, then bent down over the handlebars. "The *bike* has a brain box," he shouted back at her. "*I* don't need none."

"Don't knock yourself."

Cresting the hill, the pistons slamming, Largo stayed hunched down. Sandy cupped her body to his back, her belly pushed into the curve of his spine, her arms right around his chest, her fingers hanging onto the leather of his vest. "Why do you guys call your vests 'colors'?" she asked, yelling for all she was worth.

"WHAT?"

"Your VEST! Colors! With Iron Riders printed on it. And those patches with the other words!"

"It's for our club! Our *colors*! Who we are!"

"Can anyone get one?"

Largo slammed on more speed. "No!" he shouted. "You *earn* it!"

Sandy's fingers felt along Largo's waist and isolated the patch with Dan the Man's name, her fingers reading the raised letters. The big bike was whining down the hill now, out in the country, past the turnoff to Weed Lake, near their destination. It was getting late; the powerful Harley headlight threw a cylinder of white along the gravel. It was like they were following their own trail even as they were making it.

"Hang on," Largo said. He took one hand off the handlebar and reached back, holding her thigh to the seat.

"I won't fall."

His hand still held her as he steered the bike around a long curve and then slowed it to the side of the road. Boots dragging ridges in the gravel, he pulled it to a stop. "This the right place?" he asked.

"Yes."

"You OK?"

"Sure."

"Your folks will be pissed."

"They won't know I left the hospital until tomorrow. I can run my own life, Largo. I'm not a baby anymore."

Now that the motor was quiet, they could hear the mosquitoes. Largo swatted at his head with both hands. Clouds of loose hair and insects whirled skyward. "You don't want to camp out here or nothing, do you?" he asked.

Sandy was getting down. "Leave the bike," she said.

"Here?"

She was already walking along the edge of the road, looking inward. The driveway was so poorly marked that she almost missed it. Only the mailbox, sticking out from its post, announced its presence.

"Here?" Largo shouted after her.

"Yes." She waved her hand. He pushed down the kickstand, swiped some invisible dust off his back fender, shook his hair again. She was already going up the driveway when he caught up to her.

"Who lives here?"

She walked faster.

"Come on, Sandy. Who lives here? You want to call home? We should of done that before we left town."

She was almost running. Largo took a deep breath, pulled his colors tighter around his chest, and hurried after her.

When they finally reached the yard, Sandy was surprised at how small the house appeared at night. Just a blocky shadow. The gardens stood in their raised beds with swatches of plants sticking over the top—it was too dark now to tell what the plants were, just black irregular blobs that moved a little in the evening wind. The house looked dark too, but Lighty might be there anyway, sitting and thinking. Or perhaps she was walking too, her head full of things that worked and things that didn't and how you went on with life anyway. Which I know too, Sandy thought, rubbing her throat.

"Sandy." Largo stood behind her like a wall, one hand on her upper arm. "You gonna knock? Who lives here? This is where you want me to leave you?"

"No."

"So why did you bring me here?"

"Shhh." Sandy turned and touched his lips, the little door under his scant Indian mustache, with her forefinger. "Wait here. I'll be back."

It was dark enough, even with the starlight, that once she had moved away from him toward the house, she herself looked like something planted in the yard, only strangely unanchored. Largo leaned back against a tree, slung his arm around its trunk, crumbled off some fragments of bark. Once she'd finished doing whatever it was she was doing, he'd have to bring her back to her apartment in Littleriver. Or would she go to her parents? He wasn't sure.

Would she want to go to Moorhead with him? His crotch tightened. Goddamn.

Now he could see a light in one window of the house, so dim and yellow it could almost have been a candle or a kerosene lantern. Some bird made a series of sounds. Birds were supposed to chirp, right?—but this one sounded more like a gargle. Largo cleared his own throat behind the back of his hand. Sandy paused, then stepped up right next to the side of the house. He could see the black line she made against the light siding, even the round mound of her belly. She was still a skinny kid in lots of ways. Couldn't lay her out on a Harley in *Easyriders*, for sure, like all those glossy broads in the pictures.

But still.

Up against the house, after she'd glanced back at Largo to make sure he wasn't following her, that he'd learned "Stay" like the obedient animal she pretended he was, Sandy stood on tiptoe so she could see in the window. She knew what she'd see. Eugene grew, but you could hardly tell because he was almost always lying down or strapped in that funny chair. She could hear the music from his radio, some old blues, maybe Leadbelly. She wondered if it meant anything to him.

The real question was, did he have a soul? And if he didn't, why didn't Lighty just turn him over to the county, or forget his feeding tube, or quietly, quietly leave something burning and go for a long walk through the poplars and pines, down to the creek where you couldn't see the house even in daytime, and where the flames would just be the crackling of the growing woods.

And if he did have a soul, how could God have been so cruel?

fifteen

In the Mercy Care Center in Littleriver, Bertha sat with a thin line of drool sliding down onto her collar. While they prayed, Ed kept an eye on it. Old Frederika had such bad cervical arthritis that she couldn't bow her head properly. Hilmar muttered to himself throughout the service, the logic of his raspy syllables having escaped Ed as long as he had been coming there. The others had their idiosyncracies too, along with their persistent faith.

Ed opened his mouth and let out a solid G as the piano player—little Mrs. Anderson, who was too blind to read the music but had all the hymns stored in her fingers—took off into "Abide with Me." No one was thinking of the *Titanic*, Ed was sure. But even if they were lonely, and it was likely that most of them were, someone was still with them. That was all that mattered.

"We appreciate your doing this, Pastor Ed."

Stephanie, the occupational therapist, said it every time. "Thank you," Ed responded as he took off his surplice and watched the aide from Jacoby wheel Bertha back to her room.

"They may not seem to appreciate it, but they do."

Ed tucked his Bible under his arm. "I know they do," he said.

Once he was outside the nursing home, Ed looked up at the sky. Some kind of front was moving in, and clouds were building in the west. If it started to rain, it probably wouldn't quit for a week. September was always like that.

His eyes still raised, Ed reached down and took out the list from his pocket. "Service" he crossed out, having just completed it. "Father Paul" was scheduled for tomorrow—some kind of consultation at the rectory about the kitchen remodeling. "Alex and Burton" hadn't been accomplished, but he crossed them off anyway. They had each other. Whatever muddle they were in with Richard Hagstrom, who was back in school now and at least halfway off their hands, they could figure out together.

But then there was "Sandy." Ed stood still, moving his head from side to side. When he'd stopped by the hospital that Monday morning, she'd been gone. Just gone. Hadn't checked out. Hadn't said anything to anyone. Her apartment in Littleriver had been empty too, a disarrayed swirl of dirty clothes, twisted magazines, and exuberant houseplants, which he'd found himself watering with the teakettle before he'd realized what he was doing. And Sandy had always been so neat. The landlord said the rent hadn't been paid for almost three months, and he was evicting her and Juan anyway.

That had been a month ago.

Ed stood by his car, the Oldsmobile which his own Norwegian obsessiveness kept immaculate. Now there was a tiny ding in the windshield on the passenger's side, which his insurance would surely cover. But how could he replace a windshield which had only a minuscule imperfection in it?

"Take me with you."

He jerked around.

"Take me with you. I've got money if you want it."

The voice came from inside his car through a half-opened rear window. An ancient woman was perched on the back seat, her purse on her lap. Her white hair lay braided across the top of her head; her butternut face underneath it was drawn as tight as a drumskin. Her jaws were stretched full. She wore a strange conglomeration of pink and blue, over which she had a heavy gray sweater. The old ones were always cold. Even in Vietnam, the grandmas had had tatttered sweaters wrapped around them when the monsoon winds blew.

Ed bent down, opened the door. "It isn't far," she said to him, smiling, the enormous Medicare teeth a caricature in her old face.

She must be from Mercy, of course. He reached out his hand.

She took it, turned it over, rubbed it with her thumb. "Too many calluses," she said. "For a preacher."

"I work as a carpenter too."

"You're not the first." She giggled, a rough ripple of sound.

"Shall I walk you back to your room?"

She put the purse between her knees and pushed them together. "Thank you," she said. "I'd rather die."

"What?"

"Than go back. Yet. I need to get something."

"They'll worry about you."

She looked at him firmly. "They have no interest in me whatsoever," she said.

Truth will out. Ed walked around to the driver's side of his car, slid in, and started the motor before he turned to her, his arm on the back of the seat. "Where do you want to go?" he asked. "Just tell me."

The old woman leaned forward and ran her fingers along his arm. Then she took out her teeth, top and bottom plates, and placed them on top of her purse. "Big Loon Lake," she said, her speech blurred but still understandable. "The south side. Where the old chapel used to be. The old Lutheran church."

"All right."

It wasn't that far. And her need for the destination seemed so pure. What with Hilmar's mutter and Bertha's drool, they'd never miss her at Mercy, at least not right away. And what else was he required to do? The list was as completed as it was going to be. Yes, he should check with the authorities again about Sandy, though she was an adult and hence not high on their list of concerns. As for him, Sandy had stretched his love for her so long and so hard that he felt the cord pulled almost to its limit.

Ed turned the key in the ignition, accelerated, moved down the road past the eternal rummage sale sign. Then Silver Moon Lake and the little drive-in. Big Loon was only five miles beyond. There were always loons there; they apparently liked the rough shoreline where their nests were safer. There was no public access, but County Road 16 swooped along the narrow end, and there was a trail back to the ruins of the old chapel. They might have to walk. He glanced back, estimating her strength.

"Watch the road," she said snappishly.

County Road 16 had so many upheavals in its blacktop that the car seemed to plunge from one ripple to another. Someone had mowed the weeds on the right side, and the fallen vegetation lay browning in the early fall sun. Behind it, a ways back, stood the reeds and cattails. The old woman watched out the window. She had put her teeth on the seat beside her.

"You've been here before?"

She nodded, but said nothing.

"The chapel's been gone for ten years, at least."

She nodded again. "We burned it," she said.

"What?"

She tapped her hand against the window. "It went up just like that," she said. "Just like that."

So be it. Ed thought about fires he had known—the forest fire in Krisgaard, where he'd worked as a ranger during summer vacations from seminary. The bonfire that had burned the doghouse after Sandy had let it run out of control—but she had already rescued Ezra, scorched and whimpering, by the time he'd managed to get the hose extended far enough to reach it. And in Vietnam, after the child had blown himself up, and Mike with him. A few matches, and the thatched roofs had gone up like orange candles. He'd never seen anything like it.

The woman leaned over the seat and tapped him on the shoulder.

"Yes?"

"Are you a Christian?"

Ed coughed. "I'm a Lutheran minister," he said.

"That'll do. Most days."

They were at the south shore of the lake. In the distance, he could see where the chapel had been, now overgrown with wild grass and rampant hollyhock stalks showing through next to the old foundation. He pulled up. "Can you walk there?" he asked.

She nodded and opened the door.

Maybe I should tell her my life story, Ed thought, as he opened his own door and hurried out after her. She was almost skipping down through the waist-high weeds toward the ruins of the old chapel. Maybe she's strange enough and wise enough to give me good advice. Every mistake I've ever made is catching up with me, Ed thought, and I just keep on making them. How can I go on proclaiming the resurrection of the Body and Spirit when my own soul, if I have one, is anchored to the ground?

Grace. Sandy. He brushed a branch away from his face.

Lighty. Eugene.

By now the old woman was crawling through the hollyhocks. The back of her sweater rose and fell. It seemed to be a private mission, and Ed slowed down, inspecting the bristly tangles on both sides of the pathway—quack grass, milkweed, goldenrod. He checked his watch—suppertime at Mercy in an hour, and he'd need to get her back for that.

His fingers came up against the shredding bark of a tree trunk at the edge of the path. It crumbled, leaving a sticky residue. He brought his fingers up to his nose, but the smell was no more than the drift of earthiness. Yet there seemed to be a presence in it, or somewhere. He looked around. There was no wind; the woods stood quiet. The old woman had disappeared.

Puzzled, Ed looked upward, directly at the soles of a pair of sneakers. For an absurd moment, he thought they were some kind of paired fruit. Some farmers stuck old boots on fenceposts, a kind of folk art. Had one of them graduated to trees?

He looked further. Above the shoes, sitting in a niche where a horizontal branch joined the trunk of the tree, was a boy, a young man, one arm around the trunk, the other in a sling against his chest. His blond hair lapped down across his forehead. His face, in the dappled light, was pale.

"Hello there." Having caught his breath, Ed sought civil discourse.

The boy nodded, seriously. He said nothing.

They looked at each other. "You're from around here?" Ed asked.

The boy nodded again, then shifted uncomfortably. "I was watching for deer," he said.

"Good place for it."

"Maybe."

"Are you from Eagle Grove?"

The shingle of hair slid downward. "Yes," he said. "Sort of. My parents are. But I don't live with them anymore."

By the ruins of the chapel, the old woman was chortling happily. She must have found what she wanted, Ed thought.

"I live with Alex and Burton. They took me in after the accident." The boy took a deep breath, wobbling the limb. "I'm gay," he said.

Various pieces crashed together in Ed's head. The old woman was hobbling back toward them both, her hands outstretched, her fists closed. "The seeds were ready," she said. "The hollyhocks. They have the double pink. It's hard to find. I'm going to plant them at Mercy outside my window. It's late, but if we have a long fall, they might even sprout before frost. When I was little, I made hollyhock dolls, me and my cousin. Mine were always best because of the double skirts. The very best."

Ed reached out an arm to help her toward the car, but she ignored him. He turned to the boy. "Anything I can do for you?" he asked. Perhaps redemption was possible if you started small.

The boy moved his legs towards Ed's shoulders. "My bicycle is over there," he said. "Actually it's Alex's, but he doesn't use it. I can steer it one-handed. That's how I got here."

"That's good."

The boy smiled. "My name is Richard Hagstrom," he said. "You probably know that. Everyone in Eagle Grove knows everything about everybody." He touched Ed's right shoulder tentatively with his sneaker. "It wasn't so hard to climb up here," he said. "But you could help me down. I guess coming down is always harder than going up. I figured that out for myself."

sixteen

The terraces down to the lake were so dry that even Burton and Alex's best efforts hadn't kept the annuals from drooping. Pitiful clumps of marigolds and petunias lay wan against each other, their leaves brittle. The fall perennials—chrysanthemums, late phlox, the low spatters of dianthus, and Sweet William—were better equipped to withstand the drought, but the little annuals had no reserves. It had looked like rain last night, that was true. But nothing had come of it.

"I have, and I repeat 'I have,' given up on the grass completely," said Alex, draped in the teakwood deck chair overlooking the terrace and the unmoving lake. "There is nothing to mow. My feet leave a trail of dust even in the grass. It is no longer possible to jog, and my waistline will soon declare its natural flabby outlines."

"Pity," Burton said. There was only one deck chair, and he was squatted on the stone steps that descended to the dock. "But I will love you in any case."

"Perhaps I should get out my bicycle," Alex said, sighing deeply and crossing his ankles. "Only, pray tell, where is my bicycle? It seems to have left the garage and found a new home."

"Richard uses it."

"Richard?"

"Remember him? He's staying with us."

"Oh, *that* Richard. Why should he want my bicycle?"

"I suppose because he doesn't have a driver's license or a car, and we're too far from anywhere to walk."

"Did he ask permission?"

"He asked me."

"Good. Miss Manners would approve. If she ever dealt in bicycles."

Burton let himself down on the steps and tucked his legs under him. He picked up a pebble and tossed it into the water. The ripples it made were the only sign of movement on the lake, and they lasted only a short time. He reached for his glass of sun tea, their outdoors drink. Very little was left. He raised it to the light.

"Proposing a toast?"

"Wishing I'd made more sun tea."

"Want mine?"

Burton looked over, surprised. Alex was exceedingly fastidious about his possessions, including such small ones as toothpaste and sun tea glasses. "You mean it?" Burton asked.

"I do." Alex stood up, glass in hand. "I've hardly touched it."

"Thank you, my dear." Burton took the offered glass, brushing his hand along Alex's fingers. "I appreciate it."

Alex sank back in his chair. "The Hagstroms keep calling," he said.

"I know."

"They seem perfectly willing to talk to us. But somehow I keep expecting the Gay Police to arrive at the door with a subpoena any moment. I feel there must be deep homophobic passions foaming underneath their superficial Scandinavian politeness."

"There probably are."

"Richard talks to them too. They didn't really disown him. I think he visits them sometimes. On *my* bicycle, probably. At least he has accumulated a boombox and several other electronic devices, as well as some shirts which are not mine. The *majority* of those he wears are mine, of course, but not *every* one. I'm losing track of my own possessions."

"You're nearer his size than I am."

"Not if I don't start exercising, I won't be."

"Alex." Burton reached over, touched his elbow. "You are in amazing shape for someone who eats only red meat, smokes secretly in the garage, and will be thirty-nine years old on Thanksgiving."

"You're very kind."

"Not kind—truthful."

"Sometimes I feel absolutely ancient."

"Getting old isn't so bad. We've got a good life to age into. Even my classes this fall seem promising."

Alex sighed and shut his eyes. "Richard is only seventeen," he said.

"I know that as well as you. Each of us is more than twice his age. Were biology rigged differently, we could have been his parents."

There was a pause. Insects whined. Then Alex sprang to his feet. "I don't *want* to be his parent," he said angrily, shoving the deck chair together into its folded form. One arm refused to bend, and he slammed it back against the frame. Burton heard a crack.

"That's our best outside chair!"

"Fuck *all* our chairs!"

"Alex!"

Breathing hard, Alex backed against the stone wall, holding the crumpled deck chair in front of him like a shield. "Do you realize that he's never *done* it?" he asked, his voice harsh. "Never cruised, never been kissed, never watched a porn video? He doesn't know any of the *words*, for Christ's sake. He looks at me as if he wants to get inside my skin. No *wonder* he wears my shirts. And when he checks over my gun collection with me, he is just one fucking cute little cowboy!"

"Alex! He still has pimples, for heaven's sake!"

"But his abs are really nice!"

"He's seventeen!"

Swinging around, Alex pitched the deck chair down the embankment and into the lake, where it floated like the wreckage of some ancient boat. "So what!" he shouted as he turned and raced toward the house. "I'm not!"

seventeen

"So how's it going?"

Largo put down his beer. He was stretching it out, but Rocker didn't seem to notice. The clubhouse refrigerator had something wrong with it, so nothing got really cold. Nobody had come to fix it yet. Usually Rocker got one of the brothers to do it. That was what the president did, kept things running.

"How long before you go back to the rigs?"

Largo had been working on the oil rigs in the Gulf every winter for the last five years. No, six. One foreman liked him and always hired him on. When it got cold up north, it wasn't a bad place to be—steaks every night if you wanted them, lots of videos, enough work so that when the day was over, you could always sleep. The money was good, and there was no place to spend it. You could live all the riding season on what you'd earned.

Rocker reached over and grabbed his arm. "Man, you hear me?" he asked.

"What?"

"You're not drinking enough to be wasted. I'm talking to you and you're not answering. What's going down?"

"Nothing."

Rocker sighed and stood up. Bikers never interfered with each other after they'd spoken their mind. "You riding with us on Saturday?" he asked. "The Angels are having their taco feed up north of Brainerd. Free booze and a good band. For once they invited *all* the Iron Riders, not just their pick of the month."

Largo swallowed a large gulp of warm beer. "I don't know yet," he said.

"Partying at the White House instead?"

Largo looked up, puzzled.

"Must be something pretty important if you can't go on a run with your brothers."

"I been on plenty of runs with you."

"Not in the last month."

It was no use coming belly to belly with Rocker. Nobody had ever won a fight with him. What came out of his mouth was hard to beat too. Largo said nothing.

"You in trouble with the law?"

Largo shook his head.

"Got a broad on your case?"

Largo shook his head again, but he hesitated for a moment before he did so. Rocker picked it up.

"No broad is worth blowing it between brothers."

Largo nodded. He raised the beer again, but the thought of that thick warm liquid made his stomach turn over. He stood up.

"Leaving?"

Largo nodded again. He didn't want to piss Rocker off. He kept all the compadres together. He was a good man, and a good biker too.

Rocker looked at him hard, reached out, gave him a handshake. "Poker party Friday," he said, not asking, just telling.

"Right."

"See you then."

Already Largo was outside, so he didn't have to nod. He swung on his Softail as fast as he could, bumped over the curb and down Twenty-sixth Street to the light. With his right hand, he reached up under his colors and felt for the little pieces of cardboard in his pocket. Ivory, Vanilla, Snowflake, Country Cream. How could there be so fucking many words for white?

The motel was just on the edge of town, on the way out toward Eagle Grove and Littleriver. It wasn't fancy, but as far as he knew, it was clean. He'd done a few favors for the owner a while back, so the rates were low. But it couldn't be all that much fun living in one room, even with a TV. He was going to give it his best shot today, try to change Sandy's mind. First he'd buy some Kentucky Fried, with the mashed potatoes. He knew she liked that. Then he'd give her her choice about the colors. He could have his whole place painted before the weekend.

But what if she didn't want white? Sometimes women liked colors—pink, purple, that crazy stuff. He could use those too if she wanted. But she'd have to help him pick them out.

At room 107, the curtains were still pulled. She must have heard the Harley, though, because the door was open just a crack. As he thumped up to it, she pulled it wide. "Hi," she said, with a little smile.

"Hi."

"You're early."

Largo looked at his watch. It didn't seem early. It seemed like he'd been waiting since he was born.

"You got Kentucky Fried!"

He handed her the box. He'd been going so fast and thinking about her so hard that he'd almost forgotten that he'd stopped for it.

"Did you get coleslaw?"

He shook his head.

"If I don't eat some vegetables soon, I think I'm going to die."

Largo looked to see if she was smiling, and she was. He'd brought her a big bowl from the salad bar at Embers just two nights ago. Well, three. And they'd been out last week to Perkins, where she'd ordered broccoli. He was sure it had been broccoli because of those weird little lumps on top.

"I can go get you some."

"That's OK." She pulled a chair for him up to the little table. There was a pile of books on it. When he'd taken her back to her apartment that first day, she'd brought out a bunch of books with her clothes. He didn't read much himself, but he knew Sandy liked to.

"Were you busy today?"

Largo felt his pocket. "Shopping," he said.

"What'd you buy?" She was pulling the two sections of a wing apart.

Now was the time. But Largo couldn't remember what those paint cards were called. Consternation swept his face.

"Are you OK?"

He nodded. Maybe she'd know. He pulled out the little packet.

"What's that?"

"I forgot what they're called."

Sandy reached over and took the cards, fanning them out in her hand. "You *paint*?" she asked. "Are you going to paint something?"

Even though his mouth was full of chicken, Largo knew it was now or never. "Sandy," he said, swallowing on the second syllable of her name so that the sound choked halfway down his throat. "This motel ain't no place for you to live."

"Is it the money?"

"NO! I got plenty of money. It's just a goddamn little motel room. You sit here all day reading. It's like I got you in prison or something."

"That's not true. I go out and walk every day. Miles."

"This is no good place to walk. There ain't even a sidewalk. Some trucker could run you down and you wouldn't even have a chance."

She just looked at him.

Oh, hell. Largo took a deep breath. "Sandy," he said again, wondering why her name stayed so warm in his mouth. "I want that you should come live in my apartment. It's bigger and it's safe. I don't keep house so good, but I figured I could paint it. I brought the colors for you to pick." He caught his breath. "They got others if you don't like these." He thought about the vegetables. "I got a kitchen," he said. "You could make salads." It was his last-ditch appeal.

Sandy just stared at him. She started licking her fingers, one by one. "Where would I sleep?" she said.

"In the bed."

There was a long, long pause. "*Your* bed?" she asked.

Largo nodded dumbly.

"What about you?"

It had never entered his head. "Hell, Sandy," he said, standing up so suddenly that the chair tumbled on the floor behind him. "It'd be *your* bed. I can sleep anyplace." He took a deep breath again. "I worry about you," he said.

For a moment, a funny look passed over her face. He couldn't tell if it was positive or negative. Then she reached for another piece of chicken.

"How big is your kitchen?" she asked.

eighteen

"It's been quite a while, Ed."

"Maybe if your rectory had more construction problems, it would have been sooner."

The little priest raised his finger. "Remember, now, this is only a consultation. I suspect that the church council is going to want to hire Jim Reilly or the Polkowitz brothers. Not that they aren't good men. I simply fear they lack imagination."

Ed slashed his tape measure along the counter, jotted down the figure on the tablet he carried in his pocket. "This is a pretty adequate kitchen as it stands," he said.

"I'm not complaining. I would just like to be able to have a center island where I could chop, clean, arrange, season, and mix. The question for me is almost a religious one. A center of spirituality, if you will. All my deeper speculations dissolve in the trundling from stove to counter to refrigerator to sink."

Ed laughed. "You should have been a cook in Nam, not a chaplain," he said. Then he squatted and measured the floor. "There's room, you know. One of the new narrow islands with the little bulge at the end. You know the shape." He stopped.

"Ah, yes. Phallic, I believe."

Laughing again, Ed put his hand on Father Paul's shoulder. "I forget sometimes that the Catholics are the only Christians comfortable with sex," he said.

"Because we observe the sacraments of confessions and absolution, I have no doubt."

"And then you can go do it again?"

"Man contains original sin, unfortunately, as the vase the water." Father Paul pointed to an enormous vase on the counter into which more than a dozen fluorescent pompons of chrysanthemums were wedged. "It's a realistic philosophy, actually. Not that one doesn't try to do better. But failure is understood, even expected. Do you still like oatmeal-raisin cookies?"

"What?"

"Oatmeal-raisin. I keep a book of cooking references about my friends. Amazing how many different favorites there are. Some of them I've never heard of. Penderson, the druggist in Jacoby, yearns for something he calls Seamless Smiths. They have mashed bananas in them, and of course he doesn't remember his mother's recipe. I keep thinking it may appear to me in a dream. Not yet, however."

"Did you make me cookies?"

"This morning. I remember you getting those packages from your mother when we were in Cu Chi together. You always shared, even under the most oppressive circumstances."

Ed smiled. "And where did you hide this new batch?" he asked.

"They're in the dining room under Mrs. Terenzki's domed platter. She thinks I use it for the Body of Christ. I have never had the moral strength to disillusion her."

Ed walked through the door leading to the cookies. His smile had broadened. "When I serve communion at Englund," he said, "I use the plate I carved. Once when Sandy was playing around while I was working on a sermon in the office, she came in wearing it on her head. 'Big hat!' she said." Ed's voice softened. "She wasn't even in school yet."

"How is Sandy?"

"We haven't seen or heard from her for a month."

"Since she left the hospital?"

Ed lifted the heavy dome off the cookie plate and, after some careful thought, took three. "So you know all about it, Paul," he said. He remembered the little priest long ago in his chaplain's khakis. Back then, he had already seemed to be aware of the ramifications of everything.

"Ah yes. All is known. This *is* a small town."

"Yes, it is."

"How is Grace doing?"

"All right. I'm not sure. We don't talk much about it."

The two men, Ed in his jeans and the priest in his ragged cotton sweater with the sacred collar perched on top like a white saucer, sat down together on the two recliners in the living room. Ed brought his chair, the red one, to an upright position; his work boots anchored it on the carpet. Father Paul sat elevated like a small, tattered pope, leaning back in the afternoon light from the front window. Mrs. Terenzki's curtains were so pristinely laundered that they gleamed in competition with the glass.

"Ed."

Ed raised his eyebrows.

"I worry about you and Grace."

"Do you?"

"She's a good woman."

"Yes."

"You've been married a long time."

"True enough."

"Sometimes one has to wait for love to resume. It isn't continuous. It has its peaks and valleys. But there is an ongoing pattern."

"Apologies, Father, but how the hell would you know?"

No anger rose in Father Paul's face—in fact, it might even have become more gentle. "I've got a chore outside for you, Ed," he said, getting up. "But take some more cookies first. My housekeeper is a chocolate chip woman. They'll just get stale if we leave them."

Ed stood up. He shifted his tool belt without saying anything and started for the door. The priest looked at him as he passed, then followed him out. When Ed turned back toward him, his face was softer too.

"Tell me what you need, Paul."

"I think the drainpipe is clogged."

Ed looked up. The drainpipe plunged from the very edge of the roof a high two stories above him. "Couldn't get your housekeeper to take care of that one, could you?" he said.

"And I'm not comfortable with heights."

"Except for the final elevation, right?" Ed was smiling.

"The ladder is just around the corner."

"Will it reach?"

"Absolutely."

Ed walked over, upended the ladder, extended it to its fullest, and put it against the side of the rectory. Solid construction-designed aluminum, it held its angle firmly, and the rungs did not bend under his boots as he climbed up. "Want me to hold it?" Father Paul called.

"I'm fine."

"Sure?"

"Sure."

At the top, but not the very top, holding the final rung for stability, Ed reached up and felt for the opening of the drainpipe. His hand grasped wet leaves. "Watch out below!" he shouted.

Father Paul danced to one side.

Ed let loose the first handful, then the second. The wrist of his denim workshirt was damp. He grubbed around, got a third, then a fourth. Finally his fingers felt metal, and a sudden small gush of water came down and puddled on the stones underneath the drainpipe opening.

"Well done, Ed!" Father Paul called up, his face a small bowl of light beneath the ladder.

"Glad to help," Ed said as he climbed down. The reassuring rub of the rungs against the arches of his boot soles anchored him somehow, and when he stepped down onto the stones, he rocked back on his heels so he could retain the feeling of pressure for a little longer.

"I'll set you free now."

"Interesting expression."

"And probably an exaggeration of my powers," Father Paul said. "But come back with me for a moment, and I'll bag you up a meaningful sample of those cookies."

nineteen

"What time should I put him to bed?"

Lighty looked at Eugene, mouth open against his pillow, legs in the fetal position despite her best efforts to keep them extended. Then she looked at Elizabeth, who, at almost thirteen, took her every responsibility with the utmost seriousness, including her three little brothers, her slatternly mother, and all chances for earning spending money, of which babysitting was the most promising. In the last year, she had turned into a different person, the lumpy child with the thin blond hair suddenly becoming a tall slender Lolita, her breasts curving against her tank top, her legs long and flexible, so that Lighty kept thinking that if she looked at the right time, she would see Elizabeth tuck a toe behind her own ear as insouciantly as she might have a rose.

"Isn't he in bed already?"

Elizabeth touched Eugene on the head with a proprietary air. "I know," she said. "But I mean, what time should I read him his story and turn out the light?"

Oh, my dear, Lighty thought. You are a good young woman. "You know he doesn't understand stories," she said.

"But he might."

Lighty looked around the room. "Just leave the radio on," she said. "If you want to read him a story, fine, of course. Or sing him a song. That would be all right too."

"With the radio on?"

Lighty put her hands on Elizabeth's cheeks, marveling that the girl had almost reached her own height, that her skin felt cool even in the sticky air of the little bedroom. "Turn it off if you want," she said. "And then turn it back on again."

Smiling, Elizabeth nodded. "All right."

"Would you like anything to eat?"

A light came up in the girl's eyes, then faded. "I just ate," she said.

Could she be undernourished? Her little house on the back road didn't even have a decent refrigerator, Lighty knew, but they must have things in cans, and she knew that Elizabeth's mother kept a garden, where zucchini draped itself over the fenceposts and cabbages marched along like the bonnets of giants, big enough to be seen even coming up the path. "I'll put some cookies out," she said. "And there's some soup I made yesterday. And I have extra milk."

"I don't drink milk anymore," Elizabeth said.

Lighty nodded. "Fine. Whatever you like." She bent over the bed and put her hand on Eugene's shoulder. For years she had said, "Sleep tight," a piece of her old childhood rhyme. She didn't say it anymore.

When Lighty left the house, it was already evening. She heard Elizabeth singing as she walked through the yard, then turned and started up the road to the mailbox. In the descending dark, insects batted against her face, and she turned her head back and forth to discourage them. She'd forgotten to rub in her moisturizer, so they must have been attracted to the pure scent of her skin. In summer, fireflies would have risen out of the grass bordering the woods as well. As a child, she had never captured them in bottles. Instead, she had lain in the grass and hoped they would burn on her.

She used to be sure Eugene heard. The pediatric neurologist had said so too. But that had been years ago. As his brain shrank, as the cells imploded like collapsing stars, perhaps the auditory nerves were thinning too, sound coming fainter and fainter until it was only a twang in the great silence inside his head. Soon there would be no touching him through any conduit, no contact at all.

Ahead of her, the driveway opened like a tunnel to the light of the entrance to the country road. Chokecherry bushes, their black berries withered now, brushed her shoulders as she walked. In the dimming light, a procession of frogs leapt across the path, their hind legs extended so far that they almost appeared to be moving in two directions at once. A blue heron from the swamp, startled by something, squawked in three descending notes and took off with a splash. Mosquitoes hummed intimately from the woods. It was hard to believe one insect could separate itself from that swarm of sound and draw blood.

She reached the mailbox, stood with one hand on it. No need to check her watch; she could hear the Oldsmobile. He was always on time.

"Lighty." From his open window, he reached out and took her hand, holding it against his face.

"Ed."

"I always think you might not be here."

"I always have been here."

"I know. It's *my* faith that's lacking."

She walked around and seated herself by him, shut the door behind her. The aging car was immaculate, smelling of evergreen. Even the dashboard was free of dust. "It's a lovely night," she said, knowing that he would define it by the same terms that she did.

"Have you eaten?"

"I had a late lunch. Don't worry."

"Do you want to stop somewhere?"

"Where did you plan that we would go?"

They were already on the highway, heading west. "Maybe the little tavern in Rudolph," he said.

"They must think we have a passion for their batter-dipped walleye."

"I would hope that they paid no attention to us at all."

Both of them became quiet. It seemed impossible that no one spoke of their relationship, that there weren't signs to accuse them at every roadhouse where they might stop. It was as if they had slid into the water of wickedness without a single ripple circling out from their bodies. The town, which talked about everything, seemed to have fenced them off. Grace, who must surely have known something, never talked at all.

"What about Sandy?"

"I don't know. We still haven't heard from her."

"When is her baby due?"

"I think another month. Or a little more."

"Who is her doctor?"

Ed took both his hands off the wheel, holding it steady against his belly, and placed them on each side of Lighty's face, pressing hard for a moment before he let go. "Oh, my dear," he said, "I doubt that she has one. She'll probably deliver it in a stable, surrounded by Harley bikers." His voice cracked. "We can only hope some of them bring gifts."

They drove on. She didn't ask where he was taking her. He'd turned north before Moorhead, so they weren't going to Rudolph. She wasn't hungry anyway. Constant flicks of light passed the windshield as the whole insect population of the roadway moved through the illumination of their headlights, so many seduced and destroyed. Frogs hopped and were flattened. Lights by the side of the road raised the possibilities of eyes—deer, raccoons—all vulnerable, all at their mercy.

"Ed?"

He turned to her.

"You know I'm all right."

"I wish I could say the same about myself."

Lighty reached her hand out. It almost touched his thigh, but she held back that last inch. "Why do you stay there?" she asked. She didn't define the question further.

"Because I'm a coward, I suppose. A hypocrite at the very least."

"Perhaps no decision is the right decision." She didn't really believe that. Or did she?

"You sound like the sibyl."

"The sibyl?"

"The old woman from Mercy. I took her out to Big Loon Lake. She wanted hollyhock seeds from around the old chapel. All her statements were oblique. They made sense, but not with the geometry of this earth."

"I am not a sibyl."

Ed turned and kissed her hair. "I know that," he said.

"But I've learned to live with what I have."

The car stopped. She hadn't felt him brake; it was almost as if the Oldsmobile had done it of its own accord. She leaned back and put her head on his shoulder.

"You don't want supper?"

She wasn't sure if he'd go on. "No, I'm fine," she said.

"Aren't you tired of hearing me talk?"

"I think you talk to me in your head when we're apart and count it as conversation, Ed. But I don't hear that talk, remember?"

"Sometimes I think you do."

They were parked so near the trees that she couldn't have opened her door if she'd wanted to. "Tell me a story," she said. "About Lutherans. Or your life long ago. Or anything that changed you." They never talked about Grace.

"I don't know where to begin."

"Start wherever you need to."

"Back in Manfred, then. You know my family had always been Lutheran." His profile was steel against the side window of the car. "Or when I served in Vietnam," he said, each syllable clear.

"You never say anything about what happened there."

"Many of us don't."

"Was it so bad?" The air outside gleamed with insect life.

Ed said nothing.

"You don't want to talk about it?"

"Nothing can be done over. I did what I had to." He swatted a mosquito that had edged its way inside. "Some of it was bad enough, as you can probably imagine. I haven't forgotten any of it."

"Have you asked for forgiveness?" Lighty despised her own smugness, but the words came out anyway.

"I guess I thought the ministry would take care of that. Every nail I hammered when I worked construction summers to save money for the seminary, I looked upon as a supplication for forgiveness. Or maybe I'm just glamorizing it. I really don't know, Lighty. Eventually I came to feel that I was past it all, that God had granted me some kind of Protestant absolution." He touched her cheek with his forefinger. "But nothing is ever final."

Lighty leaned against him, thinking that they must look like aged teenagers, too shy to go all the way. "Not even absolution?" she asked.

"It seems not." Ed ran his finger down her cheek and around the curve of her chin. "There are times, and they're more and more frequent, when I feel as if I've done nothing but hurt people. How can you be absolved of that when their pain goes on?"

"You're not talking about me."

"Perhaps I am."

Lighty pulled away. "Don't be stupid," she said. "I made my own choices."

"And Eugene?"

"That is a whole separate thing."

"Only it isn't."

For a moment, neither spoke. Lighty put her hand under Ed's jaw. Men grew jowls as they got older. Women had wattles. All flesh edged downward.

"I think about him all the time."

Lighty's hand tightened against Ed's neck. "You don't have to," she said. "Leave him to me."

"I feel as if I condemned him before his birth."

"Ed! Stop it! You know the placenta separated early. His brain lost oxygen. If that hadn't happened, he would have been all right."

Ed grabbed her. She leaned into his mouth. Her body rose against his, and he pulled her against his chest. His fingers pressed into her upper arms. Slave bracelets, Lighty thought. She shifted her weight. He held on.

"Ed, that hurts."

His tongue was in her mouth.

"Ed."

He dropped his face to her breasts.

Bracing herself against the dashboard, Lighty pulled away. When his fingers loosened, she could feel their imprint.

"You have to let go of everything, Ed. Me included."

He didn't respond. Outside the car, in the dark woods, something made a guttural rippling sound loud enough to penetrate the glass. She looked at him questioningly.

"An owl."

Lighty rolled down her window and listened. Nothing. Only the trees moving in the wind. "Are you sure?" she asked.

Ed nodded. "Great horned owl."

"Aren't there legends about them?"

Ed nodded again. "The Indians thought that if you heard them hoot, someone you knew was going to die."

"Would a Lutheran minister believe that?"

With a half smile, Ed reached for her hand. "Probably not," he said. "Probably not."

twenty

"Man, you are killing yourself."

Largo bent over the clubhouse table from his chair and put his head on his arms without saying anything.

"I mean, killing as in *dead*. This is stupid, bro. She won't fuck you, she won't ride with you, she's a real wasteoid. If Juan comes back to town, he's gonna cut you up, down, and sideways. And you end up getting nothing for any of it. Get regulated, pal. Don't screw yourself with that broad."

Largo said nothing. His colors stretched across his bent back. Rocker looked down at him, then at the other two bikers leaning against the wall of the clubhouse. The ceiling fan was on high speed, but something was wrong with its motor, and it sent out a high-pitched whine that lay under their voices like a metallic platter. September had gotten out of control. Everyone was sweating. The room smelled of hot metal and salt. Even the glasses and beer bottles were sweating into small puddles on the table.

"No sense in it at all," Dinger said, lifting his bottle. Bendix nodded, wiping his forehead. They both looked past Largo to Rocker, who had called them together. The other brothers were coming as soon as they could, but it didn't take all the Iron Riders to explain things. Three should be more than enough.

"You want a woman, man? I got women from here to Grand Forks. Say the word and you can get laid by Jessie. Or her sister. The sister is hot, Largo. I mean, like in the magazines. Got hooters like basketballs. Likes it too, man. Puts out like there was no tomorrow."

Largo sat up straight. He took off his shades. Underneath, his eyes were baggy. He grabbed the beer—Bendix's glass, actually, but no one said anything. Then he poured it over his head. The raw smell of hops rose.

"Jesus, bro."

Largo shook the mop of his head. "Baptized in the name of the Beast," he said, the beer running down his neck. "Holy Harley water." He plunged his face into his hands. Beer oozed out from between his fingers.

The three men looked at each other. Largo's misery filled the room.

Sighing, Rocker sat down at the table too. He put his hand on Largo's arm. "You got her at your place now?" he asked.

Largo nodded.

"Her folks know?"

Largo shook his head.

"You could be in trouble, man. It's been a while, right?"

Largo rubbed his eyes. "She's free, white, and over eighteen," he said.

"Yeah, but she's knocked up by that Mexican dickhead, and what you going to do when that rug rat pops? Who's signing the papers but you? You'll be stuck with the support for the rest of your life if you don't pull out now. Sandy's gonna break your balls and make you pay just because you're so fuckin' *kind*."

"It's not my kid, Rocker. I ain't the dad."

"No lawyer's gonna give a shit about that. They don't do no DNA testing in Eagle Grove. What's eatin' you, man? You ain't no cherry. Sandy's OK, but she's just another broad. Cunt is the same all down the line. You know that."

Like a volcanic eruption, Largo jumped to his feet and slammed his glass against the wall. Shards scattered across the room. Rocker, Dinger, and Bendix looked at each other. Outside, the roar of Harley motors sounded in the distance. The brothers were coming. Good thing.

"Shut the fuck up!" Largo yelled, his voice hoarse. "Just fuck off, you guys. You supposed to be my brothers, right? Die for each other and all that. You ain't never had the vision! You know from nothin'. You come in and take it all away. Smallpox blankets, the booze. You . . ."

Rocker grabbed his arm and held him. "Drop that Indian shit, Largo," he said. "You know that ain't about us."

Largo glared at him as if he were a stranger. Then he rolled back his sleeve. "See that?" he said. "I got Dan the Man on my skin. When he went, I fasted. Did the dream vision thing. Cut myself. Paid four hundred dollars for this tattoo. Best they had."

"You know we all got patches on our colors for Dan after he passed."

Largo caught his breath. "Yeah, I know." He slapped his cheeks with both hands as if he were setting his head more firmly on his shoulders. "But you know," he said, his voice eerily quiet. "This is for real. You read those Cavalier poets? Those knights with the armor? All that shit?"

"Largo, what the hell you talking about?"

"Listen. I learned something in school. When I made it there. You want it bad enough, you die for it. And you die laughing. Live the day. Be a man." He put his hand alongside Rocker's cheek and patted him like a child. "Made me a fuckin' biker," he said. Then he grabbed his leather jacket off the back of his chair and headed for the door.

"Where you going, bro?"

Largo ignored him. "I love her," he said, his voice breaking. "It's stupid, and I ain't proud of it, but there it is. She can have any part of me she wants, any way she wants it. I'll cut it off and mail it to her if I can't give it to her personal. And if she don't want no part, that's OK too. I'm just a fuckin' breed biker asshole, but I fuckin' love her to death."

twenty-one

"Well, I'm sure Lutheran Missions put *all* our quilts to good use." Mildred shook her head firmly and took another stitch. It was so early in the morning that the light entering the basement at Englund Lutheran had only begun to penetrate the two windows behind the quilters.

"Is it Tanzanika? Or the Ivory Coast? In 1994 it was Nigeria. I'm sure I remember that right. Or one of those little countries that used to be called something else?"

"But weren't they all hot?" Mrs. Lund, her bad hip still a symbolic presence in her life, cared mightily about the heat.

"Even hot countries get cold sometimes."

"At Sygne Solem, they did bandages. For years. But then the wars stopped."

"We've always done quilts."

"Nineteen last year."

"But that's only because Mildred took them on vacation with her." Gertrud Chilson nodded in Mildred's direction. "To bind the edges. We could never have done it so fast on our own."

At the corner of the big quilting frame, the one nearest the door into the kitchen, Grace stitched with her head down, saying nothing. All the women acknowledged that she was the most consistent and delicate stitcher, producing tiny, evenly spaced lines that never wavered. She used any needle too, not a special one, and even on the darkest winter days of quilting, when no sun shone and the overhead fluorescent in the church workroom seemed only to stir the gloom, she inserted the thread into her needle with only one accurate thrust.

"We aren't going to make nineteen this year," Mrs. Lund said, pulling herself upright and heading for the coffeepot. "There's been too much going on. We missed quilting just last week. Once in May too. And there were two days in January when we had blizzards. Even Elrich's Jeep couldn't get through. Worst I've seen."

"It was just as bad in 1937."

"But Mildred." Mrs. Lund handed her a cup of coffee, went back for her own, her hand on the small of her back, moaning slightly. "Only *some* of us were quilting in 1937."

"Doesn't change the weather."

"That's right."

Grace straightened her shoulders. Everyone looked at her. They were ready if she wanted to talk. Half of quilting was talking—about the flaws of husbands, the harshness of climate, the complexities of money. Everyone knew about Sandy. And about other things too. But if Grace didn't want to bring it up, no one else would either. That was the rule. No one asked direct questions.

"If we don't get rain, the late corn will dry up."

"The Andersons' field doesn't look so bad."

"They live on that slough. Groundwater is almost at the surface. They'll be the last to suffer."

"The weather report said it was coming. Starting out west. Another front. If it doesn't pass us by."

"If it just would rain enough."

"Maybe we should do a little rain dance," said Rose, with a barely perceptible giggle. Her chins wobbled cheerily above her pearls and the Peter Pan collar of her housedress. "It used to work. I think the Indians still do it. Or we could ask out at the reservation."

Grace stitched on. She smiled at the idea of a rain dance. It was tempting to think of such a simple physical system for fulfilling needs. But with her head bent over her work, no one knew she was smiling.

"Why do we always sew the Garden Path pattern?" asked Ethel, who almost never talked.

"We don't always."

"Seems like it."

"My grandmother had a Double Wedding Ring. Got it from her mother."

"That's a good pattern."

"The Log Cabin is good too."

"But we'd have to make matching swatches."

"We could do that. Buy fabric. We do sometimes now."

Outside, in the great silence of the September morning, someone drove up. The basement window by the parking lot was open. It was an old car, but it sounded well tended.

"Who's that?"

"Alice?"

"She's working."

"That's right."

"The man to tune the piano?"

"He was here last week."

Mrs. Lund got up, moaning again. She went to the window, looked out, turned back to the ladies seated around the frame. Her eyes were wide.

"It's Lighty Stuart."

Automatically everyone stopped sewing. "She never comes," Mildred said.

"Last year. She came once. She knows how to quilt."

"Where's the boy?"

Mrs. Lund looked out again. "I don't see him," she said.

"She never leaves him."

"Why not? He can't do anything."

"But what if the house burned? Or a tornado came? She'd be responsible."

Upstairs, the church door opened. Mrs. Lund sat down in a flurry of fabric. No one looked directly at Grace, who had suddenly stopped sewing, her hands lifted from the quilt squares.

There was a pause. The women explored each other's faces. "Grace?" Mildred said. The others kept their eyes hidden.

"Sorry." Grace's voice rose, louder than the descending footsteps, yet very, very soft, so soft that everyone leaned forward to hear her.

"Sorry. I pricked myself." Grace touched her index finger to her lips. "I don't think it's going to bleed," she said. "At least not much. Go on. Don't stop."

The footsteps ended. Lighty, wearing a long full dress with Indian embroidery, her hair pulled back, moved towards them.

"Hello, Lighty," Grace said, standing up. "How nice of you to come join us."

twenty-two

"Jesus, Largo, all I know is somebody said he's back in town."

"Who said?"

"How can I remember? I was soused. It was at Whiskey Corners. Nobody can remember nothin' after a night at Whiskey Corners. You know that."

"He sure it was Juan?"

"How the fuck could you miss that taco bender? Everybody else here is a fucking Norske!"

Largo stalked out of the clubhouse. He hadn't been feeling right, twitchy like something was poking at him. Why would Juan have stayed south of the border anyway? If he'd even gone there. Why would he leave his kid, even if that kid wasn't born yet? He was an asshole, but even assholes used their brains sometimes.

He was pretty sure Sandy didn't want any more to do with Juan. She didn't talk about him. She didn't seem to miss him. How the fuck could she miss him? He had goddamn near killed her and the baby!

With his head down, Largo started the search. Moorhead and Fargo, its mate across the river, weren't that big. He checked with the bartender at Whiskey Corners. He parked his bike down on NP Avenue and walked from one end to the other, stopping in all the grubby little shops, the Army surplus, the dirty bookstore. A couple of guys had seen Juan, but nobody knew where he was staying. They all started out talking pretty free, but the longer they went on, the quieter they got, glancing up at Largo's face, then down at his hands. Did they think he was going to blast them away, for Christ's sake?

It was an inspiration that made him check the Dorothy Day House back in Moorhead. All the bums who came through hung out there, three hots and a cot, and no guards breaking your knuckles. A little nun ran it. All the real bikers had some kind of job at least sometimes and wouldn't suck up to a place like that. But some asshole wetback might just give it a try.

Not wanting to scare anyone when he got there, Largo cut the Softail's motor and glided the bike up the driveway. He pulled back his hair and tied it down tight. If he saw the nun, he didn't want her to be upset. Although he wasn't sure if nuns still wore those long dresses or not. Maybe he wouldn't even recognize her as a nun.

The driveway back to the front door was lined with flowers. Walking carefully so he wouldn't disturb anything, Largo thought how much Sandy would like them—especially those big tall spikes of blue. They couldn't have a garden by his apartment—there was nothing on the ground but a parking lot. He'd bought her some plant—a fern, the lady had said—and she liked that, but it didn't have any flowers. Maybe there was something wrong about the air in the apartment. He'd wanted to ask Sandy about that, but he was afraid she'd think it was her fault in some crazy way.

Deep in his thoughts, Largo stomped up the front steps, concentrating on the screened door behind which he imagined the nun waiting to make a fool of him. He didn't even notice the man sitting on the porch, back in a wooden chair in the corner. When he heard the voice, it took a while for it to penetrate, and then it exploded in his head.

"Hola, compadre."

Juan.

Largo swung around. The nun in his brain shattered. Bending a little for momentum, he flung himself across the floorboards, over the oval rag rug that some nice lady must have donated. He crashed against the corner of the porch swing, abandoned it waving wildly, and pulled Juan upright by a wad of his shirt. Juan's hands shot out at his sides and his feet scrabbled against the porch floor. "Largo!" he choked out. "Let go of me, man!"

Largo did. Then, swinging from as far behind himself as he could get his arm, he coldcocked Juan right in the jaw. As he slumped, Largo bashed him in the gut with his left hand. He had never been much good as a two-handed fighter, but today he had it all together. He got in one more fierce punch with his right before Juan hit the floor, white-faced and coughing.

Holding himself in, Largo stepped back. He thought about his piece, but that would be carrying things too far. Words had to do it, even though the fucker wasn't all that good in English. He took a deep breath.

"I heard you was in town. I figured you was over here, like all them other wasteoids. Stay here if you want, if the nun will let you. But get one fuckin' thing clear. You don't go near Sandy. You lost any chance you had with her when you beat her up. She ain't yours. And if you try to muscle in, me and the brothers will run every Harley we own over your worthless wetback body until there ain't nothing left on the pavement but salsa!"

Juan didn't say a word. His eyes were shut. Largo thought about kicking him, but he had nothing to prove. He turned around.

In the shadows behind the screened door, a small figure moved. She had something funny on her head, but her other clothes looked pretty normal. "Oh, shit," Largo said, thinking he was going to have the cuffs on his wrists any minute. Then he realized that she was smiling.

twenty-three

"Richard, you don't seem like the kind of student who would want to write a paper on guns."

"Not *any* guns. Dueling pistols."

Ralph Smithies, the English teacher for the advanced class, sighed. Then sighed again. Any sensible human being would not have required his students to seek individual approval for each paper topic. He regretted his conscientiousness deeply.

"Where are you going to do your research?"

"The library."

"I know. But that's a terribly specialized topic."

Standing in front of the desk, Richard seemed to fade in and out of Mr. Smithies' focus. His hair was straggling down below his jawline as if growing its way into what people used to call a bob. He had the usual adolescent acne. Small melancholy bristles of a beginning beard were prickling through his skin. But he was wearing a splendid shirt, a little theatrical for Eagle Grove with its loose sleeves and silken sheen, but still impressive.

"I can ask Alex. He collects guns."

"Alex?"

Richard straightened himself, then slumped down as if someone had released a string. "My friend," he said.

Like every other faculty member at the high school, Mr. Smithies knew the story. He knew Burton too, who in his quiet way managed to get enormous amounts of work out of even the most marginal students. He suffered for it too, because he always got the numchuk classes assigned to him. Though occasionally the principal did toss him a tidbit in the form of a quarter of journalism.

"There's only room allotted for one personal interview in the footnotes."

Richard slumped further. "I have two months," he said. "There's time to get material from the university if I need it." He began to twine a strand of hair around his long fingers.

"What do you think your hypothesis might be?"

It was a loaded question. Dueling pistols looked like pure historic research. But Richard spoke right up. "That even though we can't change who we are, we can still stand up for our rights," he said, eyes gleaming.

"Well, that's a possibility."

"Even if we die for it."

Mr. Smithies had never seen Richard so militant. This must have something to do with the gay issue, he thought, but the connection seemed obscure. Or perhaps Richard was simply infatuated with guns like almost every other male adolescent.

Outside in the hall, someone shoved someone else up against the lockers. A yelp, then a scuffle. Mr. Smithies got up, but by the time he had aimed himself for the door, everything was quiet again. Not really quiet, just the shuffle-and-giggle quiet of high school during lunch hour at the cafeteria. Which was where Richard should be, dueling pistols and all.

"All right." Mr. Smithies reached out to clap Richard on the shoulder, then pulled back. He didn't think Richard noticed. "Try it. Let me see the first pages of the rough draft in two weeks. The final version isn't due until the week before Thanksgiving. You're ahead of the game."

Richard nodded, shifted his book onto his hip.

"Go eat lunch, Richard. There are only fifteen more minutes. They'll have run out of tuna fish casserole, or whatever the centerpiece is today."

"Meatloaf."

Mr. Smithies waved him away. Richard departed. The back of his head looked peculiarly flat, as if his skull were retreating into his brain cavity. It must be whatever he was doing to his hair, Mr. Smithies thought. Hard to know what someone like that would find attractive.

Once in the hall, Richard shut the classroom door behind him, then looked both ways as if he were about to cross a busy street. Eagle Grove High School had joined a new building to the old building when it had had to expand a few years ago, and down the hall from where he stood, the walls narrowed and darkened. The cafeteria was around the corner, protruding from the north side of the building like a malignant growth. Richard had no intention of going there.

Instead, he walked to the front door. There were no monitors at the table. No one paid much attention to who went in or out at Eagle Grove High. The table was more for decoration than anything else.

Outside, dust rose in great billows from the parking lot as an old car pulled away. Mrs. Mendergast's little pickup, miscellaneous picture framing material spilling out of its box, was nosed in as near the door of the building as it could get. She always had lots of things to carry, and she didn't like to carry them far. The principal's restored Eldorado had its own double space by the street. The hubcaps weren't genuine. Richard knew quite a bit about cars. He hoped his folks would buy him one when he finally went home. They seemed to be softening, though they never talked about the real topic.

Of course, he might not ever go home. Sitting on the steps, his elbow against Mrs. Mendergast's pickup as if it were a large friendly dog, he raised his other arm and sniffed at his armpit. He had never used deodorant before he went to live with Burton and Alex, and he couldn't believe that it worked. But only the very faintest hint of sweat came through the silken fabric of Alex's shirt. You didn't have to stink, even if nobody came close enough to notice. Life was not totally a set of unalterable circumstances.

The bell for afternoon classes rang, loud enough to be heard throughout the parking lot. Richard rose. Alex's guns were so pretty, amazing for something that could kill you. Shiny and smooth and perfectly proportioned. Although he wasn't really going to write about those specific guns, he sort of was. Smithies could think the paper was about dueling pistols or whatever. Some feelings were private, and that was just the way it should be.

twenty-four

Sandy had known her own mind. Once in Largo's apartment, she had taken to cooking with serious intent. The kitchen, while not as large as she'd pictured, had a decent stove and refrigerator, even though the freezer, supposedly frost-free, grew an impenetrable coat of ice in one corner. The sink came with a garbage disposal, and there was a semifunctional dishwasher, which she never used. Washing dishes by hand made her feel like she was in charge of her life.

"Where's your cutting board?" Cucumber in hand, big knife within reach, Sandy turned to the table where Largo was sitting, looking out the window when he wasn't looking at her. He'll develop arthritis in his neck if he keeps spinning around like that, Sandy thought, when she wasn't thinking about the gazpacho, which was her primary concern.

"What?"

"Your cutting board. I want to chop this cucumber."

From a distance so great that it appeared to involve interplanetary travel, Largo heaved to his feet. He was wearing a new shirt, the plastic ribs still forming the points of the collar, but his jeans were filthy, and his boots so dust-covered that Sandy could have written her name on either one.

"Don't got one."

"How do you *cut*?"

Largo sighed, his hands behind his back. "You don't wanna know, Sandy," he said.

"I'll do it in the sink." She leaned over the porcelain, cucumber and knife at the bottom. Her elbow rose and fell. She was wearing one of Largo's T-shirts, motorcycle cylinders and wolf's head overlapping each other on the back. It hung down below her butt, which seemed not to have expanded at all with her pregnancy. Underneath, her legs were bare, skinny as a child's. Her feet were bare too.

"What you making?"

"Gazpacho."

"What?"

"Cold soup."

"Some Mexican deal?"

"Well, I guess it's Mexican. Or Spanish. But it's really good, Largo. Lots of vegetables and garlic. Lots of vitamins." A startled look passed her face, and she reached for her belly. "This baby kicks so hard I don't know why I think he needs more vitamins," she said, giggling.

Largo stood up. He needed to say this. "You should see a doctor, Sandy," he muttered.

"Who's got insurance?"

"They don't mind if you pay cash."

"Who's got cash?"

He walked around behind her, looking over her shoulder, circling her back. "I got enough, Sandy," he said. "From working the rigs. You don't have to worry."

"Why should I spend your money?"

Largo opened his mouth as if to give a complete and thorough answer, then jammed it shut again. He stepped back, lifted one hand against his head, looked out the window over the sink into the window with the tattered shade over the neighbor's sink, pulled his ponytail, and sighed. The chop of Sandy's knife against the cucumber resounded like Harley valves that weren't seated right. He opened his mouth again.

"Just say it, Largo. I promise not to whup you."

Largo said nothing.

Sandy waited a moment, then turned to him. In the unventilated kitchen, her face was flushed, sweat on her cheekbones, her skin dark with moisture. She pushed back her gypsy hair. She looks more like an Indian than me, thought Largo. Especially with that knife.

"You know, Largo," Sandy said, standing on tiptoe so her face came up toward his. "You are just too damn generous for a biker. You paid all those motel bills, remember? And what am I contributing to the rent here? A sliced cucumber? Do you want me to get so in debt to you that I'll give up and do anything you say? Is that it?"

"Sandy . . ."

She rose even higher on her toes until he could feel her breath on his face. "I only want to get through these next weeks, OK?" she whispered. "When I have this baby, you can grab some doctor and give him a handful of money if that'll make you happy." She started to cry, but her face didn't quiver. The tears simply slid down her cheeks as if someone had poured them out of her eyes.

Behind his back, Largo forced his hands into fists, hoping to hear the joints crack. He dug his nails into his palms. If he let loose, he'd be touching her face. She'd be mad. She'd never finish that stupid soup she was making. She'd never talk to him again.

It was like her belly was a sun, ablaze under his T-shirt. He could feel it start to burn him. He shut his eyes. In his mind, a crazy image leaped up, that her tears would wash her body away. Water and fire couldn't live together. If he didn't do something, there would be nothing left of her, not even a chopped cucumber. He leaned forward.

"Largo, why are your eyes shut?"

He opened them. She wasn't crying anymore. She had moved back, but the sink was right there and she couldn't get back any farther. She straightened herself instead, her small square shoulders cutting a bar in front of his chest, nipple to nipple.

"Largo, why are you staring at my belly?"

He couldn't answer. Instead, he brought his hands around and held them in front of her face as if he were making a spell. She stared at him through his spread fingers, her serious eyes softening.

"Largo, how did you manage to cut yourself?"

He looked down at his hands. Both palms were bleeding. "Workin' on the bike," he said, though he'd been in the kitchen for almost an hour, and the blood was new.

"You should clean those cuts, stupid. They'll get infected." She turned on the sink faucet and wet the sponge. It was the same one she used to wipe down the counters, but he didn't say anything. No germ would dare come near Sandy anyway. When she turned back to him and took his hands in hers, first the right, then the left, he could hardly breathe. She'd hung on to him in the bitch seat, sure. But that was different. Now she was looking at him.

"My God, but your heart is pounding! Are bikers afraid of blood?"

He shook his head dumbly as she wiped.

"Do you have any Band-Aids?"

He shook his head again.

"Hold your hands up."

He did.

"Just keep them there a minute." She ran her index finger along his palms, looked at it. "It's drying," she said. "You coagulate well."

"What?"

"You're not a bleeder." She touched her tongue to her finger, looked at him with mischief in her eyes. "Joined for life," she said, and Largo's heart thudded louder than any Harley as she turned back to the cucumber. When she went on talking, he could hardly hear her.

"Do you have any kids?"

"What?"

"Children. Do you have any?" The curls on the back of her head bobbled as she chopped. She'd moved on to a green pepper.

"Daughter. She's in Takoma."

"How old is she?"

Largo hesitated. He'd been seventeen. No, sixteen. Betty had been working her way through all the boys of the junior class. But once the kid was born, there hadn't been much doubt. "She's twenty-seven," he said.

"Good God! How old are you?"

"Forty-three."

"Are you in touch with her?"

"Christmas. I send her some money. She's got two kids of her own now."

"Bet your wife would have liked a little more contribution than that when her daughter was little."

Largo bit his lip. "She wasn't my wife," he said. "And I was in the joint after the kid was born."

Sandy sighed and started chopping on a tomato. "Any others?" she asked.

"Just the summer children."

"The what?"

"The summer children. Some are here, some are there."

He had never thought it all that funny. All the bikers had summer children, or thought they did. But Sandy turned and looked up at him, her eyes narrowing, and burst into peals of laughter, laughing until she choked, until she bent over her belly, until she dropped the knife on the floor, where it bounced off the vinyl and slid under the cabinet. Largo got down on his knees and picked it up. He thought about chopping the tomato for her, but he had never chopped a tomato in his life, and he was afraid he would do it wrong. In his hand, the handle against the cuts in his palm, the knife felt hot. He put it on the counter. Sandy was still convulsing.

Then he finally did it. First he touched her hair, into which his hand sank as if through smoke. Then he put his hands on her shoulders, marveling at how firm they were even though she was so small, as if they contained bones and muscles like a normal person's. Her belly pressed against him at an embarrassing level, but he ignored that, not being at all sure her belly was really a part of her anyway, but maybe just a kind of carrier, like one of those car seats, which would cough out the baby when the time came and then retreat, untouched, to be just a part of Sandy again. He bent over and put his hand under her jaw, so happy that she hadn't stepped back or slugged him or sworn at him that he could hardly believe his luck, and started to raise her face toward his. Only then he remembered the bruises from when she had been in the hospital. It had been a while, but he jumped back.

"It doesn't hurt anymore," she said. But it wasn't an invitation. She raised her finger and ran it along his Indian mustache, smiling as if she had a secret he couldn't share. "No more, Largo," she said, but her voice was soft, and he hung onto that, hung onto it hard. "And I'm not going to the doctor anymore," she said. "Or calling my parents either, in case you've thought of that too. I'm doing this all on my own."

twenty-five

"What's up, Buttercup?"

"Man, Largo, we thought you was dead."

It was a joke, but not entirely. Most of the Iron Riders were hanging out at the clubhouse, completing a project they'd started two years ago of painting the walls in the big room. Now, as they approached the delayed finish, the original new paint had already faded. The fan rattled. The refrigerator whined. Outside, the Harleys stood aligned in a triple row—ape hangers, buckhorns, drag bars. Also the brand-new Fat Boy that Red Harry owned. He'd had luck in Vegas, plus a few good deals in other areas.

"I ain't dead. But I ain't staying."

The men looked at each other. You never gave up on a brother. "Good to see you, pal," Rocker said, knocking the toes of his boots together as he hoisted himself upright. "We're making a run up to Hinckley for the Muskie Feed this weekend. Ten bucks and all the booze you can drink."

It was an invitation, and Largo knew it. He nodded, not to accept but to acknowledge that he'd been asked. "How's the chopper?" he asked Rocker.

"Good, good. Humming. Rebuilt the motor. Getting it chromed next week."

"The chopper?"

"Sure. Now it's an antique. Like an investment. Bigger and better." All the brothers nodded, and Tarzan, the newest member, nodded the hardest of all. Then they fell silent, looking at Largo.

"Gotta go."

"You just come."

"Just wanted to make sure you pissers ain't killed yourselves over me."

Rocker shook his head. "You're the one killing yourself over *her*."

The air sharpened. Largo turned. "Watch your ass," he said. His voice had an edge, but it could have been anything—the weather, the bike, his bad back. Anything.

Outside, Largo climbed on his old Softail and started it up. He knew they were all listening, but he didn't care, and no one came out to stop him. He pulled into the street, down to the light, heading toward Highway 10 and out of town. It was later than he'd thought. Sandy had been reading, the book propped on her belly, and she had given him a little wave when he'd pulled on his colors and left. She didn't ask where he was going, but it wasn't as if she hadn't cared. She'd made that crazy soup, after all. What was the point of soup if it was cold? But he'd managed to swallow two bowls of it. He could feel the vitamins, huddled in hostile territory, setting up timid outposts in his digestive track.

The sky still had a rim of light in the west as he aimed the Harley in the direction of Eagle Grove. He knew where Sandy's parents lived, just a few miles short of the city limits, not that Eagle Grove was a city, for Christ's sake. You turned at the sign for Weed Lake—all the lakes seemed to be named for some stupid piece of nature. When the actual sign finally appeared, Largo squinted his eyes and swung the heavy bike across the blacktop onto the gravel, slowing enough to keep it upright. He didn't want to lay it down on the road tonight, not until he'd finished his business anyway. Though he didn't want to be gone too long either. Sandy might finish her book, even though it was goddamn thick. She read fast. She was a smart one.

With dust rising behind the Harley, swirling far enough forward so that he coughed on it, Largo felt a surge of pride. She *was* living with him, after all. And cooking too. Her folks might be mad, but they knew she shouldn't have that baby without seeing a doctor regular now that she was big. They'd help make her do the right thing.

Balls against the wall, Largo pushed the bike down the gravel as hard as he could, then turned in and braked it inches from what looked like a workshop, with boards stacked against the doors and a cart of used shingles drawn up at one corner.

There were so many trees around that the house looked like it was behind a dark curtain. Largo dismounted, set his bike upright on its kickstand, took a breath so deep that it flopped his ponytail against his colors. He rocked back on the heels of his boots. Then, head down as if he were attacking something, he charged toward the house, hit the doorbell with his thumb, rubbed his Indian mustache, and, when Ed answered, stared him right in the eye.

"Yes?" They must have been eating late, because Ed was still chewing. "Do you need me?" They'd met so briefly in Sandy's hospital room that Largo was sure the minister didn't recognize him.

"What is it?" Ed reached out and put his hand on Largo's arm. In his leathers, Largo stood dark as a bear on the porch, his face the only swatch of white. "Are you all right?" Ed asked because Largo was gripping the frame of the door as if he intended to shred it.

Behind Ed, Grace stood, a cup in her hand. "Coffee?" she asked. "We always have plenty of coffee."

Around them, some fall insect began an insistent hum. Forcing himself loose from the frame and into some image of politeness, Largo stepped inside. He and Ed weren't that far apart in size, but Largo's bulk dominated, and his big hand swallowed the cup of coffee without even grasping the handle. Both Ed and Grace were looking at him, slightly puzzled but ready to be kind. He could tell.

No one sat down. Largo looked at the cup as if he'd never seen one before. He held his hand out a little from his body. Ed was still touching his arm. Largo glanced at him, his face distorted in a spasm of discomfort.

"Do you have something you need to tell us?"

And with that, with that impossibly simple question, Largo felt a door open on a lifetime of untold puzzlement, passions that never made their way to words, the revolution that never came and the cocaine and the meth and the tequila and the bikes wrecked across the continental U.S. of A., and the oil-smeared hands and the pretty ladies and the not-so-pretty ones. "I got her," he said. "She's with me. She won't see no doctor. She won't. I all but got on my knees. Her belly is so goddamn big. Anything could happen. I know they're supposed to look at the baby. I mean, with that machine. So they can tell if it's OK. If she's OK. That goddamn dipshit Juan! He don't deserve her. Never did!" Largo waved his arm and the coffee arched onto the counter in a brown rainbow.

Grace stepped forward. "Sandy?" she asked. "Sandy?"

Ed gently pulled her back. "You know where she is?" he asked, his voice quiet.

"Goddamn right. She's at my place."

Ed straightened his back. "Will you tell us about it?" he asked, holding his voice down.

"What the hell you think I'm doing now?"

They walked into the living room. Grace poured Largo another cup of coffee. When she offered it to him, he looked at the empty cup in his hand as if overwhelmed by the geometry of dealing with two. Then, mercifully, Ed took the empty cup from him and set it on the coffee table.

"You know we haven't seen her for a long time."

"Yeah, I know."

"She doesn't want to contact us."

Largo gulped his coffee down, sputtering. A string of drops landed on his colors, sparkled off the leather. "It ain't that," he said.

"Isn't what?"

"That she don't want you." The waters were getting deeper. "I mean she don't talk about you much." His words began to scramble with each other. "She says you sew good," he choked out, turning to Grace. "Now, Sandy, she don't sew. But she cooks."

Ed and Grace looked at each other. "She never was much for cooking when she lived at home," Ed said, keeping his voice uncritical. "But my wife does most of that, so it's not surprising."

The three of them gazed at each other. Outside on the lake, some silly nighttime jet skier zoomed by, his motor sharp as a sting. "I thought you could get her to see the doc," Largo said, gulping down the rest of his coffee.

"We've never been much good at making Sandy do anything."

It was clear that there would be no resolution. "Goddamn," Largo said, starting for the door, slamming the cup on the counter with such force that it broke into two pieces. Both Ed and Grace rose, staring at him.

"Tell me where you live." Ed had his appointment book in his hand.

"You ain't gonna yell at her?"

Ed's voice was soft. "I have never yelled at Sandy," he said.

Reciting like a school child, Largo gave his address and phone number. "It's them apartments in Moorhead next to the place with the kids," he said. "The daycare. She's always home. She don't go out much."

"Is she still bleeding?"

Largo turned bright red. "I don't know nothin' about that," he said. "She sleeps good, though."

There was a moment of silence. Largo caught his breath. "I mean, I hear her," he said. "Breathing. She don't wake up till morning." He seemed to be digging himself in deeper and deeper, and he backed toward the door as if expecting frontal attack. "I ain't *with* her, I mean," he sputtered as he stumbled out onto the porch, Ed and Grace following. "I mean, she's got the bed." He was halfway to his bike, walking sideways, his colors flopping.

Ed stepped down too, but didn't follow. "Where do *you* sleep?" he asked, unable to help himself.

Largo swung himself onto the bike. Just before its engine roared to life and his boots left the ground, he looked back at Ed, his black hair tumbling into his eyes. "On the floor," he said. "In my sleeping bag." The Harley coughed. Then, above its ascending rumble, Largo shifted his weight and swung the front wheel around. "So I'll be there if she needs me," he yelled, dust rising around him like a halo as he hit the road again.

twenty-six

Ed checked the address scribbled in his appointment book. He knew he'd never have been able to remember it, and he'd been right. Once he'd reached the city limits of Moorhead, even the location of the daycare that the biker had mentioned had completely slipped his mind. He was grateful that he'd retained sufficient organization skills to write down something to guide him.

It had been a quick trip. The roads were essentially deserted, even though it was nowhere near midnight yet. Only on the intersection with Highway 9 had there been something going on—flashing lights, a policeman in the road beckoning traffic forward with his flashlight. No way to know exactly what had happened.

And now he was in front of Sandy's building. He pulled to the curb and turned off the engine. In the heavy dark, the place didn't look too bad—a skimpy three stories, with the first level halfway underground. Brick, at least on the front. A small strip of lawn between the sidewalk and the building itself. A front door with dim lights stuck on the wall to each side.

As Ed looked at them, one blinked and went out. How often did that happen? He hoped it wasn't a message of some sort.

Bent over the steering wheel, Ed ran both his hands through his hair. The music station of National Public Radio played softly, some tune almost too sentimental to be classical. He had no idea what it was, but the small line of stringed instruments made the darkness inside the car more animated, more alive. Less lonely.

But what did he have to be lonely about, after all? Grace had stood by him through everything. With an irony so sharp that it pierced him, Lighty had too. The tragedy of Eugene seemed less and less real, his needs so swallowed and encompassed by Lighty's never-ending acceptance that, God help us, his vegetable existence seemed almost enviable. And Sandy, perhaps up there behind that blurred light? She remained his daughter through every wild, self-destructive act that she carried out. Perhaps more his daughter because of them.

And the little boy in Vietnam. Brown eyes, narrow and bright. That loose shirt, hanging down to his knees. The edge of a smile when he reached for the detonator. Then gone.

God's children. No, *his* children. The fire burning around all of them.

Ed started up the car. His U-turn brought him nearer the lawn of the apartment building. It looked as if someone had been digging near the brick facade. Surely it was too late for any kind of a garden.

On the way back, the commotion at the Highway 9 intersection had disappeared. Ed slowed at his Weed Lake turnoff, but then went on past. He drove down the highway a little farther, then edged his car down the main street of Eagle Grove, so dark everywhere that, if he hadn't known them all so well, he would have been hard put to distinguish one house from another. There was still a light in the rectory, though. Father Paul was awake.

From somewhere in the back of the main street, he heard a subdued roar. Motorcycle. The riding season wouldn't last much longer. Snow came in November more often than not.

Another U-turn. Ed drove out of town. At the highway, he turned west, toward his own road. Another turn, and he was threading his way along the gravel.

Grace would be asleep. Would the skunk be in front of the garage again? He smiled to himself. Probably not. It was getting too far into fall. She—if it was a she—would be settling in somewhere that was protected.

Like all of us, Ed thought. That's what the church does. Gives us somewhere protected to settle in.

He turned into his driveway. No skunk. No lights in the windows. Somehow, though, he didn't feel protected. Whatever his tenuous relationship with God at this moment in his life, it didn't seem as if protection had any part in it.

twenty-seven

The Church of the Sacred Nativity in Eagle Grove was bigger than any of the Lutheran churches. Built in the 1950s and faithfully remodeled twice in the ensuing years, it hugged the ground in traditional midwestern ranch style, with only the steeple erupting from the north end to give it a spiritual identity. The rectory, on the other hand, dated from the 1920s and stood two houses away. Mrs. Berneson, who owned the house in the middle and had owned it since 1932, had refused to sell it to the church, or to the diocese, and even a visit from the bishop had made no difference. She was too old to go out much now, but she had never relinquished power of attorney to anyone. Even the presence of Father Paul, of whom she was fond, changed nothing. The Catholic Church, which had waited with infinite patience for so many things in its history, was waiting with less-than-infinite patience for her demise.

This late at night, there wasn't a living being on Main Street in Eagle Grove. The only tavern was on the main highway just outside of town, and any partying, even of a mild rural nature, would take place there. No one in town stayed up late. Even the teenagers were in bed by midnight, or so far away that their absence contributed even more to the silence than their presence would have.

This is a stupid place to do business, Rocker thought, leaning against the door of the church, back far enough under the roof so that his dark figure was only a vertical streak of intensified darkness. More sense to be meeting the guy at that bar outside of town. But maybe these hick customers figure that they might as well give God a good eyeful right on his own turf.

His customer wasn't showing, though. Not the first time that had happened here. In the Cities, you kept your appointments. If you didn't, you got stomped. Out here in the sticks, customers were a whole lot less dependable. But then, he was working the lower end of things these days. If standards were falling, he had only himself to blame.

Still. In the old days, he'd have been worked up. Not any more. Even that Largo, the champion dickhead of all the brothers, didn't make him mad these days. Of course, you tried to show him a few things. That was your duty with a brother. Only it was his life. He had to walk the line the way he saw it.

And Sandy was such a squirrelly little thing. Largo wasn't even sticking it to her, so it wasn't because she was anything special in the sack. Who knew about love? He didn't have a clue.

Squinting into the darkness, Rocker looked down at the illuminated dial of his watch. Not that the world was going to end if his customer didn't turn up, but it was pretty damn late.

He didn't even need the dineros. Just keeping his hand in. And his back was starting to hurt. The Iron Riders as a group probably kept most of the chiropractors in the area in business.

He'd count to one hundred. Slow. Then he'd take off. His Harley was down the block behind the car repair shop. No need waking up the whole dumb dinky town.

And, because Rocker always counted with his eyes shut, he didn't see the small figure walking up to the church until he heard the footsteps, jumped back, and opened his eyes. The big house down the block had a light in the window that he hadn't noticed before. What was going on? He didn't usually fuck up on something like this. Rocker had a reputation for doing business right.

"Are you in trouble?"

This ain't my guy, Rocker thought.

"I saw you standing there. For quite a while, actually. Sometimes it's hard to go inside. So I thought I'd come lend my support, for whatever it's worth."

Rocker felt like he was all tequilaed up, but he hadn't had a shot in a week.

The little man stood at the bottom of the steps, his face upturned. He didn't seem the least bit nervous. In fact, Rocker would have said he was downright mellow. It didn't seem likely the FBI would have bothered to establish a presence in Eagle Grove, or the ATF either. But the guy was *not* a steady customer.

"Our lives are full of secrets," the little man said. "Mysteries are only secrets of universal proportions. And without the malice. I sometimes think people travel so much because they want everything to come clear. And perhaps it will, at some place down the road. Or perhaps it *might*, to be totally accurate. But 'might' is often good enough. In this world anyway."

Rocker found his voice. "Right on," he said. He'd been down many a road looking.

The little man smiled. "I'm Father Paul," he said. "Perhaps we were meant to meet here tonight. For whatever reason. And it isn't necessary to go inside. I do, of course, but that's what they pay me for. You earn your living in other ways, no doubt."

Rocker could only nod.

Father Paul turned and went back down the walk, his head tilted backwards so that Rocker could just see snatches of his profile. "It's there for all of us," he said. "No fuss. Just be kind, if you think of it. That's the best we can do in this world."

twenty-eight

It had not been a busy night at Memorial. But to Alex that didn't matter. Usually he started out filing patients' records that had accumulated during the day, but then he sometimes expanded into tracking down charts, tracking down equipment, reassuring the occasional frightened patient waiting to be examined. Making coffee, however, was his most useful act, he often thought. A pot was dripping right now.

"Not very busy." Missy scratched her forehead, then her neck, then one ear. It was as near as a Lutheran ever came to crossing herself. Alex waited to see if she'd finish the gesture appropriately, but no.

"We'll be busy before the evening is over. As I massaged my third client today, I had an intense feeling of anticipation."

"You should have studied nursing."

"Ah, no. I know my limits." Alex liked not being a nurse. Massage therapists were in total charge of what they did. He was not immune to the delicious seductiveness of power.

Off in the silence, someone's beeper rang. Mathison's, it must be. He was on call, though that meant nothing much in

Littleriver, where most of the crises were handled by the supporting staff.

"And I should have gone to medical school," Missy said, not quite seriously. "We are all terribly underemployed."

"Probably good for our souls." Alex pushed his collar back. He was wearing his green shirt, the color of spring shrubbery. Richard had worn it too, but apparently not for long. Only the faintest yeasty smell hung in the armpits. "But you can still go, you know," he said to Missy. "Even the ancients are doddering through clinical rotations now. Callow youth has lost its savor."

"Its what?"

"Forget it." The beeper rang again. "Even this massage therapist is feeling a twinge of the literary tonight."

His words drifted off. Mathison was striding toward the desk, buttoning his white coat, which he seldom wore. "Incoming," he said, as if announcing a bombardment.

"What?"

"They're bringing someone in. Local ambulance from Tomsville. Get a gurney ready."

Missy began her duties. Alex checked the coffee, added a dollop of crème de menthe from the bottle in the back of his file drawer. Sometimes he tossed in a little José Cuervo or a touch of Burton's elderberry wine, from the year he had taken wine making seriously. The same year Alex had begun target shooting every other night.

"What happened?"

But Mathison had hurried away to the other side of the room, where a medical student from the university's outreach program was suiting up in his scrubs. Two aides-in-training joined them. There was a flush of excitement. No one enjoyed torn flesh, spilled guts, pulverized bones, of course. What they enjoyed was the rush, the sense of possible salvation. When the doors from the ambulance bay clanged open, everything was possible.

"Did Burton go to the summer conference?"

"What?"

"The conference. At Hudson. For the language arts people."

Missy, back at her post, gestured widely, encompassing both the chart rack and the coffeepot.

"I have no idea."

Missy stooped down by Alex, one ear cocked toward the door where the ambulance would be arriving. "It's different when you're two men, isn't it?"

"*What*?"

"You don't have to keep track of each other the same way." She sighed deeply. "You give each other your freedom," she added.

"Missy, I am once again clueless. Nobody gives freedom. It floats in the air like industrial pollution. You breathe it in. Then you either choke or take another breath."

"You're changing the subject."

"I don't even know what the subject *is*." Alex waved his hands helplessly in the air. He was still carrying some remnants of Hansford County clay around his fingernails, much to his distress. In a seizure of misdirected passion, he and Richard had transplanted all the bigger chrysanthemums that afternoon, almost guaranteeing their death. Only a very late freeze would preserve them.

"Alex."

"Missy, just have a cup of coffee." In the distance, the air took on sound. "Prepare for meltdown. I hear the ambulance entering the city limits. Let us singlehandedly raise the level of Hansford County medical care. Maybe they'll subsidize medical school for you if you save one more drunk or de-limbed farmer."

"You're bitter."

"What?"

"Bitter. Bitter, bitter, bitter."

The siren sounded louder. "I am *never* bitter," Alex said, rising, a shuffle of admittance forms in his arms. "Never."

Through the glass doors, the revolving lights of the ambulance sent fractured strips of color into the room. The siren choked into silence. Mathison stood to one side behind the hospital gurney, his arms alert. "Much calmer than on TV," Alex said, then realized that might have actually sounded just the tiniest bit bitter. Missy held the blood pressure cuff in her hand. Around the corner, in the waiting room, a Norwegian exchange student with a sprained ankle watched with Scandinavian detachment. Next to him sat a fat young mother with mucus-laden twins, whom she held back, one with each hand, when the sliding doors opened.

"No! Don't try to get up! Stay flat!"

The doors let in a wall of outside air. Through the opening came the rolling stretcher, manned by Fred and Henry, this evening's paramedics. The IV bottle swayed on its rack as they plunged forward. Fred's arms were engaged in holding down the body on the stretcher, which was doing its best to sit up. Blood spattered.

"Lemme up!"

"Stay down!"

"Lemme up, goddamnit!"

Mathison moved forward. Missy grabbed the side of the stretcher. They transferred the patient to the gurney with record-breaking speed, then crashed around the corner to the examining room, Fred flung half horizontal on top of the struggling patient. Henry scrambled alongside, wheeling the IV.

"Who is *that*?"

"Biker."

"What happened?"

"Cracked up on that bad corner where Highway 9 cuts across. Someone driving by saw the bike sitting in the ditch, still running. He was scared to get out of his car—thinking

Hell's Angels or something. He called in at the tavern. When we came, we found this guy in the ditch on the *other* side, unconscious. Woke up on the way in. Broken ribs, probably some internals, the usual cuts and bruises. No helmet, of course."

Mathison shook his head, lowered his voice, checked vitals. "He might need a CAT scan of the head," he said. "That means sending him up to Fargo. The ribs aren't so bad. X-ray of the abdomen too—I don't like the feel of that spleen." He bent over the figure on the gurney. "What's your name, fellow?" he asked. "Do you hear me? I need to have your name."

For the moment, the figure seemed semiconscious. Nothing coherent came out.

"Does he have a wallet?"

"Couldn't find one."

The figure on the gurney jerked, then lay momentarily quiet. One hand lifted. "You a doctor?" he asked, coughing and wincing.

Everyone looked relieved. "Yes," Mathison said, stepping forward.

There was a pause. "What kind of doctor?" the man said, spitting blood with such force that it laced up Missy's chest.

Mathison raised his hands. "A regular doctor," he said. "Now, what is your *name*?"

Suddenly the figure sat up, scattering everyone. Missy and Mathison plunged back in to hold him down. "You know about babies?" he asked, one hand swabbing blood from his face.

"What?"

"You know about babies?"

"What *is* this? You're not having any babies!"

The figure swung his legs off the gurney. He grabbed his chest, grunted. "Shit," he said, and leaned back. Then he reached out and grabbed Mathison by the arm with both hands, holding him above the elbow, straining his own IV connection until the tube cut straight through the air.

Mathison twisted away. "What do you want?" he shouted, trying to extricate himself, trying to get the man back on the gurney before he did himself permanent damage. Missy pushed futilely at the doctor's back as if she could anchor him in some way.

"Listen," the man said. "You can do what you want to me. I've laid 'em down in the road before." He wiped the blood away from his mouth, his eyes glinting ferociously. "The brothers from the club will pick up the chopper. It'll be OK. But her now. She needs to see someone. You got to see a doc when you're so far along. And I got money too," he said, poking Mathison in the chest with a bloody fist.

"What *is* this?"

The man, the biker, Largo, eased himself back down on the gurney. "Just do what you gotta do," he said. "But call her. 291-3468. In Moorhead. Tell her to come on in. She can have her folks bring her. Then you look her over, OK? Once she's inside, you got her. Tell her it's paid for already. And tell her that soup was good. Real good."

twenty-nine

Sometimes when Largo wasn't home, Sandy just let the phone ring. It was mostly telemarketers anyway. And when it was late, it was mostly Iron Riders, usually drunk, running their mouths. They seemed to need to run them right by Largo, who would stuff the phone against his neck, sprawl on the sofa, and listen as long as anybody talked. Though sometimes he fell asleep, the phone still anchored in his hair. She could hear the husky voice yammering on the other end when she picked it up.

If she did answer the phone, and it wasn't a telemarketer or a biker, there was usually silence. Just plain silence. Once somebody, a woman, had said, "Jesus Christ!" and slammed down the mouthpiece on her end. Sandy knew Largo had a past. He hadn't spent forty-three years in a box. The woman had sounded brain dead anyway.

Tonight, in bed, she couldn't get comfortable. She had a good light for reading, but there was no place to balance her book. Sandy knew it was a joke that she was reading *War and Peace*, like she was trying to work her way through the classics or something. She had been going to take it back to the library if she didn't like it, but then she did like it. Natasha reminded her of herself, only with more money, and Russian, of course.

The first time the phone rang eight rings. She didn't answer it. It was powerful to lie in bed with the phone ringing practically inside you and still not pick it up.

Then it rang eight more times about fifteen minutes later. Was it a code? She thought about picking it up, but didn't. She had no intention of listening to some wasted Iron Rider drool into her ear.

Could it be Juan? She was pretty sure it wasn't. He'd had no interest in babies when they were together. Even if he just wanted money, he knew she didn't have any. And how would he know she was staying with Largo?

Then she must have fallen asleep. She just remembered pushing *War and Peace* over to the side because it was digging into her stomach. She pulled the blanket over herself, up far enough so she could smell it. Largo didn't smoke, at least as far as she'd seen, but there was a whiff of smoke in the wool. It had probably come from the storage closet at the clubhouse. Most bikers smoked all the time even though they knew it wasn't good for them. But when had a biker ever chosen to do anything because it was good for him?

When the phone rang this time, it came from far away. A little ding like the bell at the end of the line when you were typing. She'd taken typing in junior high—Eagle Grove was so far behind that they'd just barely begun computers, and then only in high school. The bell sounded like that, only it was ringing all the time. She always hit the return key, so what was going on? What *was* going on?

This time it didn't stop. When she came out of her sleep far enough to realize it was the phone, she grabbed it without thinking. "Hello," she said, her voice groggy. Nobody answered.

"Hello?"

There were some rumbling noises. A strange voice came on, a woman's, but not some biker broad. "I was asked to call this number," it said.

"OK." Sandy was trying to sit up, but it was hard to brace herself. The phone seemed slippery. She shoved it against her cheek.

"This is Memorial Hospital in Littleriver. I had a request to call this number."

"But the baby isn't born yet."

There was silence.

"Is it about my baby?"

More silence. "A *man* asked me to call," the voice went on, enunciating clearly.

"What man?"

Sandy could hear the crunching of paper. "I think his name is Larry," the voice went on. "I can't read the last name. He was admitted this evening. He wanted us to call this number."

Sandy couldn't remember ever knowing a Larry. None of the bikers had that for a name either. Red Harry was the nearest, but he hardly ever even spoke to her. He was afraid of women.

"Say that name again."

More crunching. "You know, I think it ends in 'o,'" the voice said.

Sandy could spell. Her heart jumped. Then the baby swung itself against her bladder.

"He said you could call your parents and they'd bring you in."

Why was it so hard to get a breath? "What's wrong with him?" Sandy asked.

"We're not allowed to give out information about a patient's condition."

Then why were they waking her up? Sandy took a deep breath, but it didn't help. Her heart was dancing. She made a fist and pounded on her chest, like in *ER*. It didn't settle down, but she managed to get some air inside her.

"If he's dead, then why should I come in?"

There was a very long pause. "He's not dead," the voice said. "He's in the OR. It was a motorcycle accident."

"Is he *going* to die?" Her voice sounded weird. She cleared her throat, thumped her chest again.

"I'm pretty sure not," the woman said. She sounded warmer. "If you get here after two more hours or so, he'll be in Recovery."

Sandy swung herself around in bed. *War and Peace* flipped onto the floor. "Thanks," she said into the phone, but it was like her hand was disconnected from her head, and she was holding the mouthpiece so far away that the woman couldn't possibly hear her. She hung up.

Where had Largo gone? What had he done? Was he drinking? Oh hell, bikers were always cracking up whether they were drunk or not. Largo was no different from the rest of them.

Only what was this stuff about her parents?

For about five minutes, Sandy sat on the edge of the bed, her toes on *War and Peace*. She wished she had a cat to pet, or anything furry. The baby did little drop kicks inside her. Her bladder sent urgent messages.

Finally she reached for the phone again and punched out her folks' number. They'd had the same one since her dad had built the house. It was impossible to forget. When her mother answered, she put her lips right next to the mouthpiece, so close that she could taste the salty plastic with her tongue.

"Yes?" This late, they must expect the end of the world.

"Hi, Mom."

Another pause. She could feel her mother getting control. In the background, she heard her father's voice, but her mom didn't give up the phone.

"Mom?"

"Sandy." She didn't even sound sleepy. "We're here. Tell us what we can do for you."

thirty

Outside the car, the night seemed impenetrable. There was no moon, no other traffic. They had passed out of Moorhead and through Silverdale, then through Jacoby. Tomsville was next. In Tomsville, the speed limit was forty-five miles per hour. You hardly needed to slow down, unlike Silverdale and Jacoby, where it was thirty.

Sandy had never felt so deliberately surrounded by protectiveness. Her mother had insisted that she sit in the front seat of the Oldsmobile. Her father used a pine air freshener, fastened to the dashboard, and Sandy felt as if her whole body was swaddled in a woodsy blanket. Even the baby had stopped moving.

"I called the hospital." Her father paused. "He's still in surgery. It's taking longer than they expected. Nothing bad, though. They thought it would be a good thing if you waited until morning to come in."

"How did you get them to tell you?"

Her father bent his head into the blackness. "Missy was on duty," he said. "She knows everything."

They were passing the Tomsville airport. Two little lights marked its beginning and end. Sandy felt for the bag at her feet, barely able to bend far enough to reach it. She'd packed Largo's newest Harley T-shirt and his razor, along with a few other things. He didn't own very much at all.

"Sandy." Her mother touched her shoulder. "Stay with us. Get some rest. We'll take you to the hospital tomorrow." She paused. "Maybe we should have the doctor check you out as well."

"Has Largo been talking to YOU TOO?"

"He came out earlier this evening." Her mother's touch tightened for just a second. "He's worried about you."

Why was her voice so funny? Did they have a conspiracy going? It was too late to figure it out. "I didn't bring my things," Sandy said. Her voice sounded funny too.

"We have everything you need."

Sandy swung herself around as far as she could in her seat. Her mother was leaning forward. The interior of the car was so shadowed that it was impossible to read her face.

"But I'm going back as soon as I see him."

"That's fine, Sandy. Tomorrow we can do anything you want. Then we have the Fall Festival on Sunday. But we'll manage."

They were approaching Eagle Grove, a festoon of lights far ahead and off to the left. Their turnoff to Weed Lake should be right about here. Ed slowed the car, put on the signal. Then they were on the gravel. Every bump seemed familiar. Even the roadside brush looked familiar.

"Watch out!"

Ed slammed on the brakes. A big doe, white in the car lights, leaped out into the middle of the road. They missed her by inches.

"Are you all right?"

Sandy had trouble catching her breath. "Wait," she managed to choke out. "There's always two." And before her words were fully spoken, a second deer, a buck this time, sprang out across the road in front of them.

"I haven't seen a buck in years."

Then the three of them sat there in silence. There was no sound from the woods. No eyes peered at them from the roadside. They went on. No one said a thing.

It didn't take long to get to the house. They all climbed out. Sandy was struck by an exhaustion so deep that she doubted her ability to make it up the steps into the kitchen. How would her parents feel if she went on her hands and knees? She put her arms out in front of her, thinking to lower herself, realizing that it was ridiculous. She had never been so tired in her life.

Then her parents were on each side of her. Her father took her elbow, grasping it with enormous gentleness. Her mother simply held her hand, intertwining their fingers. "I'll make you tea," she said. "If you want. I have jasmine. That used to be your favorite."

"Or anything else you'd like," her father said.

Sandy was too worn out to argue. She didn't even feel like arguing. The familiar kitchen surrounded her like a cloud. Her dad still hadn't gotten the doors made for the lower cupboards. Every iota of their cooking and storage life was laid open to view. It all looked pretty innocent, actually.

She sat down at the table and propped her head on her arms. No one spoke. Her mother was filling the teakettle. Her father was looking at her as if he wanted to pick her up and take her to a secret place where everything was perfect. They had used to play a game like that. A long time ago.

Sandy took a deep breath. "Why don't you ask me what you want to know?" she said. "Like why I screwed my life up. Like what I expect you guys to do for me. Like how this crazy baby seems to have two fathers. Ask me something." She tried to glare, but her eyes kept closing. "Ask me *anything*," she said.

Her father sat down next to her. He touched her arm, just with one finger. "Does your music box still work?" he asked.

thirty-one

Ed bowed his head. So did all the rest of them. "Dear Lord," he said, with a long pause following. "Dear Lord, make this meal blessed, for those who eat and those who prepare. In thy holy name, amen."

"Amen," said the kitchen crew at the Fall Festival—Alex and Burton; Richard at the cash box; Gertrud Chilson, Mrs. Lund, and Mildred in flowered percales; the young Lutherans from the Eagle Grove youth group, who would clear tables and deliver desserts; the Philipson sisters, who had served at the festival for more than thirty years; Gil Halvorsen, his hands gripped around a spatula as if it were a logging implement. And Grace, gently checking the fairground ovens for the correct temperature before the chicken rolls went in for heating. Outside the food hall, a line was already forming.

"I just hope the weather holds."

What the Fall Festival needed was sun. Early October sun was usually something you could count on. But this summer had been strange—almost too dry, then too wet, then dry again, then finally a drought-breaking rainstorm that had lasted only half an hour. It was hard to know what to expect weatherwise.

Outside, the rumble of hungry visitors increased. Burton checked his watch, checked Alex, who, wearing enormous padded gloves, was hauling the first trays of chicken rolls out of the ovens. Checked Richard, who was using his arm now, whose pimples seemed to be receding, and who, Alex said, was thinking about college after next year, or maybe the Army. Burton noticed that Richard was intensely concentrating on stacking the little rolls of silver next to the cash box, fanning the bills into their cubbyholes. The prize quilt to be raffled hung like a backdrop behind him, out of reach of grease spots and spilled food. For a creation of the Lutheran ladies, it was downright flamboyant.

"We couldn't do it without you."

Suddenly Grace was standing beside Burton. Her face was raised to his, a face that seemed thinner somehow, the dimple in her chin less obvious. How curious to be looked at so closely by a woman, his pastor's wife, yes, but not an elderly church fixture, a woman who had just spoken a gracious compliment and whose eyes were following his as he watched Alex fling open the door with a theatrical flourish to admit the first of the hungry Norwegians.

"I feel as if serving chicken rolls at the Fall Festival was prescribed in the Bible somewhere, but the chapter has gone missing," Burton said.

"Spoken like an English teacher."

"Well, I am that."

"And I'm the pastor's wife."

Of course. But why say it?

The line was moving. The paper plates were being filled with chicken rolls, potatoes, cooked carrots in their orange circles beautifully free of any seasoning. Ed's long arms reached out with a steady rhythm, sweeping chicken rolls from the trays and levering them onto the plates. He smiled when it was appropriate.

Grace inclined her head. "It looks like we'll be making money again," she murmured.

"We always do."

The two of them seemed to have created their own space. Grace took off her plastic gloves, laid them on the counter. The line was moving rapidly now, earnest and quiet, the polite voices mingling with the clatter of dishes and Richard's clinking of money at the cash drawer. In the dining room, the picnic tables were beginning to fill. The Young Lutherans peered from the corners, ready to distribute the ice cream bars as soon as the plates had emptied. Only last year, the Englund ladies had baked brownies and cookies themselves, but now the department of health demanded that the desserts be baked under department supervision if they were baked at all. Hence the ice cream bars.

"Grace, you don't look well."

"I'm all right."

"You don't look all right." Mildred, abloom in exotic flora, had penetrated their space, wiping her red hands on her apron. "Is it too hot in here?"

"It's not too bad."

Mildred took Grace's arm. "Go out where there's some breeze," she said. "Catch your breath. Don't pass out. Burton, you escort her. She's been working since five a.m. *I* only got here at seven."

Burton looked harder at Grace as he took her elbow, his fingers cradling under the angle of the joint. She never tanned like most people, but today her skin seemed unusually white, even for her. Her eyes were shaded, darker underneath. "Shouldn't we say something to Pastor Ed?" Burton asked, even as Mildred nudged them toward the back entrance.

"It's all right," Grace said.

Then they were outside. It had turned unseasonably warm for an October day, the air like clotted gray wool. At the very zenith, a white disc of sun burned into the clouds—you could see it, focus on it, but it was so cloaked with the gray cloud vapor that it didn't hurt your eyes. Grace leaned against

Burton, her weight slight on his arm, then leaned outward again. A small strand of hair had loosened itself and lay against her cheek. She turned her head and looked at him, moving back against the corner of the Chicken Roll Shed, as they called it. Burton, uncomfortable with his unclear duties, stepped back as well.

"Is it hard to be gay in Eagle Grove?"

"What?"

"Hard. To be gay. In Eagle Grove." Her voice was so soft that the words were propelled more by the movement of her lips than by the sound.

Burton thought for a moment. It seemed unlikely that she had said what she had said. She looked up at him, her eyes heavy-lidded, unblinking.

"Well." The saving word. "Well, I don't know."

"Yes you do."

He took her hand. Surely no one would mind. "It's just what I am, Grace," he said.

"Does it make a difference having Alex?"

He looked at her hard. Was she going to faint? She was leaning back against the corner of the building, her shoulders against the worn wood, her hips thrust slightly outward. She was wearing pants of some loose fabric that slid down over the tops of her shoes. Although the air was full of incipient moisture, some dust was rising too, from the passing people's feet, from the cars down the way that were bringing crafts to the exhibit hall. He saw her through that haze. "Grace, you need to lie down," he said, moving his hand to her shoulder.

"No, I don't. Answer my question." Her voice was soft, as it always was. Her eyes glowed.

But before the words came, Burton thought back. He and Alex had met in college, he a senior, Alex a freshman. It had been registration, and he'd taken Alex's pile of forms in his hands at the long volunteer table, checking through the papers to make sure they were all there, all signed, all right side up. Alex had had a bad haircut, almost pathologically bad, layered in peculiar dips around his ears, which stuck out. His skin had been as clear as an angel's.

"Yes, it makes a difference," he said.

"I thought so."

Burton considered Richard, the shirt borrower, the child of the perfect abs. "But it isn't always ideal for us," he said.

"I thought that too."

"Grace, I cannot believe we're having this conversation."

Now she put her hand on his elbow. "Did you know that Sandy's baby will be born within the next two weeks or so?" she said.

Burton tried to remember if he had even known that Sandy was pregnant. Ah yes. He certainly remembered the wedding, and Alex had passed on much information. Heterosexuals had their own problems. "Is she having a good pregnancy?" he asked, wondering if that was the proper inquiry.

"We hardly knew. She hasn't wanted to see a doctor. But now she has. She called us two days ago, and we brought her in yesterday. Jim Mathison examined her. Her cervix is already dilated a little, though that may not mean anything." Grace's voice sounded as if it had been recorded, it was so slow and clear and without expression.

"You and Ed will be grandparents then."

"Yes." She hesitated. "We will."

Her eyes had grown so large that Burton felt as if he were going to tumble into them. "There's one thing about being gay," he said, his thoughts coming up from some unexplored place. "That's the child issue. We could have adopted, I suppose. But it's almost impossible with two men, especially in the Midwest. And I have all my students. I don't think either of us is equipped for bringing up a baby. We like our own space. Although sometimes I do wonder. We'll probably both end up in Mercy Care

Center without a single relative to visit us. But perhaps they'll let us share a room. I suppose they wouldn't allow us to move in a double bed, considering the rules of propriety. However . . ."

He looked at Grace, gritting his front teeth together to keep another of his foolish words from charging out into the air. She was sliding down against the wall of the building, her feet making little tracks in the dirt as they moved outward. Her eyes were closed. "Call Ed," she said, in a voice like paper crackling. "Please call Ed."

thirty-two

Yuck. He'd stuck his fingers right up inside her!

Sandy heaved her body around in the waiting room chair. She wasn't stupid—she knew what he was doing. But there was nothing to find out. King Kicker in there was just going to keep on growing until he decided to be born. Dr. Mathison had always been a prick anyway. What had Largo thought he was going to find out with some stupid examination? Why had her folks wanted her to do it too?

The wall clock said ten. Light sloshed through the windows, so it must be morning. Somewhere along the way, she'd slept. Two nights ago, when her folks had come for her at the apartment, they had just taken her back to Eagle Grove, to her old room. They'd made a study out of it, with a photocopy machine for the church bulletin and all her mother's sewing things. It must have been way after midnight by the time they'd got there, and she'd fallen asleep on the sofa bed without even taking off her sneakers. She'd been so tired.

The next day, they'd gone in to the hospital. Her parents had met Largo before, but they told her to go up by herself. Not that she had wanted to. But it didn't matter anyway, because he was completely out of it, muttering like a drunk, yanking at his pillow. Once he'd laughed. "Fuck off, Dan," he'd said with a crooked grin. When she'd touched his hand, he'd looked at her like she was a stranger.

Then she'd gone out and had a late lunch with her folks at the Gateway. Their pasta wasn't as good as it used to be, but their green beans were still wonderful. They used bits of real bacon and sesame seeds. She'd eaten up every one.

And then it was back to the examining room and that prick physician. She felt like a victim, like some little Vietnamese woman when the Thai pirates attacked. Who was she trying to please by giving in? Her folks and Largo were both crazy.

After that, she'd just kind of chased her parents away. She'd said she'd call a friend to bring her back to Moorhead. And she could have done that too. But she hadn't.

Interesting things went on at night in the hospital. There'd been a baby with a penny stuck in his nose. The nurse had pulled it out with eyebrow tweezers while his mother pinned his arms to the table. One old lady had been carried in like she was drunk. Maybe she had been.

Sandy knew she needed to go see Largo again before she left. It just got harder and harder to do. He probably wouldn't be able to talk to her anyway. She hadn't brought him any flowers. She didn't know what he was doing in her life, but he was sitting in the middle of it like some big carved Buddha. His eyes were even a little slanty.

She'd heard that Indians had come over from China. Maybe that was why.

When she finally heaved herself up, she jammed her hands into the pockets of her maternity slacks. Her heart gave a little blip like it had when that nurse had telephoned. The baby kicked back. It must have some kind of communication system going in there.

Her hands still wedged in her pockets, Sandy tromped to the stairway and climbed up to the next floor. She could barely make it. When she got to Largo's door, she was panting. It was hard to believe she'd been a skinny Harley Mama just a little while ago.

Part of her hoped he was sleeping. Awake but delirious was OK too. But when she stepped inside, he looked at her like he knew her better than he knew himself. "You came," he said.

"I was here yesterday too."

"Did you . . ."

She didn't let him finish. "YES!" she roared, thumping on his mattress with her fist, pretending that she didn't see him wince. "YES! That prick doctor dug around inside me and decided that I was going to have a baby. That's probably worth about five hundred dollars of your hard-earned money. I hope you're happy."

Slumping down into the chair next to his bed, Sandy felt ashamed of herself. She even reached out and touched Largo's nearest tattoo. But, although his eyes were bleary, he was smiling at her like she'd won every spelling bee Eagle Grove had ever sponsored. "Sandy, babe," he grunted, his voice sounding out of practice, "I knew you could do it."

"Right."

"You know to call Rocker if you need a ride."

"I guess."

"Did you eat all that soup?"

She had no idea what he was talking about. Then it came to her. "There's still a little left," she said.

"If it don't get rotten, I'll finish it up when I get home."

thirty-three

"Isn't he hungry?"

"I don't think so, Elizabeth."

The air in the room was so stuffy that Eugene's forehead gleamed under a thin mantle of sweat. Droplets coalesced in his eyebrows. His eyes were shut most of the time, but when they opened, the pupils rolled from one side to the other, lost circles rotated by the musculature behind them.

"You always feed him with that tube?"

"He has trouble swallowing." No need to go into details. Lighty wasn't sure how much Elizabeth understood to begin with. She had always treated Eugene simply as another human being.

"But he has teeth."

"I know. He just can't chew with them."

Elizabeth bent over the bed, her hair sliding across her cheek. "He's grown since you started letting me babysit," she said. "He really has."

"I know. His body grows."

Elizabeth stood upright, pulled her shoulders back. Her little breasts popped out against her faded T-shirt. "I've been growing too," she said.

Lighty thought about the slovenly mother, the white trash diet, the crumbling linoleum on the kitchen floor, which she'd seen one of the few times she'd been invited inside. When she checked her own refrigerator after Elizabeth had babysat, the Coke was always gone, as well as anything sweet. Once the brown sugar jar had been half emptied, but once four eggs had been gone as well. She couldn't imagine what dietary passions swept through the girl.

"Do you want me to feed him with his tube?" Elizabeth asked. "I can do that if he's hungry. You could show me how."

Lighty put her hand on the girl's arm. "I did it an hour ago," she said. "But thank you. I'm glad you care about his well-being."

Her eyes wide, Elizabeth turned toward her. "I *like* to take care of him," she said. Her face suddenly looked adult. Then it slid into childhood again as she reached down and wiped the sweat off Eugene's forehead. "When I leave home I want to be a very good mother."

"I'm sure you will be."

Elizabeth smiled up at her. The enamel on her teeth seemed particularly fragile, the thinnest possible coating over the bare nerves. Then she sat down on the rocker next to the bed. "I know it's all right if I want something to eat," she said as Lighty turned and walked out of the room.

"Yes, it is."

"Will you be back late?"

"I might be late getting back."

"All right. I'll be awake."

As Lighty walked out into the yard by the raised garden beds, she thought about how Elizabeth had never once been asleep when she returned, not the whole summer, not last spring, not the late winter when she'd begun hiring her. Perhaps she felt it her responsibility never to sleep. Or was it curiosity as to where Lighty went? After all, she didn't leave a phone number. But she felt no guilt. What disaster would Elizabeth not be capable of handling? Eugene never stirred. The phone worked. Now the propane heaters weren't even on. Elizabeth probably relished the free time in a home that was neat and clean, or relatively so. Perhaps she went through Lighty's books as she did the refrigerator. Perhaps the freedom to nourish herself as she chose was a compensation for the seven or eight dollars Lighty paid her when she returned.

The sky was clear, speckled with early stars. A good day for the Fall Festival. The Englund people would have made enough money to pay Ed's small salary into the new year. Ed would smell of the fairground's kitchen, grease in his shirt, sweat and smoke on his skin. Even his hair, waving around his growing bald spot, would hint of chicken rolls and mashed potatoes.

He had asked her if he should shower first. But then it would have been so late. Better for him to meet her with his aura of chicken rolls.

Tonight, she was driving. Lighty pushed up the door into the garage, a chicken coop that had outgrown itself and become a refuge for her old Volvo, rusting in ornate gashes around its wheel wells and door handles. She changed its oil herself, her back against the compacted dirt floor, the Volvo's front tires on lifts. Nothing else was ever wrong with it, but then, she drove it so seldom. Perhaps once a week into Eagle Grove. Perhaps twice a year to the quilters at church. An occasional medical errand for Eugene. Not many.

On the road, however, she felt an excitement that had nothing to do with the Indian summer weather or the old car. Always, she had been the one lifted above her life. Even her nickname, Lighty, had been given to her by her parents because she seemed to step so lightly on the ground, to suffer so little from the torments of childhood. No one had called her by her given name, Eleanor, for decades. Whenever she thought of it, the tendrils of her mind had to push farther and farther into the past. Another few years and it would be gone forever.

Once she had passed the turnoff to Hallam, the road became deserted. This time Ed had proposed meeting at the old quarry, at the end of the scrub woods, which the teenagers, who hung out at the quarry after dark, avoided because of the snakes. The only Minnesota snake she'd ever seen was a garter snake, as harmless and ornate as a swatch of decorative fabric. But the snake still carried the connotation of evil here.

If Ed had been free, would they have married? Probably not. What she loved about him disappeared in the pulpit. Behind those strange robes—Advent, Pentecost, Lent—his body became as untouchable as if wrapped in sanitary plastic. Only his hands escaped, moving in gestures like lonely strangers as he wound his way through his sermons. His lovely square chest was gone, the fabric covering it anchored at his waist with that silly green or gold or red tasseled rope. His solid legs, the long muscles hard under the skin, were encapsulated in his Sunday pants.

The car coughed. Lighty couldn't believe it. When she pushed down on the accelerator, it coughed again, a quick intense vibration. Then it lost power. She watched the speedometer needle slide downward even though her foot was pressed to the floorboard. She was still two miles from the quarry, and in the opposite direction from which Ed would be coming. The road was quiet, so quiet that when the old Volvo delicately stopped running, she could hear the grass blades crunch as she guided the wheels onto the side of the road and into the grass.

Only she had miscalculated. The strip was narrow. The passenger side wheels moved over air, hesitated, slid downward. When the Volvo came to rest, it was hanging at such a steep slant away from the road that Lighty found herself clinging to the door handle, now strangely above her, to keep from sliding downward herself.

Damn!

Struggling, Lighty got the door open just far enough to insert her leg, then half of her torso. It was like climbing backwards through a skylight. In fact, the sky above her was the most notable feature, graying into black, one huge orange star standing by itself just over the treeline. The door frame dug into her hip, then her breast. She'd be black and blue for a week.

Angry then, angry at her stupidity for going off the road, even though it had been the car's fault and not hers, angry that Ed would be waiting for her and she wouldn't be there for the first time ever, angry that she'd have to explain where she'd been to someone—a tow truck driver, a farmer with a tractor—she wrenched herself upright, her hand against the side of the inclined car, and then pulled herself up on the grass by the edge of the road. She'd been smart enough to turn off the ignition and the lights. The Volvo looked like a dark boulder.

So. Now she needed to seek help. Straightening her shoulders, Lighty walked a little distance down the road, out to where she could stand unprotected by trees and watch for someone to pick her up. In only a minute or two, a small car went by, but it was speeding so fast, even around the curve, that they didn't see her. Late mosquitoes gnawed her ankles, and when she scratched the bites, they itched more. She wasn't wearing a bra, but even so her breasts seemed compressed against her, heavy on her chest under her cotton blouse.

The second car was a pickup. They usually stopped, but not this one. As it came out of the curve, it slid over halfway into the opposite lane, then righted itself and was gone.

Then it was silent for a long time. By now Ed would be looking at his watch. At the other side of the quarry, where the snake threat was perceived to be milder, a few brave teenagers might be leaping off the edges of the rock, splashing into the cold water far below. Every now and then, someone drowned, went down and never came up. But it hadn't happened for years.

Lighty walked back and forth on the edge of the road, one foot in the gravel, one on the grass. Behind her, she could see the tilted bulk of her car, like a stranded whale. Mars, or whatever the orange glow was, had risen slightly in the sky, and other stars were coming out around it. At the peak of the heavens, the white band of the Milky Way stretched from one side of the blackness to the other.

When she first heard the motorcycle, she didn't know what it was. The rumble of its pistons built up with its approach. The big front light rose and fell as it came nearer at significant speed, holding a more steady trajectory than the pickup had. Lighty stepped back, both feet in the grass, and held out her arm. She couldn't remember if you were supposed to raise your thumb or your finger, it had been that long since she'd hitchhiked. She balled her fingers into a soft fist and raised that instead.

He saw her, braked. The bike skidded, but he controlled it. As it passed her, he leaned to the right and brought it into the grass. His legs came down on both sides and balanced as he turned back to look at her.

"You all right?"

"Yes. But my car's in the ditch."

She couldn't hear his response. Then he dismounted, put down the kickstand. In the bits of light from Mars and the other stars, she realized that the bike was one of those astounding models from the movie *Easy Rider*—stretched-out silver with a seat balanced so far back that it appeared to be precipitating itself off the rear wheel. The handlebars stood enormously high. Even idling, the engine rumbled like a jungle creature. Lighty had had a cat once, a big tom, who purred so loud it had rattled her dishes. Like that.

The biker was walking down the road to her car, then standing at the edge of the bank above it, looking down into its slanted interior. "Getting this up will be a two-man job," he said. Then he walked back.

"Can you do anything?"

He scratched the fringe of hair under his Harley cap, then his chin under his beard. "Nope," he said. "Need a tractor. Or a tow truck. Car looks OK, though."

"I'm grateful for that."

"I can take you into town."

"On your motorcycle?"

"Seems to be the only choice you got."

He wasn't nasty about it, but he was right. Suddenly Lighty felt incredibly bulky in her heavy cotton blouse, her Mexican skirt with its yards of handwoven fabric that reached to her ankles. The biker had kicked loose the stand and seated himself, hands raised on the handlebars, leaning upwards.

"Do I hang onto you?"

In the dark, his teeth flashed. They didn't all seem to be present, but it was certainly a smile. "Best way of doing it," he said.

"All right."

"I don't break."

She climbed up behind him. He was wearing a leather vest with emblems sewn on it. "But I need to go home," she said, realizing that she could deal with a car by a telephone call, better made from her own place. Everything would be closed in town anyway. George from the Cenex could haul the Volvo out in the morning. And Ed would surely telephone her once he'd waited a while and she hadn't come.

"Just tell me where."

"Back on the road. About seven or eight miles. I'll show you."

The bike started up. Its roar pushed deep into Lighty's pelvis. She hung onto the biker's leather vest, feeling the solid body beneath it, the little gut, the broad back against her.

"Scared?" The biker tilted his head back in her direction.

She thought for a moment. "No," she said. "I trust you."

The bike took the big curve, leaning to the right. The handlebars were so high that the biker's hands seemed to be reaching into the sky as he guided it back into the straight roadway. "Thanks," he said.

"Where were you riding? Almost nobody was on the road."

"Coming back from the hospital in Littleriver."

"Someone sick?" Lighty's hair was being pulled out behind her by the wind. The skin on her cheeks felt stretched.

"Not sick. Banged up. Guy in our club. Laid it down in the road two days ago. Ruptured his spleen, and some other stuff too. Ribs, concussion. Crazy dude. Good thing he's not dead."

"Will he be all right?"

The biker leaned back, forcing her breasts against the leather. He didn't seem to notice. "Sure. We're bringing him home in a couple of days," he said. "Me and the guys in the club."

"That's nice of you."

He looked back at her with a scowl. "Nice?" he asked, the wind passing the word over his shoulder. "He's a brother."

They were coming over the hill before her turnoff. "What's your name?" she asked as she gestured him toward her property, her lips against his ear. He smelled like cheap hair tonic mixed with dust.

He hesitated. "Robert," he said finally, clearing his throat.

"You don't seem like a Robert."

The bike slowed as he turned into her driveway. "The boys call me Rocker," he said.

He didn't seem like a Rocker either, but who would? They bumped up Lighty's stretched-out drive. She should have told him to let her off at the main road, but she hadn't. Through the trees, she saw the light in Eugene's bedroom. Usually Elizabeth had left his room by now. Maybe she was reading in there.

"This is a pretty lonely place to live." Rocker brought the Harley to a stop and let it idle. The engine grumbled steadily.

"I like it."

"I'll wait till you get inside."

It had been so long since someone had expressed concern for her safety that, to Lighty's surprise, tears came to her eyes. She started to refuse him, the first sounds already pushing at her lips. Then she stopped. "Thank you," she said. "I'll come out and tell you that everything's all right."

He nodded. Such chivalry! Lighty swung her leg over the seat, muffled it in her skirt as it came free, hurried up the steps to the door. She never locked it, and Elizabeth didn't either. No one was in the living room, though the reading light by the green chair was on. No one was in the kitchen either, though there was food on the counter—a slice of bread, some peanut butter, a carton of milk.

"Elizabeth? I'm home."

No one answered.

"Elizabeth?"

A small sound came from the bedroom. Lighty went to its door.

"Elizabeth, it's me."

The girl stood directly inside. She was holding a plate and a glass.

"I'm glad you got yourself something to eat."

The girl shook her head wordlessly.

"Although I'm afraid I didn't leave you very much."

The girl was still silent.

Lighty bent down to her, to the white face, the fragile teeth, the poorly washed hair. "Elizabeth?" she asked.

"He's asleep."

"Of course."

The girl opened her eyes wider. Her lips were trembling. "But he's *awful* quiet," she said.

Lighty turned to the bed. Eugene was lying on his back, one hand stretched out on the sheet. His eyes were slitted. There were brown stains around his mouth.

He wasn't breathing.

"Elizabeth!"

The girl fell on her knees. "Peanut butter is easy to eat!" she sobbed. "And I gave him milk too. To help wash it down. It went right in his mouth. But then he made a funny noise. He wouldn't stop making it. Even when I shook him. And then he looked different. Kind of blue. And then he just slept and slept and slept."

The room had turned golden. For a moment, Lighty thought the stars had burst through the window. But of course it was her own head that was bursting.

"I thought he was hungry!"

Then Lighty was running back through the door, through the hallway, through the kitchen with its mild disorder, through the living room where all the books in the many shelves, those Ed had built and those she'd purchased, seemed to be leaning forward from the walls as if to bury her. On the porch, she caught herself as she plunged down the steps. Rocker had swung his Harley around toward the driveway, but he was looking back at her, and when he saw her stumbling toward him, he cut the motor and reached out in her direction. She tried to stop, but couldn't, and he caught her as she fell on her knees in the dirt next to his bike, clutching at his jeans.

"Jesus, what's wrong?"

But how could she tell him? She caught her breath and said the only thing that was sayable.

"Call Ed. Please call Ed."

thirty-four

Ed held her with both arms around her shoulders. They were in a private room, the counseling chamber. The Council of Service had given Memorial Hospital a special grant to have it built, and it was relentlessly nondenominational. Everything was cream-colored, even the carpet. The lights were dim.

"What happened?"

"He choked. It went to his lungs. Then he couldn't breathe."

"My God."

"He'd been dead for a little while. I didn't even try CPR." Lighty rubbed her eyes, realized she wasn't crying. "If my car hadn't broken down, I wouldn't have gotten home that early. But he'd have been dead either way."

"I'm so sorry."

"Yes."

Ed let his hands slide down her arms. "Now what?" he asked.

Lighty could smell the chicken rolls, or perhaps just the presence of Ed's flesh. "What do you mean?" she asked.

He was silent. His hands loosened.

She had never asked him to declare himself, to take the initiative. She had preferred to manage Eugene alone—with Social Services, with Medicaid, with the standard neutral assistances. If she had shared him officially, then he wouldn't have been hers in the same way.

"What do you mean, Ed?"

He sat in the chair by the door, holding his head in his hands. She could see his bald spot. If she had been on Mars, that strange orange star, she couldn't have been farther away than she felt now.

"Ed, there's no use to mourn."

He sprang to his feet. She'd heard the expression many times but had never seen it so obviously activated. "Lighty," he said. "Lighty, I want to marry you."

"You're already married."

He paused. "Grace is sick," he said.

"What?"

"She fainted at the festival. The ambulance team brought her in. She'd been seeing the doctor, but she never told me. He'd done lots of tests, but now they'll do more. We'll have all the results next week. She doesn't look good, Lighty. I've never seen her so pale. Only her smile is the same . . ."

He was running on. She felt no inclination to touch him, but she held out her hand as if she might. He turned toward her.

"Eugene's dead, Lighty."

"I know that."

"We can't bring him back."

And that did it. She stood as high as she could and pulled back her shoulders. It was almost as if the wind from Rocker's Harley was blowing her into position. Maybe Grace *was* going to die. Maybe they were all going to die. Of course they were. "I don't want Eugene back," she tore out, even though it hurt her chest to say it. "I just once, once want you to speak out about something, to tell the truth about where you've been and what you've done. Or at least recognize the truth and accept it. Whether it's about Sandy or Vietnam or about me. I don't want those platitudes anymore. I don't want your righteous Lutheran melancholy. But you can bury him, Ed. You can give me that. You can say the prayers over him like you would any other child in your congregation, and when he's lying in the casket, that's exactly what he'll look like. You can preach a nice little sermon over him. All the Chilsons and the Lundquists and the Phillipses will sit with their heads tilted to one side, listening and nodding. I'll be in the first row because I'm his mother, but I won't be looking at you. I'll be looking at him in his coffin and thinking how cold and damp the dirt is most of the year, especially in early spring, especially when the first thaw comes. I'm a gardener, and I know. Of course it won't get in right away. The wood has to rot first. But when the water does get in, that'll be the end of it. Because he didn't have a spirit, or a mind. He just had his body. Just his body."

Someone knocked at the door. She must have frightened them with her screaming. Had she been screaming? Of course she had. Well, why not keep it up? "Fuck you!" she yelled as she pushed past Ed, smelling the chicken rolls, smelling his skin, repudiating them both. "Fuck you! He was yours too!"

thirty-five

"Are you in pain?"

"What?"

The nurse glanced into the chart she was carrying. "Your roommate told us you were groaning," she said. "If you're in pain, we can give you a shot. I've got the tray here. It's prescribed."

Largo put his big hands on each side of his butt and yanked himself upright in the bed. The nurse sprang back. Fierce fingers clutched his gut, but, hell, he'd had it worse in more than one brawl at Whiskey Corners. "I ain't a *groaner*," he grunted out. His hair stood up in a great bush as if it had exploded from his scalp.

"Then you're all right?"

"I'll live."

The nurse shrugged. Across the room, the thin elderly man in the other bed shook his head. Largo kept himself upright by dint of digging his heels into the mattress, his hands grabbing the blanket in wads on both sides. He squinted at the door. "I gotta go," he said.

"Do you need help?"

Largo stared at her.

"The bathroom is right here. Do you need an orderly?"

Inside his head, all Largo could hear was an incoherent rumble, louder than his Heritage Softail, more threatening than thunder. Sandy was home by herself. He ought to be there with her. Somewhere on the edge of the rushing sound, the nurse's little voice rose and fell. He tried to concentrate on what she was saying, even though it made no sense, but both her voice and her face kept getting father and farther away. "What fuckin' bathroom?" he asked. He stared at her. She stared right back.

"What fuckin' bathroom?"

"You can't talk like that in here!"

For the first time, Largo heard his own words. It was as if a bubble of pressure had popped in his head. He yanked at his hair with both hands. A wave of pain shot through him.

"We don't have to put up with that kind of language."

She was right. It was no way to talk to a woman. He knew better. "Sorry," he said, chewing on his lip.

Her face softened. "Well, I've heard worse," she said. "But do you need any help now?"

Largo had lost track of the whole issue. The pain in his ribs and across his gut was pulling him into a knot. He bit the inside of his lower lip. His bridge crunched and loosened.

"Goddamn!"

"I'd really rather you didn't talk like that."

With his tongue, Largo shoved the bridge back in place. Dan the Man had finally thrown his bridge out. They'd been all tanked up, doing ninety over the Mississippi River bridge at Fort Snelling after a run to the Cities. Dan had spat his own bridge into the air like a missile. They'd both ground to a stop, tumbled off the bikes, and run to the edge to see if it was still falling, so full of beer they couldn't even focus. Something about losing a bridge *on* a bridge had broken them both up, and they'd hammered on each other's backs until Dan had puked. "Don't need no fake teeth for *that*," he'd said, wiping his mouth on his sleeve. It had been the funniest thing Largo had ever seen.

Somehow it didn't seem so funny anymore. And maybe he did need that shot. The brothers were coming tomorrow to haul his sorry ass back to the apartment. He didn't much like the idea of them having to do that. He'd rather do it on his own.

"Give me one of them shots," he muttered to the nurse.

"What?"

He gestured toward the tray. "Them needles," he said.

The nurse picked up the hypodermic. "Turn over," she said.

"Do what?"

"Turn over. It doesn't go in your arm."

"*What*?"

She had the needle out. "Turn over, Mr. Miller," she said, with what might have been a smile. "Don't worry. I've seen it all."

Largo edged himself down in bed again. Suspicious, he felt around his waist. Nothing. He didn't dare think what he didn't have on below. He felt the red creeping up his neck. Like a child, he shut his eyes, squeezing the lids so tight together that between his tense cheekbones and his throbbing ribs, he didn't even feel it when the needle went in.

The nurse pulled the blanket back over him. He kept his eyes shut. By now the red had reached his ears. "Give it fifteen minutes or so," the nurse said. "Then you can sleep."

But sleep seemed as far away as heaven itself to Largo when the nurse had finally left the room and he had shifted himself into an upright position again. The little old man in the other bed was staring at him. Largo tried to swing his legs down to the floor. Where in hell were his clothes? Except for Sandy's visit, the last three days were a blur in his mind, and the TV on the opposite wall made such a blather that he couldn't even think.

"Turn that goddamn thing off."

The other patient looked at him. "It's mine," he said weakly.

"I know that." Largo tried not to swear. The old man looked ready to kick off without any help. "Just turn the goddamn thing down then," he said, his voice rising. He got his feet on the floor, which was surprisingly cold. Then he saw his boots in the corner by the closet. His jeans must be in there. They'd cut his shirt off him—now he remembered that. He'd just wear his colors.

The TV clicked off. But by now Largo wasn't thinking about the television. It was all he could do to get himself to the closet. All the muscles across his gut felt like they'd been cut in half. He dropped his hospital gown on the floor, shivered, caught his breath, grabbed his jeans from the hook inside the closet door, leaned against the wall and pulled them on. The snaps at the belt-line didn't seem to match, and he couldn't suck his gut in enough to give himself any leeway. Without his underwear, the zipper sliced across his privates like a knife. Bracing himself against the wall, which seemed inexplicably to be swaying, he got his boots on, and then he pulled his colors down from the hanger where someone had put them and slid them over his shoulders. Good thing they hadn't cut them off him too.

He didn't have a comb, and he knew his hair looked like shit. His ponytail was long gone. Even if he could make a new one, there was nothing to tie it with. He held the tangle of his back hair in his two hands, willing it to hold together by itself.

The old man leaned forward in his bed. "You can take this," he said, holding out a rubber band.

His hands still clutching his hair, Largo looked over at him. "What?" he said. His eyes didn't focus properly, and the rubber band waved in the air as if it were alive.

"Take this," the voice said again.

Largo launched himself from the wall, refusing to feel the pain in his ribs, and reached the edge of the old man's bed. Before he could grab the mattress for support, the man dropped the rubber band into his palm. "Hang on to it," he said in his cracked, elderly voice.

"Thanks."

But the man went right on. "Are you a biker?" he asked.

His question penetrated the fog. "Yeah, whatever," Largo said back. "I ride a Harley. It's busted up right now, but I'll get it on the road again." It felt as if the ends of his ribs were rubbing against each other, sharp as hornets. "Guess I'm fucked up too," he said, trying to stuff his hair inside the rubber band.

But the old man didn't seem to be looking at him. "When Lucy and I got married," he said, his voice creaky but clear, "we didn't have much money. I borrowed my brother's Harley, and we went on our honeymoon riding it. Lucy was so shy she didn't even want to hang on to me at first." He smiled. "But I went so fast that she had to." The smile broadened. "We went to Itasca," he said. "Stayed in one of those cabins. A family of raccoons came out at night and begged for food. Even the babies could sit up and beg."

Largo gave up on his hair. In the fog of his brain, he sought for something polite with which to end the conversation. The man seemed old enough to be his grandfather. "Your wife visiting you today?" he asked. The old buck could chew on that while he snuck out.

But the man seemed to be thinking about something else. Then he focused back on Largo. "She's been gone six years," he said. "I live at Mercy Care Center now. But I have this clot in my leg. I think they're going to cut it off."

"Oh, man, I'm sorry."

Again the old man looked like he'd gone to another place. "I don't care about the leg," he said, running his hand across his forehead. "But I never got over Lucy," he said softly. "I always thought we'd go together."

And that was all Largo could handle. He lurched toward the door, the rubber band tangled around his fingers. Out in the hall, he pulled himself upright with every ounce of strength he had, forced his legs forward in a straight line, like the one he'd walked, or tried to walk, for the Moorhead police more times than he could remember, crashed down the EXIT stairs from the second floor, pressing his incision together with his elbow dug into his gut. In the waiting room, he thought of stopping to rest, but rest wasn't really the problem. Sandy needed him.

Holding his breath, he started toward the door, willing it to draw him in, and then he was outside in the parking lot, leaning against someone's pickup and puking onto the asphalt. Every heave made his side split apart. He looked around, desperate, knowing his bike wasn't there, hoping that it would be. His head sang.

"Are you all right?"

Largo got his head up far enough to focus on a slender figure standing to one side of him. Even in the dim light over the cars, he knew it wasn't one of the brothers.

"Yeah."

"Are you sure?"

No, he wasn't sure. Largo swabbed off his mouth with his wrist. He could get through this like he had before. He was no groaner.

The figure stayed. "I could give you a lift," it said, the head a little to one side. "That is, if you don't mind a Miata. The most impractical car on the road. However, it has proven itself such fun to drive that I indulge myself."

The words slipped off Largo like water. In the sky, the stars were each followed by a yellow streak, as if they were moving. The streaks rotated in time to his pulse. He pressed his eyes closed to try to stop them, but the streaks continued inside his eyelids. Angry, he hammered on the pickup with his fist.

"Now, now." The other man laid his hand on Largo's wrist. "No point in causing major damage."

Largo looked at his own hands. There seemed to be more than the usual number of them.

"Where do you want to go?"

"What?"

The other man took off his jacket, something smooth and soft-looking. Largo knew it was expensive, even though its shape undulated along with the parking lot light. "The wind is coming up," the man said. "You must have left your own jacket behind."

He draped the fabric over Largo's shoulders, patting it down as he did so. Something in his gesture was both off-putting and comforting.

Stumbling, Largo planted his feet far enough apart so he could stay balanced on them. "Where you going?" he asked.

The man reached out his hand. "Wherever you need me to," he said. "I'll drive you. My name, incidentally, is Alex. I'm a massage therapist, but I'm foolishly addicted to volunteering in the ER. I just put in an extra stint there." His eyes ran over Largo. "My lucky night, obviously," he said. "And I must state that, even though I suspect you're a little out of condition, and who isn't, you really have a splendid torso. The tattoos aren't bad either."

thirty-six

Usually on Tuesday nights, Sandy geared all her activities toward the watching of *NYPD Blue*, her absolutely favorite TV show. But it wasn't as simple as just curling up on the sofa with the remote at nine p.m., which to her mind would have been shortchanging the program, acting as if it were just another piece of network entertainment that you caught or didn't catch, depending on what else you were doing. There was more to it than that.

When she'd moved in with Largo two months ago, he hadn't even had a television, or rather, he'd had a tiny black-and-white set with a cracked plastic case that he'd kept plugged in on the bathroom counter so he could watch it while he was on the john. "Most people read!" she'd shouted at him, once she'd figured out why the TV was in the bathroom in the first place. He'd turned bright red, and when she'd come home from her walk the next morning (even if she didn't intend to spend any time being bossed by those doctors, she knew she ought to stretch her muscles), there'd been a twenty-five-inch model teetering on the coffee table in the living room, and Largo had been up on the roof of the building, siphoning off the power from the big cable antenna. She hadn't wanted the set on the coffee table because watching a screen so close hurt her eyes, but through the window Largo had seen her shoving at it when he was climbing down from the roof, and he'd raced around the front of the building and up the stairs while she was catching her breath. "Shit!" he'd bellowed, one of the few profanities she'd ever heard from him, as he grabbed the set in his arms. "You can't lift nothing like this!" The set had ended up on the chair in the corner, a little tenuous on the overstuffed cushion, but at the right distance.

In the bedroom, all he had was the sleeping bag. In the living room, the only good chair now held the television. When he watched with her, he squatted on the floor, his hands hanging between his knees. He was the only man she'd ever known who didn't like football. "They get too much money," he'd growled.

On the coffee table, Sandy lined up the popcorn, the lemonade, two paper napkins, the remote control, and her latest book about childbirth. This one didn't have photographs, just drawings. She liked those better.

She wasn't scared. She just wasn't comfortable with the idea that once all this got started, she'd have to keep going. When she was little, her dad had called her his zigzag girl. He said she never went straight to anything.

With one hand extended, Sandy flipped the TV on, just as the camera started leaping from one New York City shot to another. Her favorite was the building being blown up—it was neat that they still used it this season. Maybe it wouldn't have been so good if you heard the sound of the explosion, but the picture appeared on the screen in total silence. Just the big beige skyscraper falling in on itself with the dust rising.

Sandy heaved herself backwards against the arm of the sofa. Her belly arched up on top of her like a little round mountain. King Kicker in there must have got the hiccups, because the skin right next to her belly button was popping up and down. She gave him a pat, as near as she could get.

Largo was the only man on earth who would have laid his bike down just to get her to see a doctor. Even her parents wouldn't have known how to make her do it. When she'd finally talked to him in the hospital the second time, you could tell he was hurting, but he never said anything about it. He'd probably had a million accidents in his life. He was tough. And he never hurt anyone but himself.

There was no point in his having been so worried about her. That awful Mathison said she was fine. Or at least he hadn't told her anything was wrong. She'd know soon enough for sure.

Would she have gone in to see Largo on her own if her parents hadn't gotten involved? Maybe, maybe not. Probably. He always liked her cooking. When he came back to the apartment tomorrow, she might try a soufflé, since he'd be stuck inside and she could make him eat it before it fell. She'd already thrown the soup out.

On the TV, Bobby Simone was in the hospital too. Jimmy Smits was a really good actor, but they were just making him die so he could leave the show. It wasn't that simple to get rid of people in real life.

The popcorn bowl was empty. Sandy swung her legs off the sofa as soon as the commercial started, and, with the bowl hanging from her hand, went off in quest of the rest of the popcorn in the kitchen. The light was still on in the bedroom. She hated to waste Largo's electricity. He always talked like he had enough money, but unless he was selling drugs, she didn't know where it came from. She couldn't imagine him having a savings account.

So when she went into the bedroom on her way back, setting her new allotment of popcorn on the bureau, she just thought she'd check his sleeping bag. She could have rolled it up, but she didn't mind walking over it, and she actually liked its smell. Not that Largo wasn't clean, but men's skin was just different. Or maybe it was his Indian hair. She didn't really think that he hid his money under his pillow, but who knew?

Only when she knelt down by the bag, struggling to keep her balance, it wasn't money that she felt under the funny old pillow that Largo had dragged out from one of the drawers. But it was something. Several things. Sandy shoved the pillow aside and pulled out a plastic bag, then a second one. For a moment she thought pot, then cocaine, but it didn't feel right—too soft and spread out. And the bags said Garfields, the department store in Littleriver. No one would store mind-altering substances in a Garfields bag.

But even though she was pretty sure it wasn't anything illegal, when she actually opened the first bag, she couldn't believe what she saw. It was baby clothes—first, four little shirts, the kind with ties, and then three of those little suits that snapped up the crotch. They were all green and yellow—she hadn't thought Largo would know about the pink and blue thing, but maybe he'd learned about gender-neutral colors somewhere along the line with the summer children. There was even a little hat, kind of a stocking cap. They were all new, with the price tags still on them. And not even on sale.

The second bag was stiffer. When she pulled out the folded chunk of denim, she had no idea. When she unfolded it, she couldn't believe jeans could be so small. But they were big enough to have HARLEY embroidered right across the butt.

She supposed he hadn't thought about diapers. And there must be a lot of stuff neither of them knew anything about.

They'd need bottles and formula. She wasn't going to do that breast-feeding gig. And a crib. Did her mom still have her old things? She'd have to ask her.

Leaning forward over her belly, Sandy tucked the bags back under the bedraggled pillow. The floor was awfully hard. What with her big belly and Largo's broken ribs, probably neither of them should be sleeping on it.

In the living room, she could hear Bobby Simone saying something in his throaty whisper now that he was dying. She'd read that Jimmy Smits was part Indian, or Filipino, or something. But Largo had a lot more hair. He was really a pretty good-looking man for somebody as old as he was.

thirty-seven

"Would you like to talk about what's going on in your life?"

Largo had no idea what his driver meant. He was just hoping that Sandy was home, because he didn't have either his wallet or his keys, and he was pretty sure that he wasn't going to last if he had to wait on the steps. Even in the soft seat of the Miata, his ribs seemed at war with each other, and his jeans pushed into his gut and against the incision. He unbuckled his belt and leaned back.

"My, my."

Largo tugged at the zipper in his fly, then remembered that he hadn't been able to find his underpants either. Oh hell. He leaned back and shut his eyes.

"Don't give up. The night is young."

Although Largo heard the words, they didn't register in any meaningful way. The Miata was so low to the ground that he felt as if his boots were directly on the pavement, walking him at an incredible speed toward the apartment and Sandy. He'd have to call his brothers at the clubhouse and tell them he was home already. He'd have to find out what they'd done with his scooter. He figured most of the damage had probably happened to him, but the bike would need a new paint job for sure. Rocker had said that the throttle cable was broken, but that wouldn't take much to fix. Dan the Man had done his in four or five times on the old Sportster. And then both him and the Sportster were gone.

"Have you always been a biker?"

Largo shut his eyes tighter.

"I've thought about it myself. In my wildest fantasies, of course. I know the motorcycle clubs have very mixed feelings about gays. Although a well-cut leather looks smashing no matter what your sexual orientation is."

Fighting up through an exhaustion so deep it was like quicksand, Largo shook his head to clear his ears. He even pulled his hair back so the air could get through better.

"Splendid hair," the man said. "And I don't suppose you dye it either. I've always thought I wouldn't stoop so low, but once those little gray twinges creep in, you look in the mirror and simply feel so *ancient*. Burton is the only man I know who can carry it off. Wrinkles have always held a weathered charm, but gray hair allows no excuses to be made for it. And, in case you've forgotten my name, it's Alex. What's yours?"

"My name?"

"That's usually an appropriate next bit of information." Alex gunned the car at the light outside of Moorhead, then slid through just as the yellow changed to red. "And we don't have to go right home. Maybe you'd like a beer. Or something more sophisticated. I'm a Cointreau man myself. Do you have a favorite bar? I'd be happy to take you wherever you want to go."

They were slipping down the main street of Moorhead, quiet at this time of night, with a few lights along the sidewalk and a few windows that gleamed a faint yellow against the darkness. Leaves scattered on the pavement. The Prince of the Prairie was on the left, but Largo didn't spend much time in yuppie bars. Still he recognized its big sign, caught his breath. "Over there," he said. "You can park in back."

"My, that was quick. But I still don't know your name."

"Largo. And, hell, I can't find my wallet."

"Don't worry. I have plenty of money. It will be an honor. Especially now that I know who you are."

The parking lot held only a few widely separated cars, front bumpers against the wall of the building. The Miata slid in among them and stopped. "Can you make it out yourself?" Alex asked, but Largo was already standing on the pavement, hunched over but aimed forward. Alex's jacket bound tight across his back with the lines of his colors showing through.

"Maybe we'd better button it up the front."

"What?"

"Button it." Alex reached out and fastened the two middle buttons even though it was a stretch. "Not that you couldn't do it yourself. But why not be helpful? And you wouldn't want to get cold."

The path Alex's fingers had made on the fabric itched against Largo's skin as the two of them entered and turned to the right toward the bar. One blond woman sat at the end, as well as a couple of college students bent so low over the counter that their noses roamed just above the surfaces of their beers.

"Shall we take a table?"

Largo couldn't imagine hoisting himself onto a bar stool. His head was swimming. Suddenly it didn't seem like such a good idea to start on the booze, because even in his drinking days he hadn't been good at holding it. Finally he'd been court-ordered into AA after three DUIs, and after that year, if he was tired, it only took three or four beers to put him away. With his gut cut open and his ribs cracked, he was in no shape for any serious drinking.

"One Cointreau," Alex said to the waitress, who couldn't take her eyes off Largo.

"Tequila shooter," Largo said. At least it wouldn't leave a taste when it went down.

From somewhere in the larger room of the restaurant, music twined its way through the air. For Largo, it wasn't so much sound as texture, like one of Sandy's scarves or the wind in his mouth when the Softail hit some good air and everything was so perfect it was like dying. He turned his head to listen. Sound was easier without words. He felt like all the words inside his head had turned to dust.

"So you like the Schubert Chorale?"

"What?"

"The Chorale. That group is magnificent on their best days. I do think it's a little early for the Christmas concert, however. I suppose it's the only tape they had."

None of this made any sense. Largo grasped the tequila, which had appeared in front of him. He took more in his mouth than he had intended to, and it flung itself down his throat before he could regulate it. His head exploded.

"Are you all right?"

He wasn't. Alex sprang up and thumped him between his shoulder blades. Fire shot through Largo's ribs. "Fuck off!" he yelled, but he couldn't get his breath, and it came out a whisper.

"I think this probably wasn't a very good idea."

Everyone in the Prince of the Prairie was looking toward them, although, since it was so late and a weeknight too, it still didn't add up to much of an audience. Alex downed his Cointreau, only a minor look of regret passing over his face as he did so. Then he put his arm around Largo's shoulders and led him outside, dropping a bill on the bar as he passed. "Not the best night for him," he said intimately to the bartender. "But we all have nights like that."

Outside, a little wind had come up. Largo let it blow him back against the Miata. His head wobbled, but then he firmed it on his shoulders. A picture of Sandy flowered behind his eyes, not her face, but her body hanging onto him in the bitch seat as they had raced from the hospital that time, her little belly against his spine, her funny salty smell. She might not be home. She might have gone to her parents. Probably that was where she should be. The baby was due pretty soon. He didn't know shit about babies. Their clothes were so fucking *small.*

Alex came up next to him. "You weren't ready for this," he said.

"Exactomundo," Largo said back.

"Did you ever do it with a man?"

The wind must have changed directions. Anyone could say anything. "You mean take it up the ass?" Largo asked.

"Well, that among other things."

"Jesus, I was never *that* drunk."

Alex smiled. "Some of us don't need to be drunk," he said quietly.

"You mean you do that shit because you *like* it?"

"I guess you could say that, yes." Alex touched the end of one strand of Largo's hair, but carefully, so Largo couldn't possibly feel it.

"When I was drinking, I fucked about everything on two legs that would have me. But they was all cunts." Largo focused on the lights by the street next to the parking lot. "Only I don't mess around much now," he said.

"Probably a good thing. With AIDS and all."

Sandy had those freckles on her nose. She didn't wear a bra. At least Largo had never seen one in the little piles of clothing she left around the bedroom. Her breasts had been small and soft against his back. Like roses.

"That ain't it," Largo sighed.

thirty-eight

It wasn't Sandy's room anymore. They'd taken care of that.

But it still held memories.

Ed held himself upright by the photocopy machine, his fingers gripping its edges, his eyes focused on the white plastic slab covering the glass. His jacket hung open. If he let go, he was going to fall on the floor.

But of course he wouldn't. He'd keep standing, like he always had. His mouth would open, and something appropriate would come out, something with the slightest of Minnesota cadences, something with an oblique reference to the text of the day.

Something to protect him.

Anything to protect him.

They were keeping Grace overnight at the hospital. How much had she known? Everything, of course. Grace always knew everything.

Ed shut his eyes. The room was dark anyway, so it didn't make much difference. Outside it was dark too. What time? Midnight? The marker for another foolish, lying, hypocritical day opening itself before him.

Without thinking, he shifted his right hand. His thumb hit the ON button. The machine grumbled electronically and ran through its cycle. A blank sheet of paper slid into the IN container.

But how could he put them all on the same sheet? Eugene, who had never been a person. Just his body—Lighty had that right. Sandy, his heart's core, angry, funny, self-destructive. The wind had blown her into their lives and might well blow her out again.

And the wind had always been blowing. When Mike had reached out for the Vietnamese boy with the bomb, he'd been planning to give him a pinwheel, a little whirling plastic gimmick from the market in Cu Chi. Mike was always giving stuff to the kids. The boy, so slight that his shirt had hung on him like a shroud, had smiled up at the big soldier but hadn't held out his hand. When he exploded, he was simply gone, and Mike, bleeding everywhere, guts flung loose in the dirt, had never said another word. Nothing any medic could do would have saved him.

There were so many of them. People, villages, huts. Burn one, burn ten, it didn't make any difference. The wind spread the flames like the angry hand of God. Then, in a day, a week, two weeks, everything would begin again.

thirty-nine

Even though it was late, Burton couldn't stop cleaning. Two years ago he had brought their living room to what he had always considered the peak of decorating perfection—the Persian rug from an estate sale in Moorhead, the Victorian settee, the almost-Tiffany lamp rising from the inlaid rosewood table. Even their cat, Matchbox, had seemed to appreciate the results, and he spent the days when Alex and Burton both worked ensconced in the righthand corner of the settee, nestled against the pillow that Burton's mother had cross-stitched. It wasn't the right style—high camp rather than high Victorian. But it didn't show the cat hair.

In the fall, when school was just starting, cleaning became a luxury. The yard was where Burton concentrated his energy, trying to bring it down toward winter properly tended. But some bubble had broken since Alex had pitched the deck chair into the lake. The lawn seemed fragmented, less amenable to rearrangement. It was as if he saw it through a distorted glass pane, like those on the old New England houses. Their house, luckily for his standard of cleanliness, still looked the same.

At night, it was harder to be sure you got everything—every dust speck, every greasy fingerprint on polished wood, every slightly misaligned knickknack. Burton had finally gone to Doan's Hardware and bought a trouble light, the kind you could attach to your belt, or, in extreme underground cases, to your forehead. It came with four D batteries. Alex had screamed with laughter when he'd seen it. "Prospecting for the mighty Dust Demon?" he'd choked out, then given Burton a sudden, spontaneous hug.

Alex.

"Do you always clean like this?" Richard was sitting on their one modern chair, located in the corner by the front hallway door. Its more rigid lines allowed him to make a perfect half-swastika of his body—head and torso absolutely upright, thighs jutted directly forward, lower legs plunging downward to the carpet. He had left his sneakers outside on the porch, and his feet were bare. They did look clean, however.

"No."

"My mother hates to clean."

Richard's mother had visited three days ago, her square pale face as chilly as an ice cube against the floral back of the settee. In her efforts not to lose her temper, her voice had become a scratchy whisper. Burton had given them their privacy, lurking next to the refrigerator in the kitchen. Alex had begun to deconstruct the flea market chest in their upstairs bedroom, letting every board tumble with a florid crash to the floor directly over the living room. But neither he nor Alex had heard what Richard's mother had actually said to her son, and Richard was still living with them.

"It takes a certain talent to clean well."

"Actually, I'm not too interested in it myself."

In the gentle pseudo-nineteenth-century glow of the two electrically wired kerosene lamps on the mantle, Richard's complexion seemed to have healed itself. Burton bent and began to line up the fringes of the Persian rug, each thread laid delicately straight and properly related to its companions.

Richard rubbed his cheek reflectively. "When did you know you were gay?" he asked.

"What?"

"When you were gay. Did you always know? Alex said he knew from the cradle."

"Alex didn't have a cradle. I doubt he even had a crib. His mother was a geologist. He spent more time in a backpack than an Indian papoose."

"Don't be racist."

Burton sprang up from the rug. "Don't be WHAT?" he snorted.

"Racist. We gays should be the most tolerant of anyone."

The smug little homo prick. Burton swung away from the rug, deliberately disarranging the fringe with his heel. "I found out when I was a freshman in high school and the basketball coach goosed me in the shower," he said. Let the idiot child chew on that.

"That really happened?"

Burton thought for a moment. "Actually, it was the track coach," he said, realizing he had genuinely forgotten. "And it wasn't the shower. We were on a camping trip over the weekend to celebrate the junior varsity winning the regionals. I was looking at the lake and thinking about T. S. Eliot."

"Was he someone you wanted to fuck?"

"*What*?"

"Eliot." Richard leaned back in his chair. "I think about fucking Brad Pitt," he said. "But I don't guess he's interested in men."

Well, he's certainly not interested in *you,* Burton thought. He put down his cleaning cloth, already sprayed with Pledge, and sat himself in the chair nearest to Richard. It happened to be the rocker, designed with no arms so a nursing mother could easily hold her baby. The lack of arms was no problem, but the chair began to dither with the force of his collapse onto its seat. He reconciled himself to its movement, leaned toward Richard. The chair leaned with him.

"Richard," he said, looking for a response and receiving none. "Richard, I believe it's time you moved back home."

"I don't think my parents want me back."

"Your parents are legally obliged to take you back. Your mother cares enough about you to come spend half an afternoon with you. She left you a parcel of toilet articles and a loaf of cranberry bread. None of that sounds as if she despises you or feels you are not a part of her life."

"But my father is really pissed off."

"Are you worried about him hurting you?"

"My DAD?"

"Yes, your father."

"He never even spanks my little brother." Richard resumed his original half-swastika. "He's a lawyer," he said. "He knows about child abuse. He isn't going to do anything that will get him in trouble."

"So you'd be safe if you went home."

"I guess."

"Then I think you should plan on going there. Your arm is back to normal. School has been in session for more than a month. I'll call the office and get your bus schedule straightened out. It's time, Richard. It's time."

"But does Alex feel the same way about it as you do?"

So *that* was the core of the matter. Richard's cliff-hanging adult voice skidded up into soprano, and he began blinking rapidly. Burton waited for more, but no more came.

"I don't know, Richard."

"I thought you guys were lovers. Don't you talk to each other?"

"And do you think that's any of your business?"

Richard glared at him. Matchbox, who had entered the room, jumped at Richard's leg. Richard shoved him aside. Matchbox uttered a truncated yowl and scuttled under the cabinet where Alex had his gun collection. His eyes glared balefully at both of them.

"Be quiet, Richard."

"I will fucking well be quiet when *I* want to!"

Inside his carefully ironed shirt, Burton felt his heart thudding as if he had just run a mile, something he hadn't done since high school, and then with extremely moderate success. He had liked being behind in the pack, he suddenly realized, because all those sweet little tushes were right there in his line of sight. Win? He would never have been so foolish.

"Richard." Fleetingly, Burton thought of putting his hand on the boy's shoulder, but he was afraid the gesture would metamorphose into a slap. He picked up the dustrag and spray bottle. "Richard," he said again. "You have your life to live. So do we. Go home. We're not locking our door, of course. We're like your uncles, or whatever senior relatives you want to label us as, for as long as you need us. But the kids in school are going to gossip. And you need to learn to live with your folks again. They'll be in your life until they die. Parents are permanent. That's just the way the world works."

"Don't you and Alex think you can fuck each other if I'm here? Because I might be listening?"

"Richard!"

"And just where *is* Alex now?"

Burton looked around at the darkened window, at Matchbox's evil little eyes glittering under the cabinet, at the tangled rug fringe and the faded fake flowers on the fake hearthstone next to the reproduction of Michelangelo's *David*. "I don't know where he is," he said.

forty

The baby must have begun to kick so hard that she was not just feeling it, but hearing it too. In her half-sleep, Sandy grabbed her gut with both hands, trying to make him be quiet. There was a momentary pause, and then the banging began again.

This wasn't labor. Her eyes opened, then shut. Labor was supposed to hurt. And no one had ever said that it made *noise*.

She sat up, gasping with the effort. When she swung her feet over the side of the bed, the cold air reached up to her twat. Why was she still wearing Largo's T-shirts to bed when winter was coming? And the baby, fat as a porpoise inside the skin of her belly, wasn't moving at all.

Crash!

Startled, Sandy reached over and yanked open the drawer of the nightstand. Largo had warned her, but she had figured it was just the biker's paranoia. No one would try to break in, not in Moorhead, Minnesota. And who would want a woman with a belly so big she couldn't even watch her own pee come out when she went to the bathroom?

The gun was under a scrabble of papers—bills for video rentals, Powerball tickets, the new booklet about what to take to the hospital when you were having a baby. Her fingers edged it out. She hadn't wanted to listen when Largo had tried to show her how the gun worked, how to slide the bullets into the little holes. But she remembered a few things because he'd been so earnest, and he'd actually gone out and *bought* her that particular gun. "A nice little pistole," he'd said. "Made special for a lady like you. They even laid in that mother-of-pearl on the hand grip."

Now the banging had stopped. Sandy waited, the gun resting in the palm of her hand. It seemed as if she could hear breathing, a kind of wheeze. She hadn't heard the buzzer from downstairs. How could anyone have gotten up to the apartment? But half the time the big door didn't latch. This wasn't exactly upscale housing.

Stumbling over Largo's sleeping bag, she tiptoed toward the apartment door, the gun held out in front of her. Somewhere back in her mind, she thought "hammer," and she pulled that little piece of metal back with her thumb. After the baby was born, they couldn't leave a loaded gun in the drawer any more. Well, it would be OK for the first year or so. No matter what kind of genius baby she ended up having, and with Juan as the dad she couldn't expect very much in that category, he wasn't likely to be going through bedroom drawers looking for firearms during his first year.

Now she was in the living room, her toes gripping the shag carpet. Largo had even shampooed that after he'd brought her here. Sometimes she just thought he'd had a compulsive mother. Other times she wasn't sure about anything.

The hall was quiet. But someone was there. Now she could really hear breathing, harsh and quick. She stepped back until her butt hit the sofa arm and held the gun out in front of her with both hands on it, just like in *NYPD Blue*. She pointed the barrel down a little bit. How do you aim? She'd thought you had to bring it up to your eye, but maybe that was for pheasants or something that flew. Her belly was so big that she could hardly get her arms extended far enough.

Then there was one more thump, a loud one. She hadn't expected it, and she jumped. The hammer slammed back against the gun. Maybe she pulled the trigger too. She heard the clank of metal on metal, and then a bang that sounded like Fourth of July fireworks, one of the little ones. But there was enough kick so she lost her balance and plopped down on the sofa arm. A small black hole appeared in the lower panel of the door, exactly like in the movies.

"Sandy! Put that fuckin' gun down!"

Largo *never* swore when she was around. At least not the really serious swearwords.

"I ain't got my keys. Let me in. Please."

This was all a dream. Largo was in Memorial Hospital, not coming home until tomorrow. It was two in the morning. Did he have a brother with that same whiskey voice?

"Sandy, *please*." A pause. "I don't feel so good."

She put her hand to her throat. "Are you drunk?" she asked.

"You know I never come back here to you drunk."

She believed him. When she slipped the deadbolt, he practically fell into the room.

"Did I hit you?"

He limped to the sofa, wincing. "How could you hit me?" he asked. "I was in the hall."

"I mean with the bullet."

He didn't seem to register what she'd said. Then his eyes widened. "Jesus Christ," he said, looking down at his jeans where a slender fraying line crossed his right leg just below the groin. "So that was what done it!"

Sandy gasped. She flung herself down beside him, her weight sinking her so deep into the cushion that she didn't think she could ever get up again. "You take this gun, Largo," she said, shoving it into his hand. "I could have killed you."

"You didn't want me back?"

"I didn't know it was YOU! I just woke UP! I thought the baby was banging INSIDE ME!"

Largo laid the gun aside, leaned his head back and shut his eyes. In the shabby room under the blank eye of the big television screen, all of his face was in shadow. Still, Sandy could see the sparse bristles along his jawline. She thought the nurses shaved you when you were in the hospital. But maybe Largo had fought them off. He was very private about lots of things.

"Are you all right?" She kept her voice low.

Largo's eyes were still shut. He ran one hand down over his chest. "I'll live," he said. "Ribs feel like shit, but I've broke 'em before."

"Didn't they operate on you too?"

Largo winced. "Yeah," he said.

"My father said they took out your spleen. That you ruptured it when you fell off your bike."

"I didn't fall off! I lost the road!" Gingerly, Largo fingered his incision. "Something come out of here, I guess."

"Does it hurt?"

"I'll live."

For a moment, Sandy thought he'd fallen asleep just like that, instant oblivion. But then she guessed he was only resting. He was wearing a strange jacket over his colors, and no shirt.

"Where'd you get that jacket?"

"Guy give it to me."

"Why?"

"Sandy, babe, I have no clue. But at least I didn't have to hitch back to Moorhead."

She turned toward him. A bit of belly hung over his belt, but not much. The stitches in his incision were black, thicker than she would have thought, and the line of the cut was puffy. Hard to imagine that three days ago someone had been digging around inside his gut.

Largo's eyes were still shut. She reached out her hand and touched his belly as gently as she could. He didn't have much hair on his chest, but there was a wispy little pathway down his midline that started to widen as it entered his pants. She knew where it was going.

"Does that hurt?"

Largo sat silent for what seemed a long time. "Nope," he said finally.

Sandy let one finger touch the scar, then another. She shut her own eyes just to see if she could feel it better when she wasn't looking at it. She wasn't sure she wanted to watch her fingers do whatever it was they were doing. "You sure have a lot of things happen to you," she finally said.

"Guess so." Largo's voice cracked, but he still didn't move.

"I'm sorry you got hurt."

He shifted just a little under her hand. "At least I don't got to have no baby."

"I really did see the doctor, you know."

"You said."

"Everything's OK. It might be another week or so. He wasn't sure."

Largo didn't say anything. Sandy opened her eyes. He was looking at her as if he were going to eat her up.

And then she couldn't hold it back anymore. She leaned over and put her head under his chin. He had his hands around behind his back as if he could keep them under control better that way, and she just reached around and burrowed until she had one extracted. He never got his nails quite clean, and even the hospital stay hadn't changed that. His hands were browner than the rest of him, as if all the Indian pigment had gotten concentrated in them. She bent over and kissed his palm.

Largo was biting his lower lip. "Babe, there's no need for you to do that," he said.

"I want to. Without you, I'd be dead."

"No, you wouldn't. Your folks would take care of you if you'd just ask. Only problem is, they don't know how to handle a free spirit woman."

"I guess I don't know what to do with her either."

Now he was holding her hand. He took a deep breath, grimacing as his chest expanded. "*I* do, baby," he said. "But I don't know as it would work tonight, with my ribs and all."

"Largo!"

"Shit. I didn't mean to make you feel bad."

"Anything you do to me, you do to the baby at this point."

"I guess that's right." But he didn't drop her hand.

"Maybe I'll have it tonight. You could take me on the Harley and try to shake it loose."

"Rocker took my scooter so's he could put it back together. But as soon as I got it again, I'll take you on any kind of run you want."

She leaned back against him. It was so late, and her head was full of Styrofoam. She touched the little roadway in his jeans where she'd just about finished off any possibilities of a long-term relationship.

"Largo?"

"Yeah?"

"You take the bed tonight. Seeing that you're hurting and all."

"You're not sleeping on that floor, Sandy." His voice was firm.

Now she touched his bristly jawline. How could something be so soft and prickly all at once? "Well, maybe I don't have to sleep on the floor," she said. "We can share."

forty-one

Elizabeth had never realized how wet it was in the woods just before dawn. Huddled in the brush, her chin on her knees, she felt the damp rising right into the core of her body. She had her period too, and she could smell the overloaded pad jammed between her legs. Everyone else wore tampons, but her mother said pads were the right thing to wear when you were still a young girl. What did that mean? It was the only thing her mother had ever said to her about sex.

When the first lamp went on in Lighty's house, she was going to go knock. So she had to keep her eyes open. She wanted Lighty to see her at the very beginning of the day, but she didn't want to wake her.

Maybe if she'd held Eugene's head up. Then he could have swallowed better. Maybe if she'd done that.

The sky wasn't brightening, exactly, but the dark wasn't so strong. Trees stood out. Elizabeth pulled off a sumac leaf and held it in her hand. Sumac was poison. Some sumac. Some parts of sumac. Lighty made sumac jelly, though, and it wasn't poison. It tasted like a sweet mist, and you never got tired of it.

At the thought of food, her stomach growled. It was amazing how all your parts kept working as long as you weren't dead. Blood came out, food went in. You made shit and pee. You breathed. You drew breath. You drew breath like it was water from a well and you were letting the bucket down. Only that was backwards, because you breathed from the top.

In some world, Eugene was still alive. More alive than he had been. She saw him sitting on a cloud, bouncing a little, holding a golden book. Elizabeth walked toward him to say "hi." She didn't know if he'd recognize her, but he did, and he stood up to reach out. Only the cloud was so soft that he slid down into it. She flung her arms out to help him, and she started to slide too. The air swooped under her.

"Elizabeth."

She didn't know he could say her name.

"Elizabeth." Something touched her shoulder. "You're so cold. What are you doing here?"

She opened her eyes. Lighty was standing by her, bending over, touching her cheek. Elizabeth shrank back.

"What's wrong?"

"I fell asleep." Tears hung in her voice. "I was going to knock when your lamp went on."

Lighty bent lower. "I've been awake," she said, and gently pulled the girl to her feet. "I just felt like walking."

"Are you mad at me?"

Lighty stepped back. "Oh, my dear," she said. "Of course not."

"But I killed him."

The words stood in the air. In the early light, they seemed to have a physical shape, sharp on the topside, glittering.

Lighty looked down. Blood was running down the girl's legs. "Are you hurt?" she asked, putting her hands out.

"It's just my monthlies."

The strange old-fashioned word caught Lighty under the heart. "We'll clean you up," she said, moving them both toward the house. "Does your mother know you're gone?"

"She's asleep. Drunk." Another shameful secret.

They were at the door. As they walked in, Elizabeth looked toward the bedroom.

"He's not there, you know. He's at the funeral parlor in town."

"Did they take him away?"

"Yes. His funeral is tomorrow."

"I don't want to come."

Lighty was kneeling in front of her. "You don't have to come," she said, pulling off Elizabeth's soaked skirt. From somewhere she'd gotten a basin of warm water and a towel. She began to wash Elizabeth's legs.

"You don't have to do that."

"It's all right."

"Do you miss Eugene?"

"Yes. But like you miss a season when it's over."

"I think summer is gone for good now," Elizabeth said, in a strange, wise voice. She shivered.

Lighty touched her shoulder, then pulled the afghan from the sofa and wrapped it around her. "I'll make breakfast," she said. "You can have anything you want."

"Did Eugene have a father?"

"Of course."

"Didn't you want to live with him?"

"It wasn't possible."

The girl squatted down on the floor, making a tent of the afghan. Only her bare toes and tousled hair stuck out. Even her voice was muffled. "Why did you love him then?" she asked.

"Oh, my dear." Lighty squatted down next to her. "I met him a long time ago. I had just moved here, gotten this place. I'd broken up with another man not long before. Loudly. You could have heard me in the next county. Eugene's father was quiet, and he had wonderful hands. I was ready for another kind of love."

"Didn't he help you with Eugene?"

"I didn't want him to."

The girl dropped the afghan. It lay in a splash of color around her. "I'm sorry Eugene died," she said, and flung her arms around Lighty. "I'm so sorry he died."

"My dear." Lighty hugged her back. "Don't cry."

"Is his father sorry he died?"

Lighty turned toward the kitchen, Elizabeth leaning against her. "He told me he was," she said. "But I don't really know."

forty-two

"I think the full moon affects nursing homes too. Not just jails and emergency rooms."

"Well, what have we seen today? Mr. Erickson attacked Gretchen Willis. If you could call it an attack when he fell out of his wheelchair on top of her."

"*She* thought it was an attack."

"She's always thinking some man is going to get her. Pity it had to be Mr. Erickson. He looks like a wreck even when he has his teeth in."

Alice and Margaret, the two aides on duty in the sitting room of Mercy Care Center, looked at each other and giggled. They'd finished their duties early. The cleaning staff had been at work since morning, and even the hallways on the nursing care ward smelled of Lysol and fresh air, while all the bags of soiled Attends had been hauled out to the garbage. For perhaps half an hour until the first uncontrolled bowel movement, they could imagine themselves in a small country hotel, one with an unusual number of elderly guests.

"Are we having a church service tomorrow?"

"I'm not sure."

"Don't we always?"

"I heard that something is going on with Pastor Ed."

"Whatever can be going on with a preacher?"

"Did you know about the funeral?"

"What funeral?" Margaret bent down and tied her shoe, making sure the loose ends of the laces ended up exactly the same length. At first she had hated the nursing shoes, rubber-soled and shapeless, but once you weren't a kid anymore and had a job that kept you on your feet, you learned to appreciate them.

"The little boy. Lighty Stuart's child."

"The one that never learned to talk?"

"Or walk either. He died three days ago. Pastor Ed is holding the service at Englund tomorrow afternoon."

"What happened to him?"

"They're not sure. Something while the babysitter was there."

The old woman sitting on the other side of the room began to cough, a rasping hack that held her jerking back and forth. The two aides looked at her, then at each other. "Is she all right?" Margaret asked.

"Wait a minute."

After a final grinding hack, the woman subsided.

"Did you get your flu shot yet?"

"Tomorrow. If I don't go to the funeral. That's the time the nurse is giving them."

"Why would you go? Did you know the family?"

"Not really." Alice shook her head. "But I'm a little curious."

"About what?"

"Well . . ."

"Well what?"

"You know how people talk."

"About the Stuart child? It's a blessing that he's gone. From what I heard, there was nothing to be done for him. He was going to be a vegetable all his life."

An elderly man, his white hair shocked above his head, came into the sitting room on the arm of his daughter. He didn't know her anymore, because of the Alzheimer's, but he was unfailingly polite to anyone who visited. When words slipped away from him, he simply said "please" and "thank you" over and over. Deferential, leaning toward his daughter, he was saying "thank you" now.

Outside, a scutter of dry leaves flicked against the big window in the front of the building. There still hadn't been a killing frost, but the trees were giving in anyway. The grass kept growing, but slowly, so even if George the Swede fell behind on the mowing, it didn't really matter.

"What do you think about priests being celibate?"

"Whatever made you think of *that*?"

"Oh, I don't know. Yes, I do. Some people say Pastor Ed sleeps around."

"I'm sure they don't mean sleeping."

"Well, I didn't mean sleeping either."

"He seems like a nice enough man."

Alice scratched her nose, then her forehead. "The residents like his services best of all. Because he sings, I think. He has a fine voice."

The elderly man's daughter was leaving. Her father was thankyouing her as fast as he could. The sounds danced across his lips.

"I don't guess it's so easy, being a preacher."

"No shit and piss, though."

"Alice!"

"Sorry. But preaching really is a clean-handed profession."

"Pastor Ed builds too. He knows about dirty hands."

"So does Mrs. Cimerone. Did you see what she's been doing?"

"She always looks so clean to me."

"But she's not afraid to dig in the dirt." The clank of supper trays in the hallway made Alice swivel her head. Today was squash—the yellow smell lay heavy in the air. "She's a nervy old woman. Wants her way."

"I don't know how you could get your way in a place like this."

"She does all right. Have you looked out her window?"

"Her bed isn't next to the window."

"It is now. She persuaded Mrs. Gravinovitch to trade. Though I don't think it was persuasion, since Mrs. G. hasn't had a clear thought since she came in."

"Can you do that?"

"What?"

"Just change beds?"

"No. But it wasn't worth the fuss to change them back. And Mrs. G. doesn't care. She has that little pink stuffed rabbit. Wherever that rabbit is, that's where she sleeps. We could put her out on the lawn if that rabbit was there."

"So what about the window?"

The supper trays were beginning to clink in the dining hall. Mrs. Leier, hanging onto her walker, was inching her way toward her seat. She had red slippers on that were fastened around her tiny ankles with bows. Every now and then she stopped and looked at them, then shuffled on.

"Underneath her window. Outside. She's got something planted. Hollyhocks, I think. I don't know when she put the seeds in, but they've sure sprouted. Even though it's so late in the season. I've seen her pouring water on them. She takes the screen out by herself."

"Won't they freeze?"

"Probably. No, I think hollyhocks come up again from their roots. If they're established enough. They live over. Some plants are like that."

forty-three

Most of the family names in the Englund Lutheran Church graveyard reached back to the old country—usually Norway. Some of the descendants of those old farmers, however, had married out of their ethnic origins, and Smiths and even an errant McClellan appeared on the more recent stones. But almost every name fitted in with other names, and the family groups made clusters like heavy bouquets of granite. Only a few stones came unconnected—the German prisoner of war who had died before the repatriation of 1946, the twins of the Mexican family who had been field hands hoeing sugar beets for the Andersons. Though the mother had been Catholic, the father had absolutely refused to bury them in the Catholic cemetery. It had been before the days of Father Paul, and the old priest had not been kind.

But that should have made no difference at all, thought Ed, sitting on the back steps of the church in the growing darkness. Anyone can be buried anywhere. All the headstones he could see appeared coated with a universal silver. They were grouped, yes, but also separate from one another, distanced by the same space that separated every one of those temporarily alive.

If Grace were dying from whatever the tests would report, he would be free to marry Lighty. But she had pulled away. And what moral right did he have to her in any event?

And tomorrow he would bury Eugene.

Down the gravel road, the sky lit up, then faded. Car headlights had swung over the hump by the Himmelsrud farm. Ed turned his head to watch. No one drove this road without a purpose.

Now the lights were steady. It was a big car, well maintained. Ed felt his mind listing its virtues as if he were categorizing them for its resale. It approached, slowed, pulled off the gravel onto the edge of the church's well-clipped front lawn.

"Ed?"

"Yes?"

"Are you all right?"

Normally he would have answered "yes" without thinking. He was alive, his limbs worked, words ran through his brain on familiar roadways. "No, I'm not," he said.

Father Paul stepped forward, moving between the gravestones like a gentle ghost. His white collar, high and starched against his neck, gleamed in the moonlight. "I'll leave if you want me to, Ed," he said, still moving forward.

Ed waved his right hand slowly back and forth. The air it passed through lay heavy on it.

"I've heard about it all, you know."

"So has everyone in Eagle Grove."

Father Paul came closer. About six feet from Ed, he squatted on the grass, his hands dangling over his knees. "Do you want to pray, Ed?" he asked.

"Just tell me what good that would do."

Father Paul paused. Above his white collar, his chin inclined toward the grass. The moonlight glimmered off his bald spot, so round and white it looked as if his hair had been tonsured. "Perhaps none," he said.

"I should have left the ministry years ago. Not owning my own actions was the purest cowardice from the beginning. I've managed to deceive myself and everyone else as well. I've been afraid to admit to my own life."

"We're all afraid of something. I couldn't go up to my own roof."

"Paul, mine is an existential fear. Not a phobia. I watched that village burn and those people die. I helped set it on fire. Back here, I've betrayed the woman I promised to cherish. I've betrayed Lighty. I abandoned my own son. In some ways, I've killed him."

"Ed, his death had nothing to do with your actions."

"So you knew he was mine?"

Father Paul shifted his weight. His knees cracked, and he let himself down on the grass. "It was an open secret," he said.

"Why didn't they report me to the bishop? Why did they allow me to stay on?"

"Are you asking that all this be someone else's responsibility?"

Ed looked down at the little priest, his legs flat in the grass, his hands bracing himself on each side. "What are you saying?" he asked.

Father Paul didn't move. "You know what I'm saying," he said. "There's no difference between Catholics and Protestants on this one."

"That I'm responsible for my own sins?"

"Ed. You've lived with your sins for years. So has God. Of course you're responsible for them. But now is the time to let them pass from you. Accept the mercy of forgiveness. It's yours for the asking."

Ed looked over the gravestones. Their white slices faded, and he glanced up. A cloud had passed over the moon and was hesitating before moving on. "At least Sandy will be all right," he said. "She's got that crazy biker to protect her."

"Salvation comes in many forms."

"Are you telling me that, in the midst of all this shit, God is still merciful?"

Father Paul got to his feet. It took a long time. His knees cracked ferociously. "Oh, Ed," he said. "Let's just talk about tomorrow's agenda. The big issues move on without us. We can't go back. Let's just think about what you do now."

"I bury my son."

"When is the service?"

"Tomorrow afternoon. Lighty wanted it here."

"Good."

"Why do you say that?"

Father Paul stepped toward him, then stopped and looked up at the sky. "Ed, sometimes all we can do is lay them to rest," he said. "The simple things. The things that involve digging, speaking a few words, going on living. I've been both a good and a terrible priest in my day, sometimes within an hour of each other. What mattered in the end was a word here, a gesture there. Finally I just relied on my body to do the next thing. And the next thing is to bury your boy."

"We don't have a plot here."

"There'll be room."

Ed got up and stood next to Father Paul. They walked kitty-corner through the cemetery, weaving in and out among the granite slabs, heads bowed, hands held slightly out from their sides as if ready to hold on to something.

"Did you know that we don't sell the plots for money? Anyone can have one."

"That's a lovely way to do it."

"It was in the original Englund charter. You didn't have to be a member of the congregation either, though most were. You just had to die and need a place to be buried."

"A lovely way indeed."

"Christian or atheist. It didn't matter."

Father Paul hesitated. They had reached the outward corner of the cemetery by the fence. He could feel the presence of the corded wire even though he couldn't see it. "I don't see any stones in this area," he said.

"Right. There ought to be some free land here."

Both men looked down. "It's pretty dark to tell," Father Paul said.

"The moon's behind a cloud."

Father Paul looked up. He moved his foot forward. The ground gave way, and he jerked to one side, his foot sliding into a declivity. "Sheesh!" he said as he struggled to right himself.

"Are you all right?" Ed bent down to him.

"There's a hole here."

"There shouldn't be."

"Then what am I standing in?" asked the little priest, breathing hard as he hauled himself upright.

Ed bent down further. "My God," he said. "Could she have been out here digging?"

"What?"

"Digging. But of course you don't know. The little retarded woman."

"Who was that?"

Ed looked hard at the the indentation in the grass. "I don't even remember her name," he said. "She came with the chicken roll ladies. Mildred's relative, or Gertrud Chilson's. I think she'd had a baby a long time ago. She was looking for it in the graveyard."

Father Paul didn't ask any further questions. Both men stood looking at the hole, clearly purposefully made. The moon broke through the clouds, its light white as sheeting.

"She must have been trying to put things to rights."

"I'm sure she couldn't drive. How could she have gotten back here?"

Father Paul straightened up. "Maybe it was just an enthusiastic woodchuck," he said. "Maybe there is no mystery at all." He put his hand on Ed's elbow, then moved closer and embraced him. "I've got a shovel in the car," he said. "Two, actually. The moon gives enough light. Let's do what has to be done. If not this corner, another. There was a space to the right of the steps.

He wasn't very big, Ed. I saw him when Lighty brought him to the doctor this spring. Even with a coffin, he won't be that big. We'll dig it just the right size, the two of us. Our hands will lay him to rest the best way they can."

forty-four

"Do you think Sears was the best place to shop for it?"

"Jesus, Sandy, I have no clue."

"But they had a lot of baby furniture. A real lot. And they delivered it the same day. That was amazing."

Sandy's face was lit as if someone had washed it with light. She had a screwdriver and a wrench in her hand. Largo stood next to her at the door of the bedroom, waiting to see what she'd do next.

"And it's mostly put together already. Cribs come in just a few parts. All I have to do is fasten them together."

"I could do it, Sandy."

She ran her hand along his cheek. He'd shaved this morning, so there were no bristles. She had kind of liked them. "I want to," she said. "No insult, Largo. I just want to do it myself."

"Sure."

"You can watch TV. There's got to be something on besides football."

"Sure."

She patted his shoulder as she opened the door to the bedroom. "I'll yell for you if I need you," she said, slipping inside. Then her curly head stuck itself back through the slit between door and frame. "But I won't," she said, grinning. The door shut behind her.

Trying hard to do this right, though he had no idea what "right" actually meant, Largo turned to look at the TV screen. It seemed big and square and totally uninteresting. Also, it was covered with dust. He pulled out his bandanna and swabbed off the glass in uneven streaks. He picked up the remote, but his thumb hovered over the buttons like a restless gnat. It had no interest in pushing any of them.

There had been some clinks from the bedroom. Now there were a few more. Largo sat on the sofa and looked at the magazines on the coffee table. *Easyriders* and *Home and Garden* lay next to each other. He picked one up in each hand. They seemed to weigh about the same. That could mean something, but he didn't know what.

From the bedroom came the crunching of plastic. Sandy must be unwrapping the mattress. The sales clerk had talked for a long time about how important the best mattress was for a baby's back, and Sandy had listened to every word. But she'd bought the mattress in the middle of the price range. "It feels just the same as the most expensive one," she'd whispered to him.

All the mattresses had seemed exactly the same to Largo. And how would a baby know the difference anyway?

Now the bedroom was quiet. Maybe she was doing something with the sheets. Largo got up and looked out the window. Nothing was outside, just dusk. His scooter was over at the clubhouse, where Rocker was working on it. He still didn't feel so hot, but better than yesterday and the day before. He'd always been a fast healer. Good blood, or something. Maybe it was the Indian in him.

Still quiet. Largo walked into the kitchen, but he wasn't hungry. The refrigerator was full of eggs. Why would Sandy want so many eggs? He had no clue.

Still quiet. Largo unfastened the buckles on his boots, slipped them off. Sandy had darned the hole in his right sock.

He always just threw them out, but she'd gotten hold of it and fixed it. Maybe she did take after her mother with the sewing and all.

His feet muffled on the shag, Largo tiptoed to the bedroom door. He put his ear against it. It sounded like someone was breathing, and that would be Sandy. She had to breathe. Then something creaked, like weight was being put on it. Maybe she was testing how strong the crib was. If the baby was big, she'd have to be sure it didn't collapse under him.

His ear against the door, Largo kept listening. There was some little sound he couldn't identify. "Sandy?" he asked, not wanting to trespass on her, but wondering if she was OK. Sometimes those screwdrivers were hard to manage. He didn't think she knew much about tools, but, hey, if she wanted to do it herself, that was OK. He kind of liked it that she didn't lean on him for everything. Most women leaned so hard they were practically horizontal. Which wasn't always such a bad thing when you thought about it.

"Sandy?" He just couldn't shut up.

She didn't answer.

Then he heard a funny sound. It was sort of like crying, but longer, like someone was holding her breath and crying at the same time. "Sandy!" he said again, and then he thought he heard his name half caught in the strange line of sound. He turned the knob so hard it wobbled in his hand and plunged into the room.

Sandy was squatting in the crib, pressed up against the railing. Her face was wet with tears. She didn't have any clothes on.

"Shit, what happened?"

First she looked at him with rage in her eyes. Then she plunged her face into her hands. "I'M STUCK!" she roared out through her fingers.

"Stuck?"

"I can't get out! I'm afraid I'll fall! With this belly I can't balance!"

Largo was torn in two pieces. He had never seen her naked before. She was so *white*. Her breasts were bigger than he would have guessed, sticking out from her chest like soft cones. Her nipples were big too, and just as pink as in the pinup pictures. And then came this huge white belly with a brown line down the middle. He was afraid to look any lower. His whole body was melting whether he liked it or not.

"For God's sake, Largo, come help me get out!"

Then he moved himself forward. He didn't know if he should shut his eyes or not. She grabbed him around the neck over the railing of the crib, and he lifted her up to where she was half standing. Then he got his shoulder next to her and hoisted her over the rail. She still wasn't all that heavy, but his ribs grabbed in his chest. She started to sob so hard that he was afraid to put her down.

"Are you OK?"

She hung on to him as if she was going to die.

"Sandy, what's the matter?"

She was screaming. But she still hung on to him. He edged her over to the regular bed and sank down on it with her on his lap. Her screams and sobs were all mixed together. He grabbed the sheet and swabbed her face with it. Then he laid her down, her head on the pillow, and slid down beside her. She fitted against his body like the sweetest Harley on the earth.

"What were you doing, babe? Are you OK?"

Her mouth buried in his shirt, she mumbled a few words that he couldn't understand. Then she turned her head so he could. "I wanted to see how it felt," she said, gulping.

"How what felt?"

"To see if it was all right for the baby."

In some world, that probably made sense. Largo stroked her cheek, then slid his hand down across her shoulder to that amazing breast. She caught her breath.

"But why'd you take your clothes off?"

One of her feet slid across his ankle. He'd never been so hard in his life. What was this stuff about that Viagra? Real bikers had no need for any of that shit.

"I wanted to see how it would feel for the baby." She moved his hand to her other breast. "They don't come with clothes."

"And how did it feel, babe?"

She snuffled. A little drip came out one nostril, and he wiped it off. She put his hand back where it had been.

"It felt good, Largo," she said. He could feel her working at his zipper. His ribs hurt, but hell, it was worth it. A thousand times.

She was pulling his zipper down now. He felt like he had an AK-47 in there, waiting to explode the world. When she touched him, he was ready to die.

Sandy kissed his ear. It was all she could reach. "But not as good as this," she said.

forty-five

Although it was already October, the basil still hadn't frozen. Lighty sat on the raised rim around the herb bed, looking down at it.

And there were other mysteries. The bulk of her Volvo stood between her and the garage, blocking off the Russian olive trees, blocking off the rising moon. Someone had apparently fixed it and brought it back on Monday. She had no idea who.

Tonight was cool, almost cold. The air was still. Frost was certainly possible, but Lighty didn't think it would come. Her breath, even this late, didn't puff out in a white cloud in front of her.

It was impossible to believe that Eugene was dead. That Ed would hold the funeral tomorrow. That they would bury him among the Norwegians, across from the cornfield, under the Englund turf.

It was impossible to think that she was free.

She remembered his birth. The bleeding had started in midafternoon, precipitously. Ed had just left. When she felt the hot liquid between her legs, she thought her water must have broken. But she had been wearing maternity shorts, and her thighs had been suddenly stained red. The stain moved down her legs and trickled between her feet into the dirt.

The doctor hadn't been sure at first. But she had. Something about the way his body hung in Mathison's hands, flaccid as a rag doll. His cry, when it finally came, had been a mousy little whimper. "Low Apgars don't necessarily mean anything," Mathison had said. But she knew they meant something.

In the silver air, the sounds from the road were exceptionally clear. She wondered if Ed would come by. Probably he was with Grace, who had come home from the hospital the day before. She must have some kind of diagnosis by now. If not, she'd have to go to Mayos, where they figured out everything.

Well, she'd said the F-word to him. Maybe that was enough to keep him away.

The noise from the road was louder, and it seemed to be increasing. She knew it couldn't be Ed's car. Now the trees on each side of her gravel driveway were lit up by flashes of white. The police? But no one had committed a crime, not even poor Elizabeth.

Then the big Harley pulled into the yard with the roar of Armageddon. When Rocker shut off the ignition, the engine hesitated as if on the brink of a precipice, then choked into silence. He held his legs down for balance. On his head he had his little leather cap with the visor over his forehead. Lighty couldn't imagine how it stayed on.

"You all right?"

She nodded, slowly.

"You're sure you're all right?"

Despite his rough voice, Lighty found herself coming undone. She tried to nod again, but her head refused to move.

"I was taking a little run after poker night at the club. I thought I'd see if you were OK."

"The club?"

"The Iron Riders. Our clubhouse is in Moorhead."

Lighty began to laugh. Odd Fellows, Demolay, Masons, Rainbow Girls. Scouts of both genders. American Legion, VFW, DAR, AA, Woodsmen of America. There was no end to this need to coalesce.

She laughed harder, choking. Rocker raised his leg, swung off the bike, put down the kickstand. In the light from the moon, the Harley stood like a metal sparkler, throwing handfuls of silver off its every angle.

Now she was sobbing. Men always hated to have you cry.

He stepped toward her. He had a big beard that stuck out like a bush from his face. It bristled in the moonlight. As he bent over her, she put her hands out and grabbed it as if it were the only refuge available to her, the only thing she could bury herself in.

"Ouch," Rocker said. He leaned closer, his boot toes digging into the dirt. His hands circled her wrists. "Go easy there. I spent most of my misspent life growing that."

"All of our lives are misspent."

Rocker let loose of one of her hands and put his arm around her as an uncle might. "I wouldn't say that," he said. "You got a nice house here, a nice garden. Your car just needed a new fuel filter and a new belt. You were upset that night, that's all. You're in good shape."

"*You* brought my car back."

"Yup."

"How did you get it started? You didn't have the key."

"There are ways."

"Thank you."

"It's all right. A trucker helped me get it up on the road. You were gone when I came by with it Monday, so I just hitched a ride."

"Did you know my son died?"

Rocker's body contracted as if someone had punched him.

"My son. The night you brought me back. He was dead."

"Oh, ma'am, I am so sorry."

"Thank you."

"That's why you came out yelling?"

Lighty tried to think back. She could hear herself screaming at him. Had she given him Ed's number? No, surely not. But the police had come, so he must have gone and called from somewhere. Her place? The Hendricksons'? She couldn't remember.

Her head down, Lighty stepped to one side, away from his arm. Her hand brushed against his belly, rock-hard and round like a geological feature. "What did you think had happened?" she asked, more for herself than for his answer.

Rocker shook his head. "It was none of my business," he said. "I thought you were pretty scared of something. You being out here in the woods and all." His hand brushed her upper arm. "It's no good when they die," he said, shaking his head again.

"Who have you had die?"

"My mom. Sugar in the blood. Buddies in Nam. Pedro in the club, back when I was a prospect. Dan the Man."

"Who was that?"

"A brother in the Iron Riders. Got hit by a drunk in a pickup. Threw him and his Harley right across the road into a tree. The machines kept him breathing for a week, and then they turned them off. Largo took it the worst."

"Largo?"

"Another brother. I was coming from seeing him in the hospital that night I picked you up."

"That's right."

"Largo and Dan was close. Sometimes it's like that. They got wasted together, were in detox together, went on the big run to Daytona together. Dan was only about five feet tall—Largo could pick him up with one arm. When that truck did Dan in, Largo just disappeared. Didn't even come to the church for the funeral. But when the bikers made the run to the cemetery, there comes Largo on that old Softail, about 120 miles an hour, right through the middle of town. Even the cops scattered. He made one swing around the cemetery and was gone. Didn't see him for another month."

Lighty turned her face to the moon. "Eugene was brain damaged," she said.

"Somebody hit him?"

She shook her head. "I did it," she said.

"You?"

Lighty put her hands on each side of her mouth as if it would help the words come out. "I didn't take the pill," she said. "I wanted to see what would happen. Then I wouldn't get an abortion either. Ed gave up trying to persuade me. But then he wanted me to go away with him, and I wouldn't. He was married. He had Sandy. And I didn't need him. I was sure I could do it all by myself."

In the moonlight, her face gleamed white. "I guess I thought I was God," she said. "And now I'm being punished for it."

"Jesus Christ." Rocker's hand reached out and took hers. "I don't figure you're in line to be punished for anything."

But Lighty raced on. The story filled her mouth. "I didn't go to the hospital soon enough," she said. "When I did get there, they said the placenta had separated early. The baby didn't get enough oxygen. When he was born, it was already too late for his brain. Later you could see it was shrinking from where the cells had died. His skull got pointy. But when his hair grew in, it didn't look so funny. And he was always in bed anyway."

Rocker could only shake his head.

Lighty put her hand up to Rocker's beard. "When his hair grew in, it didn't look so funny," she said again. "It's amazing what hair can do."

Rocker stepped back. "We can't do nothing about it now, can we? They're all dead. It hurts, but, hell, so do a lot of things. Nobody's to blame." Then he pulled her up beside him. "You want we should go on a little run?" he asked. "We could do that. It can cure you in the head when you hit a high on a good chopper. Not too long for your first time, though. When you're used to it, we can make a run up to the clubhouse." His eyes narrowed as he smiled. "After all, you already know how it works on the bitch seat."

"Is that what bikers call it?"

"Well." Rocker swung himself onto the bike and kicked the stand up, then reached out for her to join him. "If your wife rides on it, yeah. Because she's always bitching at you. If your girlfriend rides on it, it's a cunt pad."

Lighty couldn't tell whether he was focusing on her or not when he said the dangerous word. She didn't care. Sweeping her skirt under her, she shifted her weight up behind him.

"And if it's some nice young girl, it's a pee pad."

"Thanks for sharing."

Rocker snorted. The key clicked and the motor started. It sounded like a dragon digesting the universe.

"And if it's me?" She had put her mouth right on Rocker's ear to be heard.

The bike began to move, crackling over the gravel. Rocker turned his head back to her. "We'll think of something," he shouted as they rode off.

forty-six

When he'd been a child, lying awake in bed at night had been a luxury, Burton thought. Even with his brother breathing across the room, he still had felt he owned the space around him, the lovely private space of his twin bed, even the block of air that cradled his head and upper body. His parents had wandered the house at night sometimes, peeing, flushing, drinking, opening and closing the refrigerator. Occasionally somebody had said something. But no one ever came into his room, ever whispered his or Jim's name from the hallway. He'd felt like he was in a sacred bubble.

Now, lying awake was no luxury, because the bubble had burst. Burst? No, just floated away. Unprotected, he lay on the king-size mattress, up against his edge even though no one else was occupying any of the rest of it, and hadn't for the last two nights.

Burton pulled himself upright, swung his legs over the edge of the bed, straightened the collar of his pajamas. Alex had given them to him for Christmas three years ago. An upscale, totally impractical present, which he was wearing now for the first time.

Richard had gone back to his parents that morning, as sullen as ever. How little difference sexual orientation made! A sullen adolescent was just that, period. He'd left behind most of the stuff his mother had brought, though not the boombox. He'd taken three of Alex's Calvin Klein shirts, trailing them behind him on their hangers. It had seemed to Burton that he'd flicked them with particular arrogance as he'd passed the front steps where Burton had been watching.

It was better that he'd gone. It was a lot better that he'd gone. But it would have been truly better if Alex had been there to say some kind of approving goodbye.

Burton stood up. The moon was high in the sky, leaving a silver shimmer across the lake almost to the end of their dock. He'd gotten a glimpse of it earlier that evening, but then it had been rich and golden. Now it was just a cold circle in the heavens.

He and Alex had been together for almost nineteen years. More than many married couples. It was different for gays, Burton thought—you were allowed your flings, but then you came back together and talked about them, like some mildly dangerous disease that had tested your body but left you wiser and essentially unchanged. Certainly Alex had explored a bit, and he had too. But not that much. And not for a long time.

Barefoot and on tiptoe, Burton walked to the door of the bedroom, started down the carpeted stairs. At the bottom, he looked out at the driveway, striped with silver in the moonlight. Alex's Miata still wasn't there.

Could one's heart fall? His seemed to be plummeting down from the moon itself.

It was too chilly to spend much time by the lake. But he went down anyway, after unlocking the heavy back door that had always seemed to him to be set up to prevent invasion from the deep, an attack of crayfish or bladderwort. The flagstones on the patio curdled his toes, but he didn't go back for slippers. The cold air gushed around his butt under the free-flowing pajama top.

And if this was the end? They owned the house jointly, after much complex legal maneuvering. More complex legal maneuvering could sever the ownership, Burton was sure. But who would get to keep it? He had always thought he'd grow old here, and he was doing that right now, with his gray hairs, a little coarser than the rest, fanning out from his temples. But die here too, feeble but supported by the Michelangelo *David*, the fake

Tiffany lamp, the brocaded loveseat, his mother's needlepoint pillow, Matchbox's successor.

By Alex.

The dock was framed by moonlight. Next to it, turned over on their little weedy beach, was the canoe. Usually they hauled it up in September, but this year Richard had been using it, once Alex taught him the rudiments of paddling. Sometimes the two of them had gone out together, gliding through the margins of the lake in a manner almost Victorian.

Why not? Burton launched the canoe, flipping it over and dragging it into the water next to the dock, hunching down alongside to slide it clear. Then he let himself down in it, almost stepping on a frantic garter snake that had clearly thought to winter under the helm. The canoe tipped wildly, and Burton grabbed for the dock, his feet still astride the thwart. Some of his weight pushed the canoe outward, and his legs followed it. He lay horizontal between canoe and dock, bridging the widening gap above the cold water. His arms stretched. His toes flexed. He folded in the middle and fell in.

"Help!"

Choking, Burton righted himself in the water. Had he really yelled for help? The water wasn't even over his head, and he didn't have shoes on to weigh him down. But the bottom under his feet was mucky, and he couldn't seem to get his feet properly distributed. Finally he slid them sufficiently far apart so he could balance. Unfortunately, he was just a little too far from the dock to grab it, and the canoe was bobbing cheerfully about six feet away.

Burton heaved forward on one leg, holding his shoulders back for extra leverage. The leg moved, but didn't come out. Letting his right foot sink down, Burton tried for his left. Not much better. His teeth were beginning to chatter too, because although it was only October, the temperature was probably in the forties. The water had lost all its summer warmth.

"Is this a new health regimen?"

Burton was so occupied with the geometry of his feet that he heard the voice only as a piece of the conversation in his head, the one that was telling him in perfect English-teacher sentences just what a fool he was. He didn't even look up. Then something struck him in the shoulder.

"For God's sake, Burton, take hold of it. Let yourself relax. You'll break the suction once you aren't vertical."

Alex.

Burton grabbed the life preserver, an eerie fluorescent white doughnut gleaming in the moonlight. Alex was kneeling on the dock, the life preserver rope around his waist, then extending through his hands. He gave a little premonitory tug, and Burton let himself go on the water, his arms extended, the doughnut in his hand. His feet came up with a slurp.

"I didn't think you were home," he choked out.

Alex heaved on the rope as Burton sloshed toward him. "Two nights under the pale green ceiling of the Moorhead Holiday Inn were enough for me," he said.

Overhead the moon was as sharp as a silver bullet. As Burton struggled up onto the dock, they both turned to look at it. The bright line on the water had moved a little to the side, washing the end of the canoe, which had beached itself down a little ways at the Ricketsons'.

"I'll get it tomorrow," Alex said.

"*I'm* the one who let it get away."

"But your teeth are chattering."

"I didn't think it was that cold."

Alex reached over and put his arm around Burton. "My God, you're not just wet. You're slimy as well."

"We'll have to haul in a load of sand next spring to stabilize that bottom."

"Probably should have done it this year." Alex was unbuttoning the top of Burton's sopping pajamas.

"Where's your jacket?"

"What jacket?"

"Your good one. That your mother gave you."

Alex looked down at himself while the two of them walked up the stairs toward the house. "Clearly it found a better home than I could provide for it," he said.

"Richard's probably saying the same thing."

"He's left?"

"Are you surprised?"

"It was in the air."

"Are you disappointed?"

Alex said nothing.

Then they were in the family room. Matchbox, sleeping on the sofa, twitched and opened one malevolent eye. Burton shivered harder. Alex pulled the afghan off the back of the big chair and unfolded it. "Take off those pajamas," he said. "Or do I have to cut them off like they do in the ER?"

"I can manage."

"Wrap yourself in this."

"I'm not an invalid, Alex."

"You're cold. Wrap up."

"How many did you wrap in that jacket of yours before you decided you'd be better off coming home to me?"

Grimacing, Alex stepped back. "That's none of your business," he said. "None of your business. But since you asked, I'll tell you. Richard had to be satisfied with my shirts, bless his tiny adolescent heart. He never got any closer than that. And while I'll admit to some thoughts, and even some movement, toward what I suppose one might define as a little fling, I have to admit to you, in a combination of shame and pride in my fidelity, that nothing came of it. Nothing at all. Except for some exercise with the Miata, and the loss of my jacket. Someone needed it more than I did."

forty-seven

Because Englund Lutheran Church had been designed to function in every weather condition, as most of the little rural churches had been, its entranceway consisted of several separate spaces to help filter out the cold air before one reached the safer protected warmth of the sanctuary. Once inside the heavy oak doors, a parishioner would be met by a small front hall, wider than it was long, the congregational mailboxes on the right side, the table for post-church coffee and doughnuts on the left. The windows on each side of the door were so small that they let in only two limited rectangles of light.

Then, after perhaps ten feet, the walls closed in, and six blue-carpeted stairs moved upward. At the top was another small hall, this one with an archway on the left framing the church library, where the small collection of books was shelved and the bulletins from past Sundays laid out so people could see them. To the right was a coatrack—not for the parishioners' winter coats, because they brought those in with them during that season to insulate themselves against any intruding chill. Instead, Ed's vestments hung there. There were specific religious mail order houses where robes could be ordered, but Grace had always sewn the ones Ed wore. Early in their marriage, he had found surprises in them—a rhinestone glimmering in the eye of the Lamb, for instance. He had never thought of Grace as having a sense of humor, and they had spoken so little about the nature of their relationship that he would never have thought to define these bits of whimsy as part of their intimacy. But her hands had sent small, delicate messages.

Then came another short hallway. It was the most narrow, but still wide enough for three people to walk through shoulder to shoulder. At the end was the wide archway into the sanctuary itself.

This final hall was where they put the coffins, to the right, against the wall. It had always been done that way. As an attender at the funeral entered the sanctuary, seeing before him the painting above the altar of Jesus rising into the heavens, he would have left behind the person who had died, lying in his coffin as if on his mattress, deeply asleep, but inexplicably clothed in his best.

If the death had been irreparably violent—car accident, combine mutilation—the coffin was usually closed with an oval cover of translucent plastic. Through it one could see only the shadow of the face. But some of the older parishioners had objected. In their long lives, they had seen everything, and they had no desire to be unnecessarily protected at this point.

Fortunately, since that congregational crisis, all the deaths among the small cluster of Englund Lutheran members had been peaceful. The issue had never had to be resolved.

Today it was Eugene's coffin that stood there.

In the night, the temperature had dropped. The first hard frost had come. The frozen leaves stood rigid on the lilacs, the bronzed peonies, the hydrangeas at each side of the front door of the church. When the sun got a little higher, unthawing the frozen water in the veins of the leaves, they would become heavy, eventually turning into small capsules of mush. As the parishioners came in, their cars having filled the parking lot and spilled out onto the edges of the gravel road, almost everyone would touch a leaf, assessing the intensity of the freeze, recognizing the real end of the season.

Ed sat in his chair to the right of the pulpit. He held his sermon notes on his knee, pressing the small sheets of paper against the bend in his trousers as if he could imprint them with the outline of his kneecap. Although he had filled four pages with writing, he had no idea what he was going to say.

And it was time.

The sanctuary was full. Not overflowing, but full, with even the front pews occupied. Someone was already closing the doors to the hallway. As he watched, the coffin was being brought inside, then quietly rolled down the carpeted aisle to the front. Ed didn't even know one of the pallbearers, a big blocky man wearing a peculiar vest, his face framed in a huge beard.

Ed stood up. Everyone was looking at him, but then they always did. Burton and Alex were sitting behind Lighty, both looking sleepy. Burton hadn't dusted this week as far as Ed knew. School must have disrupted his schedule. Mildred and Gertrud Chilson sat across the aisle, wearing hats, strange little bundles of flowers and leaves. Women hardly ever wore hats anymore.

Even though the piano hadn't stopped its introductory melody, Ed stepped up into the pulpit. Lighty was looking at him. Not angrily, no, he would have felt that, but directly, her eyes clear, her face tilted slightly upward. She hadn't wanted a specific text, yet she seemed to be listening for one, listening for him to put things to rights.

Or perhaps she was listening for nothing at all.

They sang "Jesus Loves Me." They always did at funerals for children. They recited the Lord's Prayer. Ed read the verses from Luke about blessing the little children because theirs was the kingdom of heaven. They sang "He Comes to the Garden Alone," something he assumed Lighty had chosen because Eugene's short life had been lived surrounded by her raised beds of herbs and vegetables and perennials. Perhaps that was a fantasy on his part. But Eugene's life had been so amorphous, so unedged, so unconnected from anything he had known.

Ed had planned to use the "Suffer the little children to come unto me" as the key for his homily, because Eugene had been as purely a child as it was possible to be, and he had surely entered whatever tentative kingdom reigned after the body died. But the next verse had gone off into laying down ground rules about who should enter the kingdom of God, and the spectre of those rules made him feel hedged in, as if he were standing inside the skeleton of a house he was constructing and the linked framing had begun to move, tightening itself around his body. Then he'd turned to the earlier chapter, Luke 17, and the opening verses about forgiveness, but even that forgiveness came garbled in the preconditions of rebuke and repentance. So he'd moved on to Romans, the old voice of Paul, who'd been struck blind and recovered, but there too it was all sin and belief, forgiveness only if the proper process had been undergone. The verses had spilled from the pages as if a box of pebbles had been overturned, small hard morsels rattling across his desk down to the floor, secreting themselves under things, behind things, as inaccessible and merciless as death itself.

"Dearly beloved," he said. He knew the words came from the marriage ceremony, and he didn't care. Lighty had lowered her eyes, but she was perfectly erect, and her head was not bowed.

"Dearly beloved," he said again. And then, "We are here to bury a little boy who was a true innocent."

The flowers on Gertrud Chilson's hat nodded along with her head. The whole congregation seemed to be nodding. His own hands were shaking on the pulpit. He stilled them and looked up.

"But what is innocence?" he went on. "Is it a kind of ignorance, that in which Adam and Eve lived before knowledge entered their lives so painfully? Is innocence a luxury that we cannot afford to possess unless we, like Eugene, are held in that state by biological necessity?"

Did they know what he meant? Sometimes he suspected that they were brighter than they let on.

"When Christ speaks of forgiving our sins, does he mean the restoration of a state of innocence? I think not. What we carry with us, even in a state of grace, is the knowledge of where we have been and what we have done. If we do not remember our acts, if we do not accept our responsibility for them, we deny our own selves. Our so-called sins are as intertwined with our flesh as our blood vessels are."

Ed looked down at his hands. As he aged, the veins rose on their backs. He could feel Lighty's tongue on them, tracing their patterns. He could feel them cupped around her breasts.

"I stand in front of you," Ed said, his hands alive before him, "as a minister ordained by God and the Lutheran Church, who is supposed to model for you, in my humble way, the pattern of Christ's church in the world. Many of you have told me that you enjoy my being a carpenter as well as a preacher. It makes me seem more like a real person to you, not someone who is trained only to transmit theology. I too have been proud of my ability to build because one builds according to a plan. One has responsibility, but one has control as well. And the results are there in one simple structure for everyone to see."

Several of the faces directed toward him now were puzzled-looking. Mildred glanced quickly over at the coffin as if to reassure herself of the central reason for their being in church. Lighty was as unmoving as stone.

"Some of you know what I am about to say. Or perhaps not. In recent years, I have often thought about leaving the ministry. Perhaps I am tired of not admitting to what I am, to what I have done. Perhaps it is only now that I am becoming man enough to accept my own flesh."

In the back of the sanctuary, Ed heard a movement. It was hard to focus, but he recognized Father Paul standing in the archway, a small man with his arm around a small woman. Grace. She had gotten dressed and come after all.

"The boy we are burying today is my son. Perhaps some of you have known that too. Now you all know. And those of you not present . . . those of you not present will know soon enough in that wondrous way of small rural parishes. I hope the word spreads everywhere. I speak without irony. And when I submit my resignation, which is on my desk, you will all be aware that for the first time in years, more years than you know, I am admitting responsibility for my acts. All of them. Forgiveness is irrelevant. What matters is that now my flesh and spirit are acting as one."

It sounded terribly florid, officious, Lutheran. Even at Eugene's funeral, he couldn't put someone else first. But perhaps it was still possible to learn how to do that. Perhaps, Ed thought, as he walked up the aisle toward the back of the church, his eyes softening even as they looked into Grace's, explored her pale face, perhaps I can see Eugene buried with decency and see Grace through whatever is coming. I am not asking forgiveness, he thought, glancing back at the coffin, marveling at how normal Eugene looked when nothing was asked of him except to be a body. I don't care if I'm to be forgiven or not. All I want is to be a man.

forty-eight

"So this is where you hang out?"

Rocker had switched on the light. The Iron Riders' clubhouse brightened, every grubby corner illuminated. No one had cleared off the bottles from last weekend's party, and the peeling bar stood spiked with them. Now the newer paint extended halfway along the fourth wall, stopping suddenly at a big dent. A couple of years ago, Largo had thrown the pizza man against that wall, hard. That was the week before Largo laid off the booze in a serious way.

"It smells pretty stale, Rocker," Lighty said. Her nose was still full of the cold wind from the run up to Moorhead. She was glad she'd had the practice on her first ride. Hanging on took more strength than you might think.

"Guess we don't pay much attention to the smell."

"Do you spend a lot of time here?"

"More than anyplace else."

"Don't you have a job?"

Rocker took her by the elbow and guided her ceremoniously to a chair, brushing it off with his hand. "Not what *you'd* call a job," he said.

"How do you live?"

Rocker fluffed up his beard and went to the refrigerator. "I guess I live like a biker," he said. With a beer in each hand, he came back to the table, pulling up a chair for himself. "I gamble," he said, popping the cap with his teeth and handing the first bottle to Lighty. "And some other little things."

"People lose money gambling."

"Some people."

"And you're not one of them?"

Rocker put his bottle next to hers, arranging them like twins. "Oh, I've had losing streaks," he said. "But poker takes some brains. It's not just luck. You can do pretty well enough of the time." He smiled. "Or at least I can."

"Do you gamble here?"

"Not much going on here in the way of serious cards. I fly out to Vegas every couple of months. A junket in Santo Domingo, maybe. Atlantic City sometimes, but Jersey stinks. The Mafia is running everything but the garbage collections. Those too, now that I think about it."

Lighty raised her bottle to the light. She couldn't remember when she'd last had a beer.

"I'm not making millions, you understand. But I can live all right. Money's just good for what it buys. That's all."

"You sound like a philosopher."

"What?"

"A philosopher. Someone who thinks about ideas."

"Well, I've been called a lot of things, but that one's missed me until today."

The clubhouse didn't seem to have any heat. Lighty shivered.

"You're cold."

"Not until now."

"I don't think the boys got the heat turned on. We got propane out back."

"I'll survive."

"We sure had a late fall this year."

But it's finally frozen now, Lighty thought. She put both her hands around the beer bottle as if to anchor herself to the earth. And the ground will be freezing soon too, and Eugene in it, in that Hansford County clay in the Englund churchyard. I watched them put him in yesterday, in that bargain basement box I was too cheap to upgrade. They had to do it without Ed, because he'd left. But that Burton Rogers knew all the right words. I don't blame Ed for leaving, though. He'd said what he had to say. I didn't think he'd have the courage. I didn't think he'd have the courage at all.

Rocker was staring at her. "You all right?" he asked.

"No."

"I figured. You need something I can get you?"

She shook her head.

"Maybe you want I should take you home?"

Lighty lifted her beer. About half was left. She drank it down as fast as she could. Lights went off in her head. She coughed.

"You want some water?"

"Just give me a minute."

Rocker nodded, rose, flipped on the television. A florid spurt of professional wrestling moved across the screen, with someone large and ponytailed hanging on the turnbuckle. "You watch that?" Lighty choked out.

"It's what's on."

"There's the History Channel."

"We don't got cable."

"Why not?"

"Some of the brothers don't want to pay for it." Rocker paused. "We vote on things like that."

"Then all you bikers are no more free than anyone else. If everyone has to choose together."

Rocker had turned off the television. He set their empty bottles on the bar, inserted a cigar in his mouth. It stuck out from the tangle of his beard like a big brown toothbrush. Then he sat down by Lighty. "What's free?" he asked.

"Like I feel now." The words came out without Lighty having even thought about them.

"You do, huh?"

"Don't bikers value freedom? Not wearing helmets? All those things?"

Rocker put his hands in his beard and parted it. The cigar waved. "Lighty," he said, articulating her name as if he were translating it from some obscure language. "We're just men. We like to get laid. We like the wind in our hair. We don't ask much. Maybe for the cops to lay off for a little. Maybe for the summer to be long so we can make more runs. Maybe a good poker hand. The rest of it is just out there happening. It's got nothing to do with freedom or deserving or any of that shit. You lay your chopper down in the road, end up in the ER. Like that blankethead Largo. Maybe you were stupid, but maybe the road was just slick. Maybe it was nothing at all. Not much you can do either way."

In the growing fog bank of cigar smoke, Lighty's eyes were watering. She sucked the insides of her cheeks. It felt funny, like eating her own flesh.

"I want another beer." She let her cheeks pop out again.

Rocker got up, walked to the refrigerator, opened it. "Good thing I'm the one who's running the chopper," he said.

forty-nine

He'd had the dream before, but the bike was different each time. A Sportster, maybe, or one of those old Shovelheads. Even an Indian, before they went out of business. Always a blast from the past.

But tonight it had been a Heritage Softail, like the one he owned. Same color, same chrome, everything. Only it didn't have him on it. Someone else was riding, someone even taller than he was. Someone with good teeth. Not a kid. With light hair, not from the tribe, his tribe or any other. And he wasn't wearing leather either, or colors, but something long and white that blew out behind him until it looked like he was gunning down through a cloud.

Largo sat up in bed like he'd been electrified. "Goddamn robe!" he yelled. "A goddamn robe!"

Next to him, Sandy jerked awake. "What?" she said, her voice blurred. "What's wrong?"

His heart was beating so hard he couldn't catch his breath. Sandy had his Sturgis T-shirt on, and all he could see in the dim glow from the parking lot was the four Mt. Rushmore faces with the Harley wings over them. For a moment, before his brain got in gear, it seemed like he was down there in the Black Hills himself.

"What's *wrong*, Largo?"

He let himself down on the pillow. A week after the accident, his gut still hurt sometimes. His ribs too, for that matter. Not that he was complaining. He reached over and put his hand on Sandy's shoulder. "I was dreaming," he said.

"Must have been some dream."

The very end of the white garment streaked behind his eyes and disappeared. "Jesus got a white robe?" he asked.

"WHAT?"

"Your dad's a preacher, right? You must know this stuff."

"Largo, I have no idea. I'm pretty sure he didn't wear Calvin Kleins. What kind of dreams are you having?"

"He was on my Softail."

"Who's he?"

Largo gave up. It was just too hard to explain. He listened while Sandy shifted in the bed, dragging her belly from one side to the other. She reached out her hand.

"Go to sleep, Largo. You were out all day. You aren't healed yet."

He really couldn't believe she cared. Maybe it was just politeness. But no, her hand was creeping down his chest on the left side, coming to rest on his scar.

"Weren't you supposed to get those stitches out?"

He tried to remember. But he'd left the hospital without talking to any doctor. Nothing was oozing. He could cut them out tomorrow.

"I can do it."

"Do what?"

"Take 'em out."

"Take out your own STITCHES?"

"Can't be very hard. I seen 'em do it."

Suddenly the light came on. Sandy had turned herself again to pull the cord. She was digging in the drawer of the nightstand.

"What are you doing?"

"Looking for something."

"You ain't goin' to shoot me again?"

She turned to him, laughing, a little pair of scissors in her hand. "Sit up," she said.

Largo obeyed. Sandy heaved herself over next to him. He grabbed the covers, yanked them up to his chest. He always slept naked.

"Pull them down."

"What?"

She started to roll the covers down from his chest. "Not all the way down," she said. "Just far enough so I can take out your stitches."

"What do you want to do that for?"

The side of her face was golden from the bedside light. The rest of her was in semidarkness. "I don't trust you to do it yourself," she said.

He turned toward her. Sometimes it seemed as if he didn't understand a single thing that Sandy did. He felt the first pull, a little ping against his side.

"Yuck," she said as the stitch came loose.

"You don't got to do that."

"You know I never do anything because I have to do it."

Holding his breath, Largo tightened his gut for the next ping. It seemed wrong somehow to have her working on him like she was a nurse or some kind of servant. He just didn't know how to prevent it.

"Move over. I think there's one more down here somewhere."

Largo moved over. Sandy's belly lay against his thigh. He supposed that when women were pregnant in movies, they just used pillows or foam rubber or something. Somehow, though, in movies they were never so big. It was just their regular bodies with a little bump.

Something hit his thigh. He jerked back. Sandy was burrowing in his skin. "Stop moving!" she said.

"Why you thumping at me like that?"

"What?"

He felt it again. "I can't hold still with you thumping at me," he said.

The last ping snapped against his skin. Sandy tossed the scissors over the edge of the bed, a tiny silver flash. Then she turned back and took Largo's face between her hands as if he were a big child who needed comforting. His skin melted where her fingers touched him.

"Largo."

"That's my name."

"It's the baby kicking."

"What?"

"What you felt. It's the baby. He wasn't kicking *you*. You were just there. That's what you felt."

Even when he'd bought the baby clothes, he hadn't believed the baby was real. He'd just done it because he thought Sandy might like it. Even when he'd seen her naked in the crib, things hadn't come clear. Now, the pressure on his thigh still alive in his skin, he truly realized what was going on. Somebody was in there. A person. He thought of what Rocker had said, months ago. He was going to be stuck with the support for the rest of his life. He'd have to go back to the rigs before Christmas. Or maybe Rocker could cut him a deal in something. But Sandy wouldn't like that.

He knew what he was getting into. He knew it. And he wanted it more than he'd ever wanted anything.

Largo caught his breath. "You know that dream?" he asked. Sandy was doing something with his hair.

"Your dream?"

"Yeah."

She was starting to braid, her fingers working behind his skull where she couldn't see, and he couldn't either.

She tapped the back of his head. "Maybe it *was* Jesus," she said. "Why couldn't he be a biker?"

"I thought maybe it was Dan the Man. My brother in the club that got killed." He wanted to show her his tattoo up close, but he knew she'd have trouble seeing it, and he really didn't want to move anyway.

"Well, maybe it could have been him too."

"Only Dan was a really short guy. This one was taller."

"Sometimes things are different in dreams."

Sandy had shifted around a little. He felt the braid growing down his back. No matter what, he'd always been able to hang onto his hair. Maybe the Old Ones were right, that the spirits lived in your hair. When you scalped someone, you took his very soul.

"And I don't think Dan never had no robe."

Sandy made a little sound. He thought it was a laugh, and he tried to remember what he'd said that was funny. Then he realized it wasn't a laugh. She pulled her hands into her lap.

"What's that?" she asked.

"What's what?"

"Something's coming out of me."

Largo didn't know much about childbirth, but he was pretty sure it took longer than that. And it was supposed to hurt. Then he felt a wash of warmth under his butt.

"Jesus, Sandy."

She was trying to get out of bed. The mattress rolled under her. When she stood up, he could see that the bottom of her T-shirt was darker than the top. She had her hands in her crotch. When she brought them up, they were dripping.

"What's happening, Largo?"

How did he know. But she needed him to know. Forgetting about his ribs, his incision, his abysmal ignorance of everything, he rolled over to her side and stood up. His brain was a scramble. Then something came in, something from the television, or maybe what one of the brothers had said. Dan the Man had had at least six kids, here and there. Maybe he'd talked about it.

Largo took Sandy's hands in his. "Don't be scared," he said, although his own heart was beating so hard that his ribs hurt. "You know, I think it's the baby. They float. I heard that somewheres. Like in a bubble. And then the bubble breaks."

Her voice shook. "Will he die?" she said. She was hanging onto Largo's wrists like someone had put the cuffs on him.

"It's supposed to be like that," he said, not sure at all how it was supposed to be, but figuring it was a likely thing to say. "So he can get born. Out here, he has to breathe the air. He's got to practice that. He can't breathe the water no more." It sounded pretty good for having been made up on the spot.

Sandy looked up at him. "Should I go to the hospital?" she asked, her voice sounding very, very young.

Largo was struck with enormous gratitude that she hadn't insisted on having the baby right there in the bed. "You sure do," he said, a crazy joy spinning through his head. "And ain't it a good thing Rocker got the Softail back today?"

"I'm going in on the Harley?"

"You sure are, babe. I'll make the run real careful. We can tell the little guy about it afterwards. He'll be real proud."

A small smile came up across Sandy's mouth. "Only first," she said, letting go of Largo's wrists just the moment before the circulation would have been cut off forever. "First I want to write down my phone number for you. My mom and dad's number. You can call them when the baby's born."

"You don't want them now?"

Sandy was putting things in a little bag. She shook her head and smiled again. "They'd worry," she said.

fifty

It hadn't really been so bad moving back in with his folks, Richard thought. They just didn't talk about the Big Issue. The breakfast cereal was the same, Rice Chex, and the stiff warm smell of ironed shirts in the kitchen. His mother was the last woman left on earth who ironed, even though she was a teller in the bank too, and on the guidance committee for the PTA in Richard's little brother's school.

His father was the lawyer in Tomsville, a tall stooped man who knew so many secrets about the local citizens that the responsibility of keeping quiet about all them had made him unable to speak freely about anything at all. He doesn't like me much, Richard thought. But then he never had.

School was different. The move back hadn't changed his bus route, just put him on the bus a little later because his family lived so near the school. His driver was still Jessamyn Manhair, a half-Chippewa woman from White Earth who had taken five tries to pass her licensing exam to drive a bus. She had appeared at the driver's license bureau so often that it had begun to be a joke, but each failed test had taught her a little more about maneuvering and braking until finally there had been no excuse for not passing her. Everyone knew the story. Richard had always felt a kind of sneaking sympathy for what she'd gone through.

The tormenting had begun about a week into the school year, when he still lived with Alex and Burton. A Kotex on his seat, the seat he always took. The next day a pair of woman's underpants appeared, laid out on the floor right where his feet usually rested. No one looked at him, but he could tell by the way the rest of them held their shoulders that they were all giggling. Then someone shoved him when he went down the steps, a neat little push between his shoulder blades that made him fall off the bottom step and dump his homework in the dirt. It happened almost every day. He learned to hang on to his homework. And even now with the new pick-up time, he was still major garbage, and he knew it.

When he'd visited Alex and Burton last weekend, making it look like a casual drop-in, they'd asked him how things were going, Alex in the rocker, Burton on the sofa, Matchbox lying belly up on the Persian rug like a hunting trophy. He'd said "OK" because there was nothing they could have done anyway, and everything was just going on as it had since school started. But he hadn't realized that even the tenuous friendships he'd had when he was a sophomore would disappear, that this year he'd be so miserably lonely that he felt like his body had evaporated to another, colder planet.

And his classes were the worst they'd ever been. Even American literature, which he'd thought of as a padded jewelry case with Emily Dickinson glittering in the middle of the plush, had turned into multiple choice questions and rowdiness. The other kids hated poetry.

He knew Burton was at school today; he'd seen him in the lunchroom, reluctantly eating the taco salad. Where else would he have been? He was a teacher, after all. And Alex massaged people in the afternoon. He wasn't a morning person, he'd told Richard. Not a morning person at all.

Of course, he didn't have any transportation. Even though he was sixteen, he didn't have his driver's license yet. But that didn't make any difference, because his parents wouldn't have let him use the car anyway. In the chilly air, after the frost, Richard pulled his jacket up around his neck and started walking, his backpack slung across his shoulder. There was nothing in it, but no one had to know that. It held its puffy, weighty shape all on its own.

Some farmer from Jacoby gave him a ride out to Weed Lake. He had a wad of snuff in his cheek and spat into a tin can down by the gearshift. Somehow he got it into his head that Richard was looking for a job, and he offered to take him on in the spring when planting started. Richard wrote his address and phone number on a scrap of paper and gave it to him. His folks would be surprised, brokenhearted, when that old Norwegian called.

At the house, the key was in the flowerpot to the left of the door like always. Neither Burton nor Alex locked regularly, but they kept their options open. Richard slid inside. Matchbox lay halfway up the stairway, ears slid back on his triangular head. It was a bad sign, but Richard didn't intend to try to pet him in any event.

It was funny where Alex kept the guns, in the bottom of the china cabinet as if they were fancy plates or something. There were only four. "At first I thought they were absolutely charming," Alex had said, rearranging them on the padded velvet in the box that looked as if it should house an oboe or a French horn. "And they are, I suppose. So delicate. So deadly. But then I realized that I didn't like collecting something that had to be *covered*. And one couldn't just line them up inside the glass like goblets. Even without children in residence. One might visit. So I stopped after four. But they are delightful, aren't they, Richard?"

Richard had nodded. "They're nice," he'd said, not liking the word but not finding another.

Alex patted each one before the cover closed over them. "They are *not* nice, dear heart," he'd said. "But they *are* interesting. It's a vital difference. Keep it clear under that blond thatch of yours."

Well, he'd been right, Richard thought as he opened the case, slanting the top halfway back as he made his choice. They weren't nice, but they were interesting. A great gulp of misery rocketed up his esophagus as he took out the biggest one, the Beretta, and tried to slip it into his pants pocket. It felt cold and bulky, and the back of it stuck out. When he moved, it grated against his pelvis. He pulled it out again, holding the hand grip in his fist like he might have a fishing rod. He kept his finger far from the trigger. He knew how to pull back the slide and drop the bullets into place. It wasn't that complicated, really.

He'd thought a long time about whether he should write a note. Burton, as English teacher, would probably feel compelled to give it a grade. And he didn't know exactly what to say. The two of *them* were happy enough. They had little squabbles, but they were actually more complacent than his parents. Richard himself had absolutely no idea what happiness might feel like.

Instead of writing a note, he went upstairs to their bedroom. Matchbox hissed on the steps, shrank to one side, but didn't vacate. Richard took his time looking through the big closet. Alex must have sent his nice jacket to the cleaners because it wasn't there. It had always felt like the soft skin of some friendly animal. And it looked like he'd bought some more shirts, though Richard wasn't sure. Alex had so many anyway.

This time he took a blue one, with little gray stripes. It felt like it had been worn, but it still had its tags. He left the hanger and tucked the shirt under his arm as he walked downstairs.

Alex's bicycle was still in the garage, draped in cloths they used to protect the fall flowers from frost. It was stupid to bother to fold them, but Richard couldn't help it. He piled them neatly on the shelf next to the weed spray, of which Burton had several bottles. He must have thought it worked really well.

Richard rode off. Big Loon Lake was about five miles. He hadn't been there since summer, since the minister had seen him in the tree and some old woman had come limping back with her hands full of seed pods. He hadn't been looking for deer like he'd said either—just jerking off. He knew it was stupid, but when you did it up high, in a tree, on a ladder, anything that got you off the ground and above anyone who might be passing, it was like, no matter who you had in your head, you might actually be able to reach up and touch him.

fifty-one

Now that winter was approaching, his garage workshop was cold. By this time last year, Ed thought, I'd split the firewood and cleaned out the creosote from the old stove. Last year I was ready.

He'd been working since morning. Since dawn, when he'd woken up as if somebody had shot him. He was out of bed and on his feet before he'd even looked back at Grace, who slept as she always had, on her stomach, her white shoulders against the goosedown pillow with the embroidered case from her mother, from whom she'd learned all her sewing skills. Before Mrs. Gurlack had died, he'd watched the two of them, usually at the kitchen table, heads bent, stitching threads in patterns so delicate he couldn't separate them out even when he'd finally gotten glasses for his farsightedness. Grace had always been nearsighted, and as the muscles of her eyes relaxed when she'd reached her forties, she'd been able to discard her glasses. Released from behind the frames, her eyes were as clear as a child's.

Usually when he built something small, something for the household, Ed followed a pattern. But there had been no patterns for what he was constructing now, a sewing box designed like a miniature tower, with levels for the supplies, the works-in-progress, the patterns. Grace had always been casual in this regard, with small gatherings of embroidery cotton or fabric on the bedside table, the bookshelves in the living room, the old pine cabinet for dishes in the kitchen. She knew where everything was; there was no accident about where she put things. But, Ed had realized, she didn't own even one of those cheap wicker sewing boxes with the glittery finish and the cracking plastic inserts. She didn't even own one of those.

The phone rang. They'd just had an extension installed in the garage because of Sandy. Now that the baby was almost ready to be born, Grace had felt that they both ought to be easily available.

The phone rang again. It was sitting on his workbench next to the gradiated wrenches for which the box had long been lost. Across from it was the little window, so high that through it one could see only the tops of the trees toward the lake. Now, even so soon after the frost, the remaining leaves had plunged into their fall colors, though many had already fallen.

Ed picked up the phone, thinking of Lighty's voice, knowing he wouldn't hear it. They had never waited this long to talk to each other.

"Pastor Ed?"

"Yes."

"Pastor Ed, it's Alex."

"Hello, Alex."

Alex had been in church the day of Eugene's funeral. Burton had too. So they would know everything.

"Ed, I need your help."

That was the last thing he had expected. What help could he possibly give? Even Alex, with his off-center irony, his silly job rubbing people's bodies, and his sarcastic infatuation with chicken rolls, was in a far stronger moral position to give help than he was.

"Are you there?"

"Yes."

"The phone sounds funny."

"I'm in the garage." Ed carried the phone toward the center of the workshop, scuffing through the sawdust. The crunching on the line diminished. "Try again," he said as he reached toward the sewing box. With the phone tucked against his face, he began to sand the top tier.

"You know Richard, don't you?"

"Yes." Ed buffed one corner with his thumb. "But I haven't seen him since the Fall Festival."

"You know he spent the summer with us after his accident?"

Ed felt the corner, testing for splinters. "Yes, I do know that," he said.

"And that he finally moved out? To live with his parents again?"

"Yes."

"Well, I think he was here today. While we were gone."

"It's nice that he feels comfortable coming back."

"Fuck that," said Alex, the first time Ed had ever heard the F-word from any of his parishioners. "We're not talking about comfort here. My bicycle is gone. My new shirt is gone too. All the frost coverlets are obsessively folded."

"Alex, what are you talking about?"

"For Christ's sake, Ed, I'm calling you because I need some help. I don't care about what you did with that woman, and neither does Burton. Anything's better than that substitute preacher you had them bring in on Sunday. To be bored to death and assured of hellfire afterwards is too much for even your gay Lutheran contingent."

Ed choked. "I couldn't preach," he said.

"Fine. It's your life. But we're talking about important things now. It isn't just the bicycle and the shirt that are missing. One of my guns is gone too."

Ed moved the phone a little ways from his ear as if the extra space would somehow form Alex's words into coherency. "Guns?" he asked.

"I showed you my guns last Christmas when we had the brunch."

He had, that was true. But in the juxtaposition of needlepoint, omelets with Brie, Burton's red coverall apron, and that small vicious cat gnawing at the tree stand, the guns somehow had not registered as anything significant at all.

"We have to find him."

From the house, Ed heard a door close. No one was there but Grace. She must be coming to speak to him.

"Ed?"

"Come over. I'll think about what to do."

"We could call the police, I suppose. But Einar Hilsrud couldn't find his own prick if it were wanted, which I'm quite positive it never is."

Well, why not use the word that was meant, Ed thought, straightening his shoulders, gripping the phone along the side of his face, taking both hands and moving Grace's sewing box to the end of the bench, out of the traffic, where he half-covered it with a swatch of muslin that they'd used to protect the strawberries two summers ago. What had happened to the strawberries this last summer? He honestly couldn't remember.

"Come over, Alex," he said again. "I'll be home. We'll go look for him together. I'll think about where he might have gone."

"I was going to call his parents."

Ed looked out the garage window on the side toward the house. Grace, in her bathrobe, had bent over the little herb garden stuck in against the hedge of honeysuckle. Nothing like Lighty's garden, but a few things were still growing. She was picking leaves, putting them in her pocket. She straightened.

"I wouldn't do that, Alex. Not yet. Bring their number with you. We'll call if we have to."

The phone went dead. Alex must have been truly upset. He was the last person in the world to disregard the amenities of a telephone interaction.

"Ed?"

He hadn't heard the door open. But of course he must have left it ajar. Grace had said nothing that mattered since Eugene's funeral. He knew it had to come sometime.

"Ed?" She had her arms hugged around herself, pushing the bathrobe against her narrow belly and her breasts.

He turned to her. No words came.

"What are you building?"

Somehow the words didn't come now either.

She waited, then stepped forward. When her hand touched his arm, he couldn't even feel it, but his eyes focused on the way it looked, white against the plaid of his work shirt. It seemed to have lost dimensionality, to have become an aberrant part of the pattern. Then he felt the pressure. "Show me," she said.

He moved the muslin aside. "It's a sewing box for you."

Ed wasn't prepared for the red color that rose from her throat to her cheeks, then slid back again almost as fast as it had come. "It's walnut, isn't it?" she said, her hand running along the wood.

"Yes."

"Walnut has the loveliest grain."

He couldn't put his arms around her, couldn't allow himself to move against her body with that false intimacy, but he was able to lay his hand along her cheek. Her eyes had dark circles under them, and there were a few tiny purple dots against her skin. "Did the doctor call?" he asked.

"Yes. We need to see him as soon as we can. I said tomorrow."

"All right."

"It's something to do with my blood. The stem cells in my blood. I don't know exactly what that means. He said it wouldn't just go away."

"Grace, I'm so sorry."

She raised her head, pulled her shoulders back. He had never seen her angry, and she didn't look angry now. But her body had taken on a different line, as if a small firm wire was running through it. "But it will take a long time to kill me," she said.

"Grace." He couldn't think of another word to say beyond her name.

"I'll get to see Sandy's baby."

"Yes."

"And perhaps a good deal more than that."

"Grace, forgive me."

She stepped back from him, her bathrobe loose against her neck. "Ed, I'm going to say this now, and not again," she whispered as if she could bring him to a more intense listening if she kept her voice low. "I don't understand how things happen. I don't understand what journeys we're placed on, either you or me. Or Sandy. You think that you've lost your call to the ministry because of what you've done. I don't know about that. I wouldn't want to presume. But I do what is given me to do, as much as I can determine it. Like pick the sage to dry for Thanksgiving." She lifted a few crumpled leaves from her pocket, the smell sharp in the air.

Ed felt the dampness rise in his eyes.

Grace slid the leaves into her pocket again. "Perhaps what we do has a meaning," she said. "Does it matter in the end? I will be grateful for your help in the next months. I know that." She ran a finger over the back of his right hand, stopping at the scar from the drill bit, then moving on. "And I would be happy to have you grateful for mine."

fifty-two

It was Burton's day to clean the church. He'd missed last week, and he didn't want to miss again. It was strange how much he enjoyed shaking out the robes on the hangers, dusting the windowsills, straightening the altar cloth. He was grateful that the board had asked him.

Actually, it had been his idea. He couldn't stand disorder. He assumed God felt the same way.

The weather had become truly colder. He could feel the air pushing in along the edges of the windows and through the cracked leading on the stained glass. The back door was always blowing ajar. Only Burton didn't think it blew open. He was sure it was teenagers, driving down the country road, taking advantage of Lutheran innocence to do a little destruction. Never very much—they were Norwegians, after all. Just enough to run up the heat bills.

And they were probably his very own students. He supposed they laughed at him behind his back. For his styled graying hair, his serious affection for Tennyson, for eulogies, for interior decoration. For his sexual orientation, if they got that far. Which they probably didn't. They were taking it out on Richard instead.

He was the one who had seen the gun was missing. He'd been dusting. He hated those guns. It had been Alex's butch period. Alex was no butch. Not nelly either, of course.

Just Alex.

And now, now, the both of them, Ed and Alex together, were out there somewhere trying to find Richard before he killed himself. Or maybe he intended to kill some others, like the kids who were undoubtedly making his life miserable. But Richard didn't seem like a killer. And how far could he go on a bicycle? It was a long pedal back to school, and it was already almost suppertime. No one would be there.

Burton realized that he'd been dusting the central window-sill for what must have been five minutes. It positively gleamed. He emptied out more lemon oil onto the cloth and gave it a final glittering swab.

He could have gone too. But he hated racheting through the woods even more than Alex did. And, if he were truthful, if he were absolutely truthful, he had no desire to go looking for Richard. Part of him hoped Richard was already dead.

The next thing to deal with was the altar. Burton stepped up to it on the bright carpet, his feet leaving little flattened prints. The communion railing curved around in an exaggerated semicircle where everyone knelt. Whenever he and Alex took communion together, Alex would line his body up so that their shoulders were at exactly the same level. He never chewed the wafer either, maintaining it was sacrilege. "Cannibalism," he'd called it once, then giggled.

Burton was so deep in dusting the railing, on his own knees now, that he didn't hear the church door open. Only the cold air alerted him. He turned around. A woman was standing in the archway, half in shadow.

"Did you want Pastor Ed?"

She said nothing. She was wearing a heavy sweater so long that it reached to her knees. She began to walk toward the altar.

"He isn't here now. I could leave a message for him."

About halfway to the front of the church, she stopped, put one hand on the back of a pew, rubbed it, looked at her fingers. In her other hand, she held a paper bag. For a moment, Burton wondered if she was checking his dusting capabilities. Few people had ever challenged them, but there was always a first time.

She stepped forward again. Then Burton knew who she was.

"Lighty." Like almost everyone else, he didn't even know her real first name.

She looked up at him. "You know me," she said. She didn't smile.

All he could think to say was "Yes."

"You all do."

"Well, it *is* a small rural Lutheran church." He hadn't wanted to be flip, but it just came out.

However, she wasn't insulted. She laughed. It was a strange laugh, almost a cough at first, then expanding. He thought of hysteria, but it ended far short of that.

"I know I'm known," she said. "And I don't care. Don't we spend all our lives on exactly that quest?"

Burton had never thought of it that way. But of course she was right.

She stopped again, by the first pew. "I need a shovel," she said.

Strange fantasies filled his brain. He didn't say anything.

Smiling, Lighty reached out. The gesture completed itself through the air. "I want to plant some bulbs," she said. "Before the ground freezes. I won't be here in the spring, but they will be. Even this far north, the daffodils are beautiful in the spring."

Burton dropped his dustcloth. "I'll help you," he said.

Together they walked back through the archway, down the steps, out the front door, along the side of the church to the storage shed where all the tools were kept. Lighty said something about the late frost. Burton knew she was, had been, Ed's lover, and the little boy their son, but the whole relationship seemed beyond him, so much a part of the ravenous heterosexuality with which he'd been surrounded his whole life. "Love is impossible to explain," he found himself saying, and then suddenly he was babbling on about Alex and Richard. During the summer, the infatuation had seemed the stuff of novels. Told in a few inarticulate paragraphs as he fumbled with the door of the potting shed, it would hardly have made a letter to the editor.

"What do you think he's going to do with the gun?" Lighty was looking at the shovels, several of them, lined up against the wall.

"I imagine he's having thoughts of suicide."

She picked the oldest one, warped but sturdy. "Are you glad?" she asked.

Burton was so taken aback that he let the door slam behind them. The shed blackened. He stumbled backwards and flung the door open again, apologizing.

"I wouldn't blame you if you were," she said, hoisting the shovel. "But there's no point to wishing. Things happen as they happen."

He followed her out to her son's grave. She handed him the paper bag of bulbs. She was an amazingly efficient digger, slicing a quick deep hole, holding back the turf while he set in the bulb, tamping it down on top. "I'm afraid I don't accept things so easily," he said.

She had arranged the bulbs in an extended oval at the head of Eugene's grave. When the daffodils bloomed, they would tumble toward each other and fill the center with yellow cups. Even now, with winter not yet begun, Burton could imagine their spring opening.

Lighty finished. She took the bag, rolled it up, stuck it in her pocket. "Did you ever hear of Nostradamus?" she asked.

"Who?"

"Not a Lutheran. But a philosopher. From long ago. He believed that everything was planned. You live it, but you don't make it happen. So there's no need to feel guilty or angry about it."

"Where did you hear about him?"

She pressed down the last irregularity of dirt with her foot. In the distance, there was a strange sound, throaty and rough. It seemed to be getting louder.

She raised her head. Her eyes were wet, but she was still smiling. "From a friend," she said.

fifty-three

At first they hadn't known where they ought to look. When Alex pulled into Ed's driveway, the Miata crunching through the dry leaves, Ed had simply gone out and gotten in without a word. He had been swept with a great release, as if he'd come out from a tornado to find the roof of the house gone but the sky as blue as God's own breath.

"I have a feeling he'd go somewhere secret. Woods, swamps, whatever." Alex swung the car off the gravel onto the blacktop, hugging the right lane. Three semis in a row passed him.

"When he stayed with you, did he have a favorite place?"

Alex rubbed the bottom half of his face, then his forehead. He pushed back his hair. "In my closet, actually," he said. "The child was insane about my shirts."

It wasn't funny, given the circumstances. Yet Ed had to suppress a laugh. Even he had noticed Alex's splendid collection of shirts, most of which certainly had not come from Garfields in Littleriver. "We have to focus on someplace," Ed said, pushing his mind back to the business at hand. "Someplace he could go with a bicycle."

Alex shook his head. "Maybe Richard was just trying some target practice," he said.

Ed had been looking out the window, thinking quarry, Hall's orchard, the big swamp, the ridge. Now he turned his head and focused on Alex, foolish and hopeful, as the Miata swerved to avoid a dead raccoon in the road. "If that's what you think, Alex," he said, "then why are we racing out to find him?"

There was no reply. Then Alex spun his head around. His eyes were wet. "I really screwed up," he said.

"What happened?"

Alex speeded up. "Stupid little me," he said. "I'd forgotten what it was like to have a young one around. Their bodies are so luscious. And they don't even know it. So I suppose I said a few things to indicate appreciation. Reached out a hand now and then. Had some talks that went a little too far in the direction of affection." He bent low over the wheel, his chin almost against the windshield. "Direction of affection," he moaned. "What a stupid expression. Burton would have a cow."

Ed sighed. "Where are we going, Alex?" he asked.

Alex slammed on the brakes. The little car plunged to the side of the road. "I wish someone would wash my mouth out with soap," he said, his voice cracking. "I have absolutely no idea where we're going."

And then Ed felt something move through him, some sense of what had to be done and how they were going to do it. "We have too many choices," he said quietly. "But let's start to eliminate them. Did Richard ever go swimming at the quarry?"

"Never. He hated all the kids who went there."

One down. "What about the ridge?" Ed asked. "It's only a mile long, and open. But there are some hiding places in the rocks on the way up."

This time Alex hesitated. "I don't think so," he said. "He was a tree person, actually, not a rock person. He liked greenery." Alex smoothed back his hair. "He was childish about it, I fear," he said. "But then he was a very young person."

The past tense caught Ed by surprise. He recognized Alex's desperation. And he also remembered Richard the first time he had seen him during the summer, perched in the tree out at Big Loon Lake while the old woman from the nursing home had plunged through the foliage to rescue her hollyhock seeds. He remembered the feel of Richard's sneakers as he'd helped him come down out of that tree.

"Big Loon Lake!"

Alex looked at him.

"He rode the bike that day," Ed said, musing. "And it's clearly a place he knows." He turned toward Alex. "I met him there by accident one day this summer. Head for Big Loon Lake."

"Is that the lake out past Rudolph?"

Good God! Didn't Alex live in Eagle Grove? "No, that's Fish-eye," Ed said. "Big Loon Lake is where the old church was. The one that's all in ruins now. The story is that when the congregation got too old and sparse to support a church, they just burned it down."

Ed stopped. The Big Loon Lake Church, now that he thought about it, had become a warning parable for small Lutheran parishes. Preachers had worried it to death—how people had felt the excess of ownership and pride, how they were unwilling to let things take their course, how they took God's will into their own hands.

But really, Ed thought, remembering the old woman, there was much to admire in those Big Loon Lake parishioners, those old men and women who had now mostly passed away. They had known what had to be done. They had accepted the responsibility for doing it.

Alex had the car moving down the road at a good speed. Ed checked his seat belt. "We'll be there soon enough," he said. "Let's plan our strategy."

"How far in can we drive?"

"Not far. But there's a trail." He grabbed Alex's shoulder. "The next turn," he said. "Then a little over a mile."

Alex manhandled the Miata around the corner onto the gravel. The little car shrieked, settled back in on its haunches, surged on. Ed found himself with his head bowed. Unfortunately, none of the glib religious words seemed applicable.

"Is this where we stop?"

Ed came back from a far place. "Pull over," he said. "As far as you can get. There's no ditch here."

Alex edged the car against the shrubbery. "I don't see any bicycle," he said.

"Don't you think he'd bring it in with him?"

Alex rubbed his forehead with both hands, like a child himself. "Ed, this is all beyond me," he said. "I feel like Judas Iscariot. I've betrayed Burton. I've betrayed that poor, dumb kid."

Ed slid out, closed the door behind him, walked around and took Alex by the elbow. "I'm not the one to give spiritual comfort at this point," he said. "But I've won all the prizes in betrayal, to the point where I wouldn't have the nerve to ask for forgiveness even if I wanted to. I don't even know who to ask anymore. We just have to do the next thing. *This* is the next thing."

Close together, Ed's taller body sheltering Alex's from behind as they edged through the sparse bayberry and sumac, they headed down the trail. It was impossible to know if anyone had been there earlier; the leaves under their feet were loose and moved in irregular patterns as they passed. But a bike could have been taken along; the branches were high enough. And there was the sense of a conduit, perhaps only because of the narrow opening, the deepening darkness on each side, the slight sense of illumination toward the end.

"Wait." Alex hesitated.

Ed braced himself so as not to fall over him. "What?" he asked.

"I saw something." Alex reached into the branches. "My God, Ed," he said. "Look at this."

It was the gearshift of a ten-speed bike, its wired attachments dangling. "He must have torn it off," Alex said, wonder in his voice. "It was never any good. It must have given out, and he lost his temper at it. I've thought about throwing it away a dozen times myself."

The little collection of silver metal edges lay in Alex's palm like a distorted jewel. He seemed unable to drop it. "Richard's here," he said, his voice low.

The two men stood silent. Nothing moved. There was no sound. Ed didn't know what to expect—a scream, a shot, a plunging through the underbrush. "We should go down to the church," he said, touching Alex at the back of his neck.

"Where?"

"There's another path."

The two men walked across the little clearing onto the second path. Through the opening branches, Ed caught a glimpse of the church's chimney, which of course hadn't burned. In the summer, when he'd last been here, some wild roses had climbed halfway up to the top. Now only the thick ropes of vines wound along the bricks.

"We should really let him know we're here," Alex whispered.

Ed thought about shouting—Richard's name, his own name, Alex's name. Some unknown series of words. But instead he began to sing, the old church hymn "There's a Wideness in God's Mercy." He didn't know why. It didn't even have a decent rhythm, and the key was too high for a baritone. But he sang it anyway. He remembered his mother singing it a thousand years ago, the year before she'd died. Her hair had already started to fall out, but she had been totally unashamed. When she'd sung "There's a kindness in his justice," her eyes had been absolutely aglow.

After a brief hesitation, Alex joined in. He even knew the second and third verses. Amazing. Perhaps he'd had a mother too.

Belting out the hymn, crashing along toward the ruins of the chapel, stumbling over fallen branches in the growing dusk, they didn't hear anything at first. It was Alex who reached back his hand. When they stopped together, they realized that someone had been shouting "Stop!" at them for any number of times.

"He's there."

Ed shut his eyes to widen his pupils, held them that way, opened them again. Over by the edge of the overgrown churchyard, Richard was standing. He was holding the gun in front of him with both hands, but the barrel was turned toward himself.

"Stop right there!"

They were already stopped.

"Don't come any closer! I'll shoot!"

He was standing around the corner from the chimney near where the old woman had rescued the hollyhock seeds. Now the dried stems of the plants stood like stiff brown rifles tilted in all directions. Against the darkening sky, Richard looked unusually pale. The low light glinted off the barrel of the gun.

Ed and Alex looked at each other. "Jesus!" Alex whispered.

"I'll shoot!"

So this is it, Ed thought. This is the supreme moment, the holocaust where all the little shanties are swept away. And there's no one here but the three of us. We have to do this without any help at all.

"Richard." Ed spoke quietly, not wanting to sound as if he were preaching.

Richard didn't say anything. Then he put the barrel of the gun in his mouth. It looked as if both of his thumbs were on the trigger.

Alex choked. "He's going to do it," he whispered. "My God."

And he *may* do it, Ed thought. He may. He may.

For a moment, more than a moment, the three of them stood unmoving. Alex had his hands pressed to his own mouth as if he were holding in his words. Or perhaps he was willing the gun away from Richard's mouth, protecting that young flesh from the bullet. Who could tell?

Ed took a breath, stepped forward. He could see Richard swaying. "I want to say something," he said, took another breath, waited. There was no shot.

"When I'm done, you can do anything you want. But I want you to hear me first. I won't preach. But I deserve this chance, I think. Richard? Richard?"

There was a crunching beside him. Perhaps there *were* deer in this place, Ed thought. Maybe the kid had been right when he'd been looking for them from up in the tree last summer. He turned his head silently, wondering what was happening. Behind him, he saw Alex plunging back down the trail, retching. Vomit splashed out from between his hands.

Ed turned forward again. Richard was looking at him. Over the gun, his eyes gleamed. He did not move.

From Nam, Ed recognized what the gun was. A Beretta. Six bullets. He was sure Richard had already pulled the slide back and sent them into the chamber. So he would have to work on the geometry.

"Richard, I know you want to do this. I won't prevent you. It's your call. I won't try to take that away from you. But there's something I want you to do first."

He thought he saw Richard's wrists tremble.

"There are only two of us now. We're both outsiders. Only I'm the one who has *put* himself outside. You're simply the person you are. Everything is still to come for you. Good and bad. I can guarantee there'll be some of both. I've already committed my defining sins, if I may use those words. And it's too late for me to take them back."

Through the absolute silence that comes when twilight is lowering, Ed heard the barrel of the Beretta clink against Richard's teeth. It clinked again.

"Richard, turn the gun around. Point it at me."

Silence.

"Richard? Point it at me."

Nothing. A small wind moved through the trees. Against the old chimney, the vine rustled. Some bird squawked. What one? Most birds had already flown south. Something unglamorous and unafraid of winter, like an indestructible crow.

"Richard?"

Very slowly, very, very slowly, Richard slid the barrel of the gun out of his mouth. Very slowly, he readjusted his hands on the hand grip. Holding the gun out from his body a little ways, his elbows against the chest, he rearranged his finger on the trigger. He pointed the barrel at Ed.

The bird rasped again. Ed straightened. "Good," he said. "Good. You know you can pull the trigger anytime. I'd even be grateful. And then, afterwards, you can do what you want. There are enough bullets. It can all end here."

Richard was biting his lips. His shoulders shook. But the gun was surprisingly steady, and Ed could see the little black hole of its barrel as if it had been cut permanently into the landscape.

"Richard," he said. "Richard, I'm going to walk forward. I won't move fast. You can do what you want. Whatever you do is all right. I want you to know that. All right. There are just the two of us, just we two men. I'm in your hands. Whatever you do is all right."

He stepped forward.

fifty-four

Largo didn't know how it worked. There was a big difference between their ages, sure, more than twenty years, but Sandy had somehow never seemed exactly young. And Gypsy had married Trina, who was seventeen, when he was already an old man. That had turned out OK, as much as anyone could tell.

But now, through the hours and hours and hours they'd been in this stupid hospital room, Sandy just got younger and younger. He expected her to ask for a lollipop, to pee her pants. Actually, she'd already done both. There weren't any lollipops either, not in the machine at the end of the hall or the one downstairs. Largo had gotten Life Savers instead, fed them to her one at a time. Her lips were dry, and she didn't seem to pay attention. Once she'd squeezed his hand, though, her eyes shut, her face disappearing in concentration. Then the nurse had come in and yelled at him because Sandy wasn't allowed to have anything to eat. How the hell was he supposed to know that? The nurse had brought him a bowl of ice cubes to give her. They were so cold. He'd tried holding one in his hand first, thinking maybe he could warm it somehow, make it easier for Sandy to suck. Of course it melted. I mean, he *knew* that ice melted. Exactomundo. What the fuck else was ice supposed to do?

Now Sandy seemed to be sleeping. Only it never lasted long. Largo squatted at the foot of the table she was lying on. It wasn't even a real bed. There must be some reason that it wasn't a real bed, but he couldn't figure out what it was. Nothing made sense anymore.

It had been crazy from the beginning, starting with that dream. Once Sandy had gotten her bag sort of packed, he'd taken her downstairs and onto the Harley, lifting her up onto the bitch seat, sliding in front of her as fast as he could so she'd have an object to lean against. Rocker had done something funny to the transmission, and it grabbed when he started the bike and shifted into gear. But then it kicked in, and they'd wheeled out through the parking lot smooth as silk. He could tell by Sandy's breathing against his back that things weren't like usual, but she was gutsy and didn't say anything. She just held tight onto him all the way in. She couldn't of known what she was getting into.

"Largo!"

He must have dozed off. When he jumped, his foot was asleep. He stumbled up beside her.

"Something's wrong."

"What?"

"I don't know." Her face was knotted. "It hurts!"

"You want I should get the nurse?"

But she wasn't listening. Or didn't hear him anyway. Her face turned inside itself, a hard line crossing her forehead. She was breathing in that funny way, like a dog panting. She'd done that before. But then she had stopped and gone to sleep for a little. Now it just kept on and on.

"Sandy, you want I should do something?"

Sandy didn't appear to hear him. Her upper teeth were digging into her lower lip. There was even blood.

Largo plunged to the door. "Something ain't right!" he bellowed out into the empty hall. During the day there'd been lots of people around, but now that it was night again, they must of all gone home. He thought about yelling "Help!" but no biker ever yelled for help. Behind him, Sandy was groaning, only it sounded like some animal with a piece of meat. He'd had a Doberman once, long ago. It sounded like that.

"Fire!" It was the only word he could get out of his mouth. "Fire!"

A door slammed. Two nurses were running toward him. Someone in funny green pajamas followed. He must be a doctor.

"Fire!" They were looking around. He stepped inside. They raced into the room. Sandy opened her eyes, then shut them again.

"There ain't no fire. She needs you."

One of the nurses was walking around the edges of the room, probably checking for smoke. She must not have believed him. The other one, with the doctor, bent over Sandy. He pulled back the sheet covering her, took something from the tray on the bedside table. He leaned down. Sandy screamed.

"She's finally in transition. That baby is coming down fast. Let's get her into delivery."

Sandy was throwing herself back and forth on the bed that wasn't a bed. One of the nurses leaned over her, grabbed her arms. Sandy kept fighting. Largo wanted to knock the nurse onto the floor, but he had never been much for hitting women. And something told him that he didn't really know what was going on. He felt a desperate need to be outside, to fling himself on the Softail, to roar off down to Texas with both cylinders thumping, stopping just to take a piss and have a beer. More than one beer.

But he didn't go. He leaned against the wall. The doctor hurried past him, banging against his chest. His ribs throbbed, but he didn't even swear.

"Get her into delivery!"

What did that mean?

Two more men raced down the hall. Their rubber-soled shoes slapped against the tile until it didn't sound like running at all, but some kind of soft drumming, fancy dance drumming, hands against the skin, on and on and on. They grabbed Sandy off the table, rolled her onto a second table that they'd pushed in. She was screaming and kicking.

"Stop it, Mrs. . . . ," one of the nurses said. She looked down at Sandy's chart. "Stop it, Mrs. Vasquez," she said louder. Largo had forgotten Vasquez was that prick Juan's last name.

Sandy raised her head a little. Her hair was a wild wet rainbow around her face, her skin flushed into a funny color that made Largo think of a Chinaman. She balled her fists and punched one nurse right in her fat tits. "Fuck you!" Sandy yelled. "Fuck you!"

Largo couldn't remember her ever saying the F-word. He would have grinned if things hadn't been happening so fast. Where was the baby in all this? It seemed like it might have fallen out on the floor, but when he caught a glimpse of Sandy's belly from among the bodies swirling around her, it was still as big as a mountain.

"Put on the restraints!"

Largo leaned forward. The men were grabbing at Sandy's arms. "No!" she yelled, arching her back.

"Don't put the cuffs on her!"

All the faces swung around toward him. Even Sandy, her eyes glazed and open so wide that they looked like holes in her face, turned her head in his direction.

"She didn't do nothing!"

One of the nurses detached herself. She looked furious, but as she came toward Largo, her face softened. "It's all right," she said. "It's to keep her from hurting herself. The baby's head is crowning. She's almost ready to give birth."

Largo nodded, wordless.

The nurse reached over to a bureau by the door and took out a bundle of green. "Put these on," she said. "We like to have the fathers in delivery."

Largo swallowed so hard that his ribs hurt. His elbows moved forward, but his hands stayed at his sides. "What?" he asked.

"Here." She held out an enormous pair of pajama pants. "Put them on. Then the jacket. Take off your boots. The slippers go over your socks."

They had gotten Sandy anchored on the other table. Somebody was holding the door. The two orderlies, or whatever they were, shoved her through it and down the hall. As she passed Largo, she looked back at him. Her face was wet. Her hands were strapped down. She looked about ten years old. He thought she was going to say something to him, but then she bit her lip again and dug her chin down into her chest. He couldn't tell if the high whine he heard was from the rolling bed or from her.

"Come this way."

He followed the nurse, still hitching up the enormous green pants and trying to anchor them over his jeans. When he had pulled the shirt over his head, he'd gotten it tangled up somehow on his colors, and it hunched together in front in a big ball of fabric. The hall floor through the paper slippers felt incredibly cold. He hoped no one walked off with his boots—they still had a lot of wear left in them.

"Will this be your first child?"

Largo had no idea what to say. The nurse guided him around a corner of the corridor behind Sandy's bed. The nurse was young too, Largo realized, pushing back his hair from his loosening braid. Maybe she didn't know much more about this than he did. But they must teach them something in school. Pictures for sure. Maybe they had videos too. But it was nice she wasn't making fun of him.

"Your wife is young. That's good, though, for having a baby. If you wait too long, it's harder to get pregnant."

The sentences sloshed through Largo's brain like a tequila shooter. He opened his mouth to set her right. She put her hand on his arm for just a second.

"Be brave for her," she said. "She needs you."

His mouth still open but as effectively stopped as if someone had wedged a large cork in it, Largo went with the nurse through a heavy pair of swinging doors into a big cold room, so bright with fluorescent lights that there were no shadows at all.

Sandy was lying almost naked on the table, a white sheet half over her chest, her legs pulled up and her feet stuck in some metal cuffs. Her hands were still tied down. Between her legs, that part he'd known in so many women, it looked like a huge melon was splitting open.

Largo bent over. He thought he was going to puke. It was worse than a night at Whiskey Corners, worse than the party they'd had the last time at Sturgis.

"Stand over here."

It was the nurse. She had her hand on his arm again, and when he didn't move, she began to shove at him until he couldn't help but follow her directions and come up next to Sandy. He didn't think she could see him, but she was wrenching her hand against the restraint, all of the muscles in her arm standing out like ropes against her pale skin.

"Largo! Help me! I need you!"

And with that, it all changed. His stomach rearranged itself. His hands stopped shaking. This was serious business, and he was an honorable man. No matter what winds were blowing through his life, he'd always managed to earn a living one way or another, and he'd paid for his Harleys with honest money. Well, mostly honest. Even in his drinking days, he'd gotten his DUIs without killing anybody, and when he'd been serious about guns—the Beretta, the Magnum he'd won when the Iron Riders had their spring shoot-out contest, the Colt .45 from the flea market—he'd come nearer to doing himself in than to offing anybody else. The Harley had always come first, as it should with a real biker. And he'd kept the honor of his tribe as much as it was possible in a world where Indians were fading into the horizon and breeds like him weren't worth shit to begin with. He'd paid four hundred dollars for Dan the Man's tattoo. He knew about honor.

He grabbed Sandy's hand. "Hang in there," he said, squatting down against the frame of the bed or table or whatever the fuck it was so his mouth could be next to her ear. The doctor down at the end had some scissors in his hand, but he must have given Sandy a shot of something because when he bent down and started to snip, she didn't act like it felt any different from before. For just the briefest moment, he wondered if it all grew together afterwards, and if maybe he'd have to figure out a different way to do things. But, hell, he could manage.

Sandy was screaming again. "Push, push, push!" the nurse yelled, and Sandy twisted up her face so tight she didn't look like the same person and dug her nails into Largo's hand right down through his skin. "Here he is!" said someone, and Largo tried to swing around to see if somebody had come into the room, but his ribs hurt, and Sandy felt like she had grown onto the end of his arm, and then suddenly they were holding up a wet red piece of work that was yelling too, and wiggling, and Largo realized, in a snarl of wild awareness, that this must be the baby.

"A big one," said the nurse, holding up a blanket. "Just like his father."

fifty-five

"What do you think of the baby?"

Largo jerked awake. He couldn't imagine how he'd been asleep to begin with, because just a second before he'd been looking at snapshots from Sandy's mom's purse that showed Sandy when she was a little girl, tough as they come, her wild hair forced into pigtails. No wonder she knew how to braid.

Largo cleared his throat. "He's big," he said. That must be the right thing to say. Actually he'd thought the baby unimaginably small once he'd had a chance to really look. When Sandy had insisted he hold him, it had been like a Harley carburetor in his arms.

"Almost nine pounds." Grace looked happy. Her face was pale, but maybe it was just being up in the middle of the night. Largo figured she wasn't that much older than he was. The very thought made him uncomfortable.

"Ed will be here any minute. He called just before you came in."

Largo couldn't figure out if she thought he was Sandy's new husband, or if she was just being polite, or if they didn't want Sandy to come live with them, especially with a kid, and figured he'd be a good alternative. None of the possibilities seemed right. When he'd met them before, they'd seemed good enough people, wanting their daughter to be safe, not having a shit fit about what she was doing with her life, nice enough the second time to keep shoving all that coffee at him whether he wanted it or not. Damn good for a preacher's family.

Grace looked at him gently. "Have you known Sandy for a long time?" she asked.

It seemed like centuries.

Grace reached over the arm of the plastic chair and touched Largo's hand. "We're so grateful to you for taking care of her," she said.

He nodded.

"Sandy has always picked her own friends. I didn't always appreciate her judgement. Now I've gotten better at trusting her."

Her hand was still touching his. What was all this business with hands? Her skin was really whiter than Sandy's, and Largo realized that, even in the peculiar light, he could see the slight coloration of blood in the veins above her knuckles.

"You all right?" he asked.

"What?"

"Are you all right? You don't look so strong."

He thought she'd pull back with that, but instead she put her whole hand on top of his. It didn't weigh anything. "I'm strong enough for now," she said, and then they both turned their heads toward the door, where her husband was standing.

"I came as soon as I could."

Grace stood up. "I'm so glad," she said. "You know she's all right? And it's a boy."

"They told me at the desk."

"She's sleeping. The baby is in with her."

"I'll wait until she wakes up."

Largo stood and held out his hand. The preacher took it. "You were with her?" he asked, but it wasn't so much a question as a statement.

"Yeah, I was." His hand didn't feel like a preacher's.

"I'm grateful," he said, and put his other arm around Largo's shoulders. He looked over at his wife. "I'm truly grateful," he said again.

Largo checked over the two of them. There was something strange about them, he thought. They were too polite to each other, like dogs sniffing each other's butts. But maybe preachers' families were just like that. And they were nice enough to him. Tired right down to his bones, his head swimming, he was downright happy to have people be nice to him.

"I need to tell you what happened tonight." Largo turned, but the preacher was talking to his wife.

"What did happen?" She seemed to be having a hard time getting her breath.

Ed sank down into the chair next to her. "In the end, very little," he said. "Alex drove by his place before he dropped me off. Burton was standing by the mailbox pretending to be painting the rust spots, if you can imagine. With a huge flashlight for illumination. Alex got out, gave him a hug, climbed back in, and took me home."

"And the boy?"

"He's home too. Safe."

"So it was a good night's work."

"I guess so."

They both sat in silence. Largo had no idea what they had been talking about. He tried to think of another topic, but he'd completely lost track of the weather, and he was afraid if he said something about Sandy, it would be the wrong thing. He sat in silence too. But he was worried he was going to fall asleep again if he didn't move, because his whole body seemed to be sliding downward toward the vinyl flooring. He shook his head violently back and forth.

"What are you and Sandy going to name him?" Ed asked.

Largo looked up.

"I don't know if they've decided yet," Grace said.

Names! In the Iron Riders, they gave you a new name after you finished being a prospect. Something that fit you in some crazy way, like Big Bang for the way he always rigged his exhaust, or Wrapper because he was the one who always had a rubber. Or Comanche, because he went bowhunting that once and shot himself in the foot. With a bow, that took some doing.

"You know, I'm not sure I remember your real name."

Largo opened his mouth, then shut it again. He'd been Largo since before the club, since before his first Harley. They hadn't even tried to change it. There wasn't any reason for his name that he could remember. He'd always been just Largo.

"I know you were at our house before, but that was a rather strange night. And in the hospital too. Perhaps now is the time to do the introductions properly. I'm Ed Olson. And this is my wife, Grace."

Largo held out his hand for what seemed like the fiftieth time that night. His mind was plunging back, past the Doberman, back to the trailer they'd lived in when he was a kid. He hadn't forgotten his given name because you couldn't forget that, but it was so far back in his past, so unimaginably far, that he had to rummage in his brain for it, track it down to a corner, hold it in place, and then extract it with a pop that he almost thought they could hear.

"William," he said. "My name's William."

fifty-six

"So this is a Harley."

It seemed so obvious to Largo that he didn't know what to say.

"They're certainly big."

Largo nodded. That was pretty obvious too. He looked behind him at the house of Sandy's parents, where he'd gone after they'd all left the hospital. They'd invited him for coffee, and he'd followed their car, holding down the rems of the Softail until he thought they were both going to burst. He'd drunk three cups, knowing he wasn't going to be able to sleep anyway. He was going back to see Sandy as soon as he could get away.

Behind both Ed and Largo, over the lake, the sky was lightening. Not lightening, exactly, but losing its hold on the darkness. It was going to be a clear day. No wind either. The birds that hadn't left already were starting to say a few things. It was so quiet that you could hear every one.

"How long have you had it?"

Largo couldn't tell if Ed was just being polite or what. He knew the preacher was a polite man. When his wife had gone to bed, he'd lowered his voice when he talked. Largo had lowered his too.

"It looks new."

Largo's Heritage Softail was thirteen years old. But what was a preacher supposed to know?

"It ain't new. But I keep it up. I got it in '85. Harley-Davidson started making them then."

"You don't have a car?"

"I buy some old beater if I need one."

"Can you ride a motorcycle in the snow?"

Largo remembered last winter, before the rigs, before Sandy, before his life had begun. The Harley did OK with snow as long as there weren't finger drifts, which were shit if you hit them at an angle. Ice was shit all the time. But he'd held out longer than most.

"Sometimes," he said, and let it go at that.

The preacher patted the seat. "I hear there are Christian motorcycle clubs," he said.

Largo hated those guys, with their Jesus colors and their creepy ways. But maybe if you were a preacher, they seemed like a good thing.

Ed patted the seat again. He was a pretty solid man, Largo realized, but somehow now in the beginning of dawn, he seemed to have shrunk a little. He was wearing canvas sneakers. Largo looked down at his own boots, safe on his feet. Nobody had walked off with them, and he was glad.

"I want to thank you again."

Largo felt like he was the one who needed to be thanking people, only he wasn't sure who. He slung his leg over the seat and stuck his key in the ignition. But before he turned it, he looked back.

"Wanna ride?"

The preacher straightened his shoulders. A few leaves drifted down at the edge of the driveway. "Sure," he said.

"You hang onto these metal bars. Keep your feet up. It's noisy, but I'll hear you if you yell."

Largo turned the key. The motor awoke. Some bird squawked like its throat had been cut, then got quiet. The big bike rumbled down the driveway and turned onto the gravel.

In all the hundreds, thousands of mornings that Largo had started out on the Harley, this was just another one. A little morning run. Before the day got started and you had to do stuff. Sometimes you saw a deer if you were in the country. Lots of paperboys in the city. Sometimes people opened their windows. You'd think they'd be angry with all the noise, but lots of times they were smiling. There was something about a big bike, even for people who had never been on a motorcycle in their lives.

The preacher seemed pretty loose. Largo could feel his weight switch a little on the curves. He seemed to know how to go with things.

Largo turned his head back. "We'll take a run around the lake," he yelled, his hair blowing over his eyes. "So you can feel how it goes. I won't lay it down in the road. Just stay mellow and hang on."

Ed nodded. Largo revved it up. They tore through the gravel, damp dust rising behind them. Through the gaps in the trees, the sky was turning silver as the night pulled away.